THAUMATROPIC ROOT — BOOK TWO

BONES
OF
CENAEDTH

STEVEN J. MORRIS

Bones of Cenaedth

Book 2 of Thaumatropic Roots
Steven J. Morris

Copyright © 2024 by Steven J. Morris
All Rights Reserved.
1st Edition

This book is a work of fiction. Any references to historical events, real people, or real places, are used fictitiously. Any resemblance to actual events or locales or persons, living or dead, is entirely coincidental.

The scanning, uploading and distribution of this book via the internet or any other means without the permission of the publisher is illegal and punishable by law. Please purchase only authorized electronic editions, and do not participate in or encourage electronic piracy of copyrighted materials. Your support of the author's rights is appreciated.

No part of this publication may be reproduced in whole or in part without the written permission of the publisher. For information regarding permission, please email grundlegatekeeper@gmail.com.

Cover design by Deranged Doctor (www.derangeddoctordesign.com).

ISBN 978-1-956105-24-7

I dedicate this story to aunts Ella & Sandy... and Janelle... Without them keeping my wife (relatively) sane, this book would have taken a lot longer!

Thanks to Intel Corp for all the years of interesting challenges, and for paying me to retire early (and finish this book)

Books by Steven J. Morris

The Guardian League series

The Guardian of The Palace

Stars in the Sand

We're Going on an Elf Hunt

The Song Unsung

Thaumatropic Roots series

Mother of Trees

Bones of Cenaedth

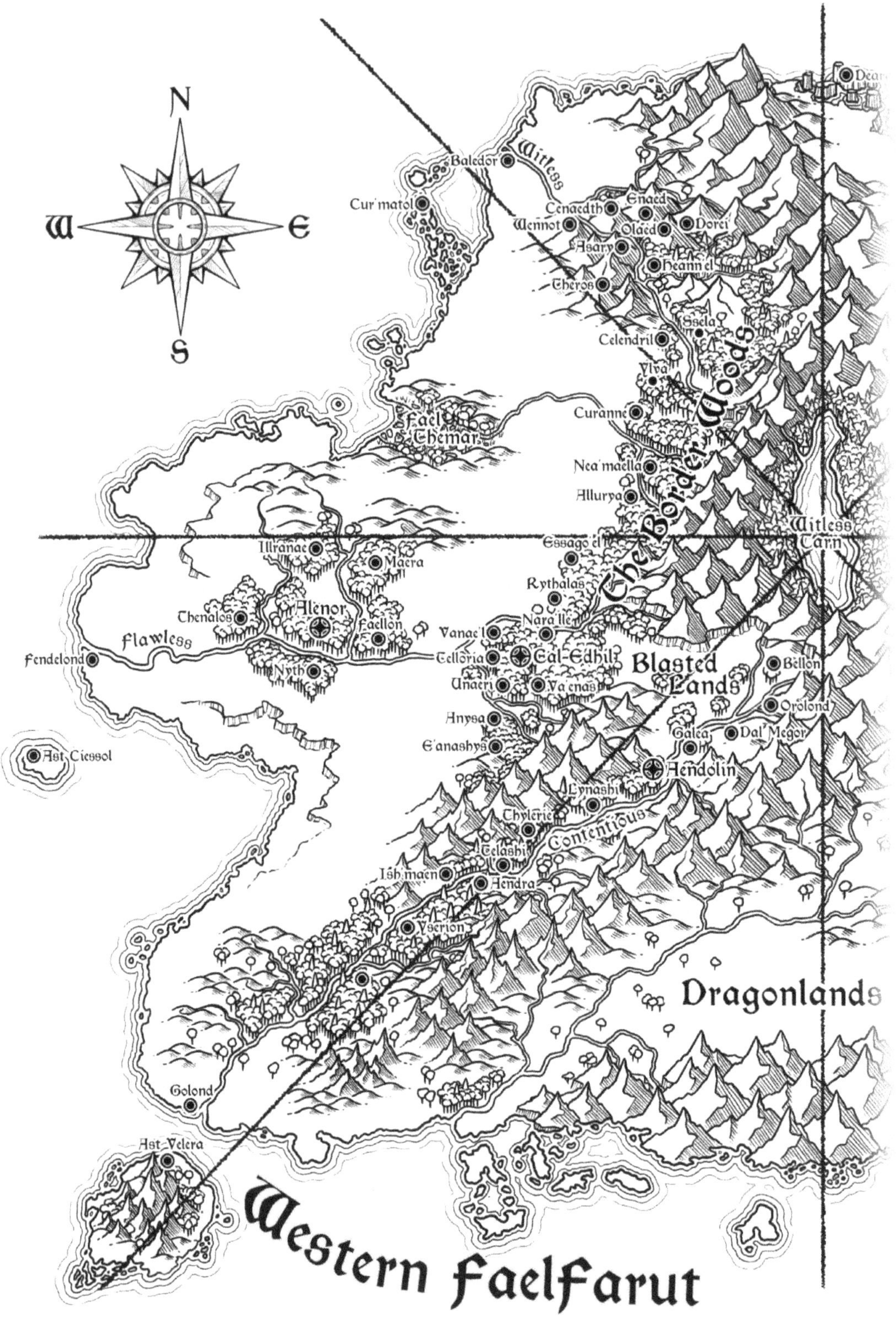
N
W
E
S
Baledor
Witless
Cur'matol
Cenaedth
Enaed
Wennot
Olaed
Dorei
Asary
Heann'el
Theros
Ssela
Celendril
Ylva
The Border Woods
Curanne
Fael Themar
Nea'maella
Allurya
Witless
Tarn
Essago'el
Illranae
Macra
Rythalas
Alenor
Thenalos
Nara'lle
Faellon
Vanae'l
Flawless
Fendelond
Telloria
Cal-Edhil
Blasted Lands
Bellon
Nyth
Unaeri
Va'enas
Orolond
Anysa
Galea
Dal'Megor
Ast Ciessol
E'anashys
Aendolin
Lynashi
Thylerie
Contentious
Telashi
Ish'maen
Aendra
Yserion
Dragonlands
Golond
Ast Velera
Western FaelFarut

Eastern Faelfarut

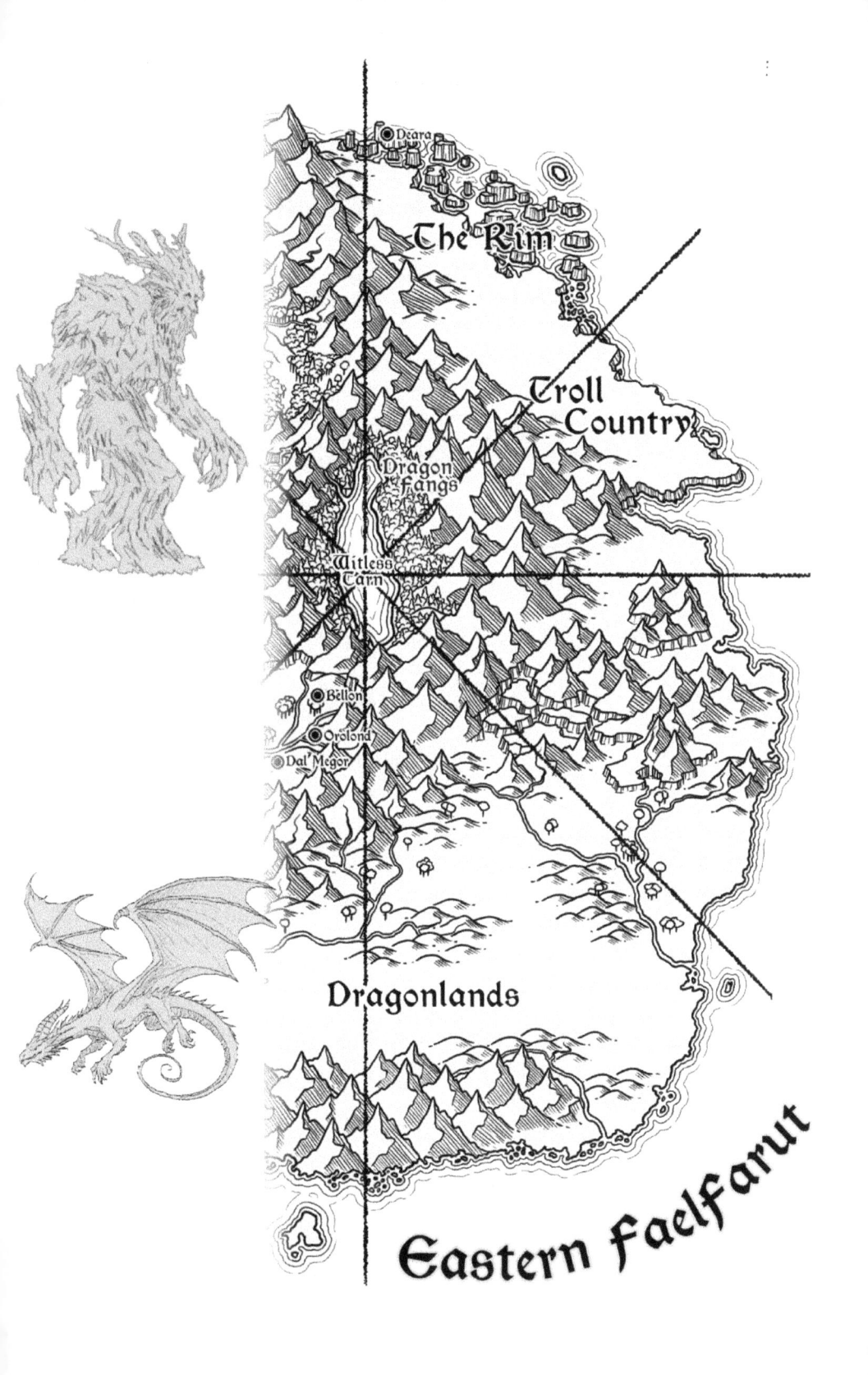

- Deara
- The Rim
- Troll Country
- Dragon Fangs
- Witless Tarn
- Bellon
- Orolond
- Dal'Megor
- Dragonlands

Prologue

"Why won't it melt?" the boy asked, frustrated and glaring at the white pipe like it personally offended him.

"You tell me," I said calmly, patiently, not wanting to rile young Othorion. A weighty name for a child. But the name fit—his life would not be easy.

I had us wrapped in a protective bubble of sorts—Othorion was too young to be trusted with our lives in addition to the repairs. The bubble wasn't like the Shields of the Warders, which would fail to keep out what we needed out. No, I whisked away the heat in a circle around us, providing time to work without burning up. I glanced up at the thick silver rod climbing far into the chamber, noting the ice patterns creeping down it. We wouldn't be able to stay long. But we didn't need to.

"Have I got enough heat?" he asked. His brows furrowed as he tried to pour on even more.

"Easy," I said, impressed despite myself. He had power. "You have enough heat. What else could it be?"

"It melts in class," he said, exasperated, but backing off on the spell to think.

I let him consider it for a few seconds, then nudged him along. "What's different about the pipe in the classroom?"

"It's the same metal," he responded quickly. He said it as a statement, but his eyes flicked up to mine and I nodded my agreement. He nodded in return.

It was his first trip into the bowels of the magma chamber. I liked taking our promising mages on their first practical applications of the magic we taught them. I put my hand on my belly, wishing.

Finally, his eyes searched up and down the length of the pipe, and he smiled. "The pipe in the classroom is short."

I smiled back, and his eyes flicked to me again, looking for confirmation, so I gave him a nod.

He revised his spell, creating boundaries for the heat. It was tricky, but not unlike the spell I used to keep us from burning up on the floor of the chamber. Unlike my bubble, he didn't need to provide an escape route. Quite the opposite.

"Careful," I warned him. If he went back in at the same level he'd attempted without the insulating barriers, he would melt the pipe beyond hope. Then we would have to replace it. That wouldn't be the end of the world, but I had something else to do. My eyes wandered up to the balcony far above. Dark-skinned Alluvium walked along it here and there, dark dots on the other side of the black glass platform. I sought out anyone looking over the ledge. There were always watchers, mostly children, when we did repairs. But several adults often stopped to observe, and I imagined I found the one I was looking for. I had a date.

My hand went to my belly once more. *Do I really want to risk the pain again?*

I shook my head, getting my thoughts and eyes back onto the problem at hand. Othorion's tongue stuck out the side of his mouth as he focused on melting the pipe just enough to repair the break. Small breaks like these were normal. The rock shifts, with the intense temperature changes between the magma and the water or steam, caused cracks. This one was relatively easy, at a juncture outside of the magma. Perfect for a first lesson.

He looked up at me with a question on his face, pulling back into his mouth the tongue he hadn't realized he'd stuck out. Children were so cute. I smiled and nodded at him. "Now let your insulators free up gradually, so that the heat equalizes."

He nodded, excited at his success.

I winced. "Slower," I told him sternly.

His tongue jutted back out as he focused on a gradual return to equilibrium. It didn't matter so much for a repair above the magma, but the consequences of blowing a pipe in the magma were grave. While it was a better lesson to learn in a non-lethal condition, such as the one before us, I didn't take the time to teach it—I had a date I was determined to keep.

At last, the repair was done, and Othorion relaxed.

"Okay, let's open the valve," I said.

"Yes, Miss Brittanie," he sang, smiling and running ahead. It was a foolish move, and I would correct him later, but for the time being, I split my bubble and kept him safe. I didn't want to overburden Othorion. His life would be hard enough. He would have the same problems as me—too strong in Fire magic for his own good. I looked up again, my eyes not searching for my date, but zeroing in on our caves for neonatal intensive care. Though it was not visible from the magma chamber, I knew right where they were. Behind *that* wall of rock. I'd been there too many times.

Othorion spun the valve, letting the water head back to his repaired pipe, and the screaming began.

***

The Pyre's Reckoning

As the Winter of Eternity casts its shadow upon the world,
The fires of the ancients shall be the last beacon of hope.
The Flame Bearers must gather, their hearts alight with the Fire of Cenaedth,
For only through their burning can the unending cold be held at bay.

In the heart of the storm, a single spark will turn the tide,
Igniting the ancient pyres to push back the creeping gloom.
But beware the rise of the army of the Bereft,
For when the Destroyer awakens, the Bones of Cenaedth shall be consumed.

— Elandra, Red Prophet

The Silent End

In the final days, when shadows stretch long and deep,
The doors of fate shall be sealed, their hinges rusted and still.
Guardians of the gates shall stand silent,
As the keystones of destiny remain untouched.

When the stars refuse to guide and the moon's light falters,
Entrances to the future shall be barred,
Their thresholds covered in dust, never to be crossed.
The portals of hope shall be shuttered, bolted from within.

Whispers of ancient locks echo in the twilight,
As the world's passages close, one by one,
And the corridors of time stand vacant, their echoes hollow.
The end shall come, not with a bang, but with silence,

As every door to tomorrow remains forever shut.

— Elandra, Red Prophet

Fire lies.

— Wynruil Embergrove

Illiara - 1

Shoving my bare hand into a pit of vipers frightened me less than Beldroth's declaration. My very bones chilled, ignoring the uncharacteristic heat of the spring day. All hopes of fleeing, of stealing away from our captors and disappearing into the forest, vanished like wisps at dawn.

"We will reach Alenor soon." Those were the words Beldroth uttered that had sent shivers down my spine. I'd recognized as much myself. Yet his words made it more real, choking off the sprouts of my daydreams.

My eyes returned to my daughter, who lay unconscious upon a cart pulled by a mucker, a great beast snatched from the grasslands and made to serve the High Elves. As the High Elves thought all things were made for. I'd lived amongst them long enough to know. I'd spent decades with them, raised by Zoras, the elf who lay beside my daughter, wrapped in bindings to preserve his corpse. For the last eighty years, I'd run from him, the elf who raised me into adulthood, hiding my daughter from him, fearing for her life. Yet they lay side by side, my daughter's mind in who knew what state, and my adopted-then-estranged father dead. And the cart rolled inexorably toward the place that birthed all our troubles—Alenor.

Elliah had not awakened since our visit to the slumbering goddess. To my delight and horror, the Mother of Trees had awakened at Elliah's touch. Reviving the Mother justified my daughter's existence as well as the years I'd spent hiding her from sanctimonious elves with agendas.

"You need not worry," Beldroth said, his mighty form looming at my side. Once he yanked me from my dark meditations, the chirping of the birds grated, the light breaking through the trees stung my eyes. What right did the forest have to be so cheerful when my daughter lay unconscious? "The Mother said she would live."

I cringed. The Warder trusted the Mother, trusted her beyond measure. I did not. Nor did I understand his faith. The goddess might have been powerful once, and was still dangerous, as evidenced by Zoras's corpse, wrapped in herbs and cloth beside my daughter. But the goddess *slept*! Slept while the trolls grew stronger. Slept through centuries of war, of elves dividing and segregating while their bickering slowly escalated until racial divisions tore apart the army that held off the trolls.

Yet I didn't have the heart to utter the reply that sat on my tongue. *I don't trust her.* Beldroth's faith was child-like, and uttering those words would be equivalent to slapping a child. Unable to control my tongue, I made a noise, a sound my daughter had begun to make, usually irritating me like a bug bite, though I knew where she'd learned it.

"Your daughter will live, and we will go to the Alluvium and raise an army," Beldroth replied to my noise, a smile slipping through the stern facade he kept up for the somber trek through the low hills of the forest.

The High Elf riding atop the mucker stiffened. There was no love lost between the High Elves and the Alluvium. I looked at the High Elf guards behind us. They either hadn't heard, or pretended not to have. Hughelas, Beldroth's half-Warder, half-Salt son whose heart belonged to my daughter, marched along just behind the cart, lost in his own thoughts. The guards in front, I couldn't see well because of the cart and mucker—the thin trail limited visibility. Almost on cue, the cart's wooden wheel scraped a sapling that had dared to lean into the cleared trail, and I cringed at the scrape of wood on wood.

"You never even uttered your plan to the Mother," I said. "How can you be so confident?"

"She Blessed it," he said, unable to hide his smile, though he quickly wrestled it back under control.

And he was right. I'd heard her. Though her Blessing had not been all blooms and honey. She'd said his plan would succeed, but also that everyone else in the room except my daughter would die. Not exactly the most reassuring words from a goddess.

Trying not to think about the doom we marched toward in Alenor, I poked on his beloved mission. "So raising an army of the Alluvium? That's your big plan? I know that you know the Alluvium used to fight on the front. You lived in the Blasted Lands. Fire magic and the woods don't play well together."

Beldroth's stony veneer became darker with a narrowing of his eyes. But only for a moment. Then his stoic mask returned and he answered. "There's more to my plan than that."

"Glad to hear it," I replied mockingly. "At least its foundation is something easy, convincing a people who have exited from a war to return to it."

Beldroth smiled like I'd agreed with the imminent success of his plan. Truth be told, I didn't care about his plan. I wanted my daughter to wake up. I'd spent decades hiding her away, and we both deserved a chance to rest, out in the open, with no one hunting us. Instead… she lay strapped upon a cart pulled by a mucker, resting beside the corpse of the only High Elf I might have trusted to revive her. I grimaced at the thought. Had Zoras lived, would I have trusted him to repair Elliah's mind?

No.

Only his death had convinced me of his sincerity.

I recognized that, if it took his death to convince me to trust him, I might have been better suited for a life of necromancy among the Alluvium. I was broken.

Still, Zoras had broken me, so he could only blame himself for trusts born of death—were he alive to blame anyone. He'd raised me from a child to adult, scheming and manipulating others, and I thought myself safe from his machinations as his adopted Wood Elf daughter. But when I'd stepped out of line, taking a High Elf as a lover and conceiving Elliah, he'd convinced her father we would be better off if our child silently disappeared.

If he'd lived, would Zoras even have been able to help? Though our High Elf captors had separated us after our adventure with the Mother of Trees, they'd undoubtedly tried to repair my daughter's mind at their outpost. It clearly hadn't worked, but I wouldn't expect the elves kept at a forest outpost to be experts in healing minds.

I stopped walking, sighing as the abused beast pulled my daughter and her deceased companion ahead. The mucker's webbed feet weren't built for the mountains. Only the mind control spells of its High Elf driver kept it on task. Made for the grassland and swamps, winged but flightless, muckers had become tools for the High Elves… they used them just like they used Wood Elves. Controlling domesticated beasts was about the strongest mind-related magic I expected the High Elves from the fortress to be able to muster.

"I can carry her," Beldroth said, stopping beside me, repeating what we'd already discussed and dismissed, "or I can fend off the High Elves." He couldn't do both. I couldn't do either. Nor was Hughelas sufficient for the tasks. Together Hughelas and I might briefly deter the High Elves while Beldroth made a break for it, carrying Elliah over his shoulder. But Beldroth, though he knew how to Heal, would not be able to keep Elliah alive in her comatose state on his own.

"No," I said, shaking my head. "It's into the vipers' nest for us."

Our original plan had been for Zoras to return in the company of the guards who had witnessed our encounter with the Mother of Trees. We had all bet on *my* words. *My* explanation of the events from eighty years before, when the Mother of Trees had prophesied that Elliah would live. We had bet on my daughter's second brush with the goddess ending on a positive note. Zoras would travel with the High Elf guards back to Alenor and clear our names. Elliah and I would gain our freedom, and I'd be at liberty to join the Warder on his quest... of my own volition instead of due to an alliance of convenience.

Yes, Zoras still traveled with the High Elf guards, but his capacity to convince the High Council had diminished greatly with his inability to expel breath. At one time, I hadn't thought even death would stop Zoras from his manipulations. I'd been wrong. In Alenor, we would find High Elves stronger in mind magic, able to wake and heal Elliah, though I cringed at the necessity.

"We will emerge from the pit," Beldroth answered, confident, but lacking his usual smile. He reined it in for my sake. He knew that worry ate at me, even though he had no doubts.

Staring into his light blue eyes, I let his surety wrap me like a warm blanket. A corner of his mouth lifted ever so slightly, his forced earnestness wearing thin.

My eyes flicked to my daughter, and I kicked the proverbial blanket off. Unable to let the mood lighten, because—*Mother of rotting Trees*—my child would not awaken, I poisoned the well I drank from. "*She* said we were all going to die."

Beldroth's mouth twitched with humor. "You didn't know that?" he asked. I glared. "You thought you would live forever? Time would not best you as it did everyone else?"

Put that way, I felt silly. I didn't like feeling silly. "Don't be daft," I snarled.

His face brightened with his characteristic smile.

"And don't pretend to be daft!" I snapped.

He continued to smile beatifically. *Goddess, why does his smile call to me?* I found my hand on my belly and moved it away, unable to discern whether I'd answered my own question, or just emphasized it.

Mother, I thought, *if you answer prayers, let this one's life be simpler.* The rear guard had almost reached us, so I hurried to catch up with the cart, Hughelas, and my already-birthed-daughter's unconscious body. *You owe me.*

Beldroth didn't hurry, only slightly increasing the pace. He gave me some breathing room. I took it. With focus on my breathing, I inhaled slowly, then held my breath, trying to calm my body. I listened to the... *wait ...*

I crouched, reaching for my absent dagger, peering deeply into the forest on one side, then the other.

Beldroth's heavy footsteps accelerated, and our action pulled Hughelas out of his daze. "What is it?" Beldroth whispered, putting his back to mine so that each of us had only one side of the forest to watch. My side led slightly downhill. His? Up. The trail followed the curve of the hill, remaining relatively flat. The High Elves, not surprisingly, had confiscated our weapons, and I felt silly with my fists in the air, despite the training Beldroth had beaten into us.

"Listen," I said. "The birds." They'd gone quiet. Something was out there.

The four High Elves behind us had tensed, also searching the forest, but one kept his eyes on us, like we might be up to something. Meanwhile, the High Elves in front, and the cart itself, pulled on ahead.

"Hold!" Beldroth shouted, and the High Elf riding the mucker looked back.

A great green snake shot out of the trees like a missile fired from a ballista, knocking the High Elf clear off the mucker and into the other side of the forest.

"Dragon," Beldroth hissed, sprinting toward the cart and the panicked mucker.

Dragon? What in the fiery pits of Cenaedth would my fists do against a dragon? But I couldn't leave Elliah on a cart attached to a mucker scared for its life. So, like Beldroth and Hughelas, I sprinted and then leaped onto the cart. The High Elves in front had scattered into the trees as the mucker and cart charged through. Even as I watched, one of them went down under a flash of green scales.

From the glimpses I'd caught, the dragon was the thickness of a plate, but it had to be as long as the cart. And faster. I'd never encountered dragons before traveling with the Warder and his son. Since then, drawgs had attacked my home; basilisks had paralyzed me; and black dragons tried to sink the ship we'd boarded. But they hadn't been able to track us ever since Elliah carried the...

"The hammer!" I shouted. The dragon had tracked us because we hadn't kept the hammer with Elliah. But Beldroth was already at the front of the cart, squatting to jump to the mucker. I grabbed his hand.

"Don't be daft." The mucker flapped its wings crazily, charging down the trail in a desperate hope of getting away from the dragon. The cart jolted and bumped, and I yanked Beldroth back so he wouldn't fall off, but he stood rooted, not at all in danger. He was using magic to steady himself. "Let me," I said, pushing him ineffectually.

He let his spell go and recast it to secure my footing as I climbed to the lip of the cart. I was lighter and more agile, more likely to make the leap successfully without crushing the mucker or breaking an admittedly vestigial wing—muckers flew as often as I did. Hoping he would release his binding spell at the right time, or else I would flop about like a fool with my feet stuck to the cart, I crouched and timed my leap to get me to the mucker's saddle without hitting any wings.

Time slowed as I jumped, eyes on my target, but catching the glint of light off of green scales coming in from the downside of the hill. Defying physics, I spun and tucked so that the dragon struck only a glancing blow against my feet, knocking them toward the uphill side of the forest, where the dragon disappeared back into the foliage. Despite my best effort, the dragon knocked me into the mucker's wing. I latched one hand on the saddle and my grip magically tightened. Beldroth. I used the wing of the careening mucker to roll myself onto its back… only I came up facing backwards.

Beldroth's spell released my grip, pulling my butt tight to the saddle instead. "My hammer!" he shouted.

Yes, the very reason the dragon had shown up. We had evidence that dragons somehow tracked the hammer whose head was crafted from the tooth of an Ancient, a gargantuan white dragon. Though we'd figured out how to neutralize its "scent," the High Elves hadn't believed us, and had kept the hammer with our other weapons, in the saddlebags of the mucker.

Crouched low, I easily found the right bag and withdrew the hammer. Beldroth held out his hands, and I swung it to him.

The dragon shot out of the trees to intercept it.

But Beldroth was ready—the hammer shot forward like I'd fired it at him instead of tossing it, and the dragon missed its chance. The woods thinned out, leaving the dragon less opportunity to hide. The spell holding me to the saddle released when he'd yanked the hammer to his waiting hand. I carefully turned myself around, fished my dagger from the saddlebags and sheathed it, then gathered the reins.

I looked over my shoulder at the downhill forest, spotting the movement of scales between the trees. Looking to the uphill side, though the trees were thicker, I also caught the gleam of lights bouncing off green scales. Two. At least two. *On the bright side,* I thought with a touch of insane humor, *we've gotten away from our captors.* I had my daughter and our weapons. If we could survive the dragons, we could at least approach a High Elf to wake Elliah on our own terms.

We burst out of the trees into a clearing hosting a squat stone fortification with a wooden wall extending from either side of it. The trail became a dirt road that pierced the center of the building. I yanked on the reins. The mucker fought me, plowing ahead in panic.

A dragon must have realized it had run out of woods, for it jumped out to catch the wagon. High Elves ahead and dragons behind, and I fought the wide-eyed mucker to stay with the dragons.

Glancing over my shoulder, I caught Beldroth leaping off the cart with a mighty swing of his hammer. Hughelas stayed crouched between Elliah and Zoras, protecting her. Determined to stop the cart, I switched tactics, casting a spell I'd learned during my upbringing with the High Elves to calm the beast I straddled.

With a mighty sigh, the mucker turned its sprint into a jog. Huffing, it slowed further, and I risked turning back. Beldroth fought with speed and strength that belied his simple smile. He'd trained generations of Warders to fight trolls and the occasional dragon in the Blasted Lands—he knew what he was doing.

The mucker slowed to a walk while Beldroth delivered a crushing blow to the dragon's head. Within feet of the gate, I pulled the mucker to the right, taking it off the dirt path to halt just beside the gate.

I watched as Beldroth backed slowly away from the dragon he'd beaten. The green dragon was longer and thinner than the black dragons that had attacked our ship. I'd never seen one before. More snake-like than its obsidian cousin, it lacked bulk but made up for it in speed. Where was the other—or others? *Dragons collect their dead.* Sure enough, another green dragon stalked out of the trees. It gave Beldroth a calculated look, then used its teeth to drag the corpse of its brethren and disappear back into the woods.

Inwardly, I sighed. We'd done it.

"That was quite something," said a voice behind me.

I spun, startled, to find a whole troop of armed High Elves outside the gate, surrounding the cart. Even as I readied the reins for a desperate escape, what remained of our High Elf escort came rattling and panting into the clearing at a run. Given their state, knocking them aside was a possibility, if the mucker would charge through. The mucker dropped to its knees, exhausted or under the duress of magic from the High Elves. I made a clicking noise with my tongue, disgusted that we'd come so close, could have died, and had absolutely nothing to show for it.

Elliah ~ 1

"The rest of you," said the Mother of Trees, looming over me, shrouding me in menacing darkness. "… everyone here…" came her heavy words comprised of roars, chirps, clicks, purrs, and leaves rustling. "… dies." She faded into darkness. "I'm so sorry," her words whispered from the far side of eternity. Sorry. The goddess was *sorry* everyone I knew and loved would die.

It was too much.

So I continued to hide.

My encounter with the Mother of Trees had gone very differently than I'd planned. When the Warder and his son appeared in our lives, I hadn't truly believed the Mother was real. As though she knew his belief in her hadn't been enough to convince me, my mother revealed she'd met her, and so had I. As a baby. I hadn't been a complete fool about it. I knew there was a chance she wouldn't vindicate my existence, freeing me from those who hunted me down for being different. But I hadn't expected to be flooded with memories from a goddess… things I couldn't name or truly even describe in the way I'd seen or felt them.

The memory of excitement flared at the light of a star blinking into existence, though not by the will of the Mother. Another being creating, while she merely watched in wonder. Worlds coalesced. That's when the Mother would intercede, forming plants and creatures of all shapes, sizes, and colors from seemingly nothing. The two of them repeated the process, over and over, and over again. Memories of memories haunted me—a thin silver disk with a hole in the center and a translucent ball of purple dangling beneath, gliding on drafts of air with nothing around save clouds, a world of water with creatures composed of nothing but tentacles dancing through the ocean. And then something had changed. Some kind of dissonance on a scale I didn't fully grasp. That in itself had frightened me.

But the truly gut-quavering fear took hold when *something* had intruded on the Mother's thoughts. A being like the object with which the Mother had fought—*He Who Creates Stars*. Maybe the very same. The monster was horrible, with its flaming eyes and mental claws that scraped my brain. I'd fled.

I'd been fleeing my whole life and knew well how to do it. Well, *almost* my whole life. Eighty years had brought me to the cusp of adulthood, running from the outskirts of one village to the next whenever my condition became a problem. I wasn't just weak in magic; like a troll, I absorbed it. Bereft. Our time in any village was limited by the religious fervor of the Wood Elves in it, once they found out about my state. Then I embarked on a journey of self-discovery and belief in myself—that had proved to be a colossal failure. Tucked away in a corner of my mind, I licked my wounds and protected myself, building walls and walls… and more walls.

But things came through anyway. Because I couldn't even do *that* right. Voices. My mother, whose disappointment in my ability to use the protective mental exercises she'd spent decades teaching me must have been eating her alive. Beldroth, who had used me to awaken the Mother and achieve his own goals. Others I did not recognize. Hughelas.

I'd sent my watcher peeking out for Hughelas. If there was anyone I wanted in the darkness, hiding alongside me, it was Hughelas. He always found a way to comfort me. But my watcher found a crowd of unfamiliar High Elf faces. They frightened me, and I sank deeper into my hiding space.

Darkness was safe. Safe from the dreamlike memories of the Mother of Trees, dreams of creation and life, but also unfathomable pain and sorrow. More importantly, walls and darkness separated me from the *thing* that had found me when I'd communed with the Mother of Trees. The creature whose burning eyes and mental barbs had torn through my mind.

Illiara - 2

Alenor's teeth had yellowed. True, Alenor proper still lay a half day's walk from the outpost, but I'd traveled the same path many times almost a century before. It was one of the waypoints between Heartshield Hall, where Zoras had raised me, and Alenor, where he served on the High Council. Dirt and decay marked the stone buildings that had once been pristine. All things aged. Even elves, in their way. But I wondered, had it really been as pure as I recalled, or had it simply been marvelous to my childish eyes?

"What are you pondering?" Beldroth asked.

Only then did I realize I had halted in my tracks, the cart that carried my daughter sneaking away on the trail which had converted to a cobbled road without my realizing. I hastened to catch up, and Beldroth jogged beside me, but we returned to a walking pace a little behind Hughelas, who resolutely followed the cart with his eyes fixed upon Elliah. Our "escorts" would have urged me forward soon enough. It irked me that we'd come so close to escaping, but at least the new group of guards treated us less like prisoners and more like honored guests. They'd let us keep our weapons, though Beldroth had set his hammer down between Elliah and Zoras, retrieving his sword from the mucker's saddlebags. The High Elves eyed him strangely, but didn't stop him, and we didn't want to attract more dragons.

"I was younger than Elliah when I first saw Alenor," I told him. "At least I think I was." My childhood, though emotionally rough in its own way, was significantly easier than Elliah's. I might have seen more days than her, but Elliah had lived harder and aged faster. There again, age showed its strange proclivities. "It was a wonder to me at the time."

I tried to place the splendor of my memories atop the scene before me, and, if anything, Alenor grew uglier.

Why had stone facsimiles of trees intrigued me? They were horrid! Had there always been so many? I thought I remembered the trees being alive. Surely they'd lived. Yet, more stone impersonations than live trees dotted the landscape.

Fairly sure.

The more I tried to convince myself, the less certain I became.

The buildings of my youthful memories stood magnificent, with sleek lines and steeples decorated with lightning, phases of the moon, and similar celestial paraphernalia. Proud windows providing glimpses of spinning wheels that pulled massive chains. The constructs had appealed to me as a child, promising secrets and wonders.

After eighty years in forests, those same structures and assemblies appeared unnatural… artificial… wrong. I sighed. Under my breath, I mumbled. "They haven't changed. I have."

How much of that difference was due to my breaking away from Zoras's influence? How much of my fascination with High Elves was from Zoras nudging me with his magic? Staring at the scene before me, I suspected quite a bit of my sentiment hadn't sprung from me. Yes, my nature was to be curious about things, but had magic manipulated that? Would I have fallen for Felaern without a push from Zoras?

My stomach knotted at the thought of Felaern. Zoras and Beldroth had traveled to Alenor before meeting us in the Mother's Den to awaken the goddess. I hadn't had the guts nor opportunity to ask Zoras before he died whether he'd run into Felaern. But if Felaern lived, the news of Zoras's visit would have reached him, and I doubted avoiding him was an option.

I tensed every time I thought about it. Felaern had been pivotal in my life. Without Felaern, I would not have broken free from Zoras's spells. Without Felaern, I would not have had Elliah.

Without Felaern, I would not have lived my last eighty years on the run, hunted, afraid… angry.

"And now?" Beldroth asked, making me jump.

"And now what?" Was Beldroth reading my mind? What had we been talking about? Oh, Alenor. I tossed my head at the city. "Pit of vipers."

Beldroth grunted. "Even vipers break their teeth on stone." I looked askance at him, broad and tall and solid as a rock.

"It isn't their physical prowess that threatens me," I said, tapping the side of my head.

"Yes," Beldroth replied, as serious as a boulder. "Their silky golden hair intimidates me as well."

A burble of laughter escaped me, drawing the snooty attention of the High Elf walking beside the mucker. I didn't care. "How are we mere mortals to compete?"

Truth be told, I'd always been a bit jealous of High Elf hair. It wasn't enough that it shimmered like precious metal. I'd witnessed that it was infinitely more malleable than my brown mop. They reshaped their locks with so little effort that it almost seemed like magic was involved.

"Perhaps hair stores their charm magic," Beldroth posed.

"To think," I replied with a hint of playfulness, "we could counter their magic with a pair of scissors."

Beldroth inhaled and let his breath out slowly. "If you grew up around here, surely you must have had friends. People you trust?"

He'd eased me into that with a bit of humor. Smart.

I sighed, grimacing.

"I had friends. For the most part, just folks to burn hours with. A few real relationships. Only one that I would trust with my life, and we left her behind at Heartshield Hall."

Beldroth thought deeply. "Axilya?"

I nodded.

"The one with the golden hair?" he asked, stroking his hair as though his bristly light-blond mane were long and silky.

"That's the one." I smiled, but it faded quickly. "She protected me in small ways, though I didn't understand until I met Felaern. The mental exercises to protect from mind magic? She taught them to me, though she never explained their purpose. She kept me busy with books and adventures, away from Zoras as much as possible." We walked a few steps in silence. "I don't know it for certain, but I suspect I owe her my life."

I clicked my tongue, irritated with what I'd just said. It painted the wrong picture. "I don't think Zoras intended to harm me. I think he thought he was protecting me, in his own misguided way." Beldroth's eyes opened wide with mock incredulity. "Yes, I know. A month ago, I would have assured you his every move had been pure cold calculation." My eyes strayed to his covered body on the cart. "But I misjudged him."

Beldroth walked beside me in silence, letting me process and speak. "But to answer your question, Axilya, I would trust. The rest of this lot, even the ones I called friends? Brood of vipers."

"Hm," he grunted. After a few steps, he elaborated. "I met one I liked."

"When?" I asked. "On your trip here with Zoras?"

He nodded agreement.

"Then he was probably tricking you," I said. How had I once thought it exciting to ply my magic against theirs? How many times had Zoras or Axilya plucked Hooks from my mind that I'd not even noticed?

When feelings of parental love washed over me, I pushed them away, questioning whether they were even real or simply dregs of spells I'd imbibed decades before. "Using a spell to encourage you to lower your guard."

He pondered my statement, patient as a stone, and I wanted to kick him. He had no mind magic. None of my feelings for him were fake or planted. I'd had a depressingly bad history with men: a father who sent me away because he wanted a son, a paternal guardian who hacked my emotions for decades, a lover who wanted our child dead. *Oh, let's not forget the arranged marriage I walked away from to choose said prized High Elf lover.* Beldroth was open and honest. It was why I loved him. And why it infuriated me that he obsessed about the Mother of Trees and his "mission." But that was on me—he'd always been true. Kicking him was an okay response, wasn't it? It wouldn't hurt him at all. Inside, I laughed at the imagery, and it almost made its way out.

"No," he said. "No, I really don't think so. It doesn't matter. I can't recall his name." Mischief danced in Beldroth's eyes. "But if you see a High Elf with golden hair…"

I smiled, tucking away my fears for my daughter, my angst about Beldroth's obsession, my dread about running into Elliah's father, and focusing on our most immediate hurdle: how to find a High Elf who had the skill to help Elliah, without getting ourselves bespelled. "I'll let you know when I spot him."

Beldroth : 1

I stood straighter for having drawn a smile from Illiara—plucking her from her dark mood had been harder than fighting the dragon. But my shoulders drooped at the sight of another cadre of High Elf soldiers hastening toward us from Alenor.

The elves from the border fortress had sent a messenger ahead. Just as the hideous stone replica of a silvervein they used as their seat of governance poked its top into view, the soldiers surrounded us. Without a word, they blended with the old guard, doubling the number of soldiers in the party.

"Did they increase their guard because we've become more fierce as we approach their capital?" I cringed, chagrined at the lack of faith in my words. I knew more guards meant nothing; the Mother's plans moved like a boulder down a mountain. Yet I'd spoken with hollow empathy in an attempt to sound concerned.

"Honor guard for Zoras," Illiara said, once again grim as granite.

I wanted to connect with Illiara. Not only did she carry our child, she didn't put up with nonsense. Occasionally she introduced it, but she never put up with it. She had convictions, even if they didn't always align with mine, and that drew me to her. It made me say things I would not normally say, like trying to show concern for a seemingly dire situation as though the Mother weren't in control.

A High Elf shuffled back from in front of the mucker. "Ho!" he shouted. Then he turned and with a raised voice, said, "Captain, it's that Warder!"

He received no response, and he visibly deflated as everyone, including me, marched on. *That Warder?* Could it be?

"But Captain?" the High Elf continued, and I grinned when I placed his voice. The Mother had a reason for everything. "You said you wanted an opportunity to show the Warder what's what."

"Shut up and get back in formation, Trentius." The cart and driver obscured my view of the speaker, but his voice also sounded familiar. They were the guards I'd confronted on my trip to Alenor with Zoras—a spectacle crafted to draw attention to Zoras's arrival.

The dejected High Elf hurried back into formation, mumbling, "I was really hoping to learn what's what."

As he disappeared from view, I said softly to Illiara, "I remember the name of the High Elf I liked."

"That's nice," she said, her thoughts somewhere dark.

"Hmph," I grunted, recognizing that I had another dragon-slaying battle ahead to win back Illiara's joy. "Hughelas?" He looked away from the emerging town to see what I wanted. "You should go walk with that fellow. Trentius. I think he would enjoy telling you about Alenor."

Hughelas looked down at Elliah.

"She's not going anywhere," her mother said. Hughelas looked hesitant. "Okay, she *is* going somewhere, and the more you learn about that somewhere, the better chance she has of leaving it again. Now, scoot."

Hughelas scooted.

We walked in silence for ten paces, then twenty. Finally, I asked, "Couldn't you have told Hughelas about Alenor? You've been there. You lived nearby." Relatively nearby—Zoras's mansion, Hearthshield Hall, lay several days walk away.

"I spent months at a time in Alenor when I was younger than Elliah," Illiara said. "When Zoras was active in the High Council." She frowned like I'd dug into an old wound. "Yes, I could tell Hughelas more. But, firstly, it's good if he makes a friend here. From the sound of it, that elf has been on the receiving end of too many compulsion spells. And, two, I don't feel like talking."

"Hmph," I said, in lieu of, *"That was a long speech for someone who doesn't wish to talk."*

"A pit of sodding vipers!" she spat out, gaining no more than dismissive glances from our High Elf guards.

I let her walk a few paces, then I added, gently, "But we need them." My tone lifted at the end, asking more than telling. I didn't understand her vehemence that Elliah needed the ministrations of a High Elf. Illiara, the sharp-tongued Wood Elf who'd grown roots into my rocky and sun-bleached heart, cast Heals with a tenacity that bordered on the impossible. But bumps to the head were tricky, and Elliah had smacked hers when she'd passed out at the end of our encounter with the Mother of Trees. Still, I'd seen warriors awaken from head wounds after long periods of rest. Yet Illiara was convinced Elliah needed High Elf mind magic to awaken.

We carried on a few more steps before she answered. "I know. And I know we talked about this already, but it tears me up to think of one of them messing around in her mind. I've spent her *life* keeping her away, teaching her how to guard her head, and now I'm walking her right into their open arms. Will they kill her outright? No. But will some complex set of events lead to her death through what looks like coincidence?"

"We won't let that happen," I said, determined to help, even if I didn't understand Illiara's convoluted reasoning.

"We're going to outsmart the High Elves? The game masters?" Her words, both angry and scared, sounded… final. Yet she walked her daughter into the trap. Admittedly, I didn't see another good choice. Fighting our way out without killing any of our High Elf honor guards would be tricky. But the Mother had Blessed my mission, and said Eliah would live, so whatever path we chose would be okay. If only Illiara accepted that, she would find peace. But telling her that directly only provoked her anger.

"You've done it once," I reminded her. "Your daughter lives because you got her away."

She pursed her lips but said nothing.

"You will do it again." I didn't smile, as much as it pained me. I wanted to smile. "And this time you have friends."

She barked a chuckle of disbelief. "Brawn won't get us out of Alenor, Beldroth."

"Maybe not," I said. "But don't forget, we have Hughelas."

She raised an eyebrow at that. Hughelas was smart. As smart an elf as I'd ever met. I could tell my son had even impressed Zoras. The Mother only knew where he got it from… not me. Hughelas was also clever, not just book-smart, though he chewed through every book that survived the destruction of Bellon. But he wasn't sneaky. Would he be able to see through High Elf plots and plans?

"And I have more than brawn," I said. It wasn't all about strength, or brains. Despite myself, I couldn't hold my tongue nor the joy that came from the certainty of having the Mother's Blessing. "I wield truth."

Hughelas #1

I ground my teeth, unleashing my anger in a form more acceptable than hitting the imbecile I'd been sent to for information. I kept reminding myself he was just simple, and my father appreciated simplicity. Yet I had so much to think through, and I needed quiet. The Mother of Trees, the goddess my father had sought for a Blessing, had been *dying*. Unlike elves, who physically never aged beyond adulthood, the Mother had seemed old, even feeble, and most definitely out of her mind. What did that mean? What had she done to Elliah? What did it imply for us? She'd said I was going to die, and while my father was prepared to sacrifice his life for his cause… I no longer felt the same.

But I still cared about Elliah. While strapping Elliah to the cart that morning, I thought she'd stirred. I couldn't shake the feeling she was closer to wakefulness than we believed. With more time, might we have been able to rouse her from her comatose state? It wasn't that I didn't think the High Elves were capable of helping. I'd read enough about their magic to trust they might be able to wake her. But would she ever be free of them again?

"That old inn has been there as long as I can remember," Trentius commented as we passed a building just inside a crude stone wall that stretched out of sight in each direction. The wall deterred random creatures of the forest from entering the outskirts of Alenor, or so Trentius had informed me, though, "some still found their way in." In truth, most trolls would have stepped right over it, so it obviously hadn't been built to defend Alenor from attack. Nothing like the wall my father and I had witnessed the trolls building.

"And how long is that?" I asked, my words seeping in bitterness. I'd quickly realized something was not right with Trentius. Undoubtedly, that was why my father and Illiara had sent me to talk with him—to learn what I could from his simple mind while the other High Elves kept quiet. Of course, the only reason the High Elves didn't stop him from talking was because he said nothing of import.

"I don't remember," Trentius answered.

Of course you don't. He had the mental depth of a turnip.

Unlike Zoras.

Despite what the others thought, I'd *liked* Zoras. He'd shared knowledge with me, and a thousand years of knowledge was nothing to scoff at. As much as I loved books, they were no substitute for a living teacher. Plus, if he'd lived, he would have had the authority to keep Elliah out of the lion's den. That had been the whole point of our endeavor with the Mother of Trees. Not from my father's perspective, of course, but for Elliah and her mother, they merely wanted to live without fear of being hunted.

"That pile of rubble used to be a shield factory," Trentius said, pointing to a blackened heap of stones off to our left. Simple, small homes and shops dotted the terrain, the spaces between them larger than what I expected to see in Alenor proper. "Runeguard Forges, or something like that. They claimed they'd worked out how to imbue magical protection into their shields. Of course, charlatans have been claiming that forever. I mean, why build your business waaaaay out of the main part of town if you had something so valuable to sell?"

Perhaps to keep their secret? I was reminded of the protection at the entrance to the wall surrounding the Mother of Trees. *Something* had bespelled us. If not for Elliah, the magic would have stopped us. "What happened to it?" I asked.

Trentius shrugged like it didn't matter. "Probably just an accident. Forges get hot after all. Perhaps a dissatisfied customer?"

"A dissatisfied shield bearer would likely not be alive to take revenge," I pointed out.

"A relative of said purchaser then," the High Elf suggested, nodding his head in agreement. Getting into the discussion, he continued. "Or perhaps they had figured out how to imbue spells, but the process was inherently dangerous." His voice took on a singsong quality. "'On the cusp of riches, Runeguard Forges incinerates their future.' or 'Their passion for shields consumes them.' You know, because it burned up."

I stared, open-mouthed, for several paces. "What are you doing?"

"What's that?" he asked.

"Why did you say those things... the way you said them?" His statements sounded so odd.

"Oh," Trentius said, a sharp intensity in his eyes darting away, making me question what I'd seen. "There's this new thing. They're calling it a newspaper, because it has daily news on it, and, well, it's on paper, I suppose. They put events of interest in it, and I quite like the way they create catchy titles at the top of each section. 'Runeguard Forges all fired up.'"

"That's terrible," I said.

"No, it's not," he responded. "I think I might have a career opportunity."

"Definitely," said the High Elf up front who I believed to be their captain. "You should pursue that. You certainly don't lack for words." Yes, the way the others' eyes tracked him and their ears perked when he spoke—he was their leader.

It was obvious to me and the others that the captain poked fun at Trentius, yet Trentius struggled. His eyes pinched as he warred with himself over whether to be complimented or offended. He quickly recovered and moved on, ignoring both possibilities. "'The secrets of Runeguard Forges go up in smoke,'" he said. "I mean, what if they *had* discovered the secret to imbuing magic into shields? That would have been a tragic loss."

"No one has figured out how to imbue magic into shields, Trentius," the captain said, his voice harsh with impatience. "If they did, they would be famous."

But that's exactly where my thoughts had gone. To what extremes would someone go to protect such a secret? I mumbled, "In a world of the blind, the one-eyed man reigns."

"And you thought mine was terrible," Trentius said with a laugh. "That's not on theme at all."

The captain turned and appraised me with an eyebrow raised. "I'm new to your game," I said, looking down like I was embarrassed. The last thing I wanted was attention. I knew I was smart, a trait uncommon among Warders. I wanted to use the prejudice of our captors to my advantage. Particularly when they were armed with mind spells and I was not.

We moved past the remains of the structure and headed into a busier district. It reminded me of Telloria'ahlia, only on flat ground and with greater order. Smoke poured from chimneys, and intricate and mighty chains spun wheels on mechanical devices whose purpose eluded me. The scent of burning oil grew stronger, though not thick. Ornate designs decorated the buildings and streets: beautiful statues of dignified High Elves stood before curved stone bulwarks decorated with tile frescos. The detail was fantastic—I reached out to touch the statue of a stern-faced woman and felt the weave of the fabric carved into her dress. The structure and order came in the form of the spacing, all well-thought-out, so that each block took the same number of steps, no storefront blocked another, and everyone went about their business quietly. Very quietly. An unnerving tranquility blanketed the city, even the noise from the chains and wheels remained hushed as though afraid to wake a parent.

Before long, my hackles stood on end; the quiet fed my fears. It wasn't the quiet that got to me per se. I cherished sitting with a good book for hours in a silent huddle. The ruins of Bellon, where I'd grown up, seeped with muted history. But Telloria'ahlia, the river-port city of mixed-breed elves, hummed, chirped, thumped, and cheered with noise. The people and the noise went together. The streets of Alenor weren't as busy as those of Telloria'ahlia, but the lack of appropriate noise weighed on me. Children followed adults politely. Adults nodded to other elves as they passed, or they ignored each other altogether. Even the other muckers in the streets kept to themselves. Were the elves communicating with each other through their minds? Did they have laws against chatter and clatter? I wanted to grab Elliah and pull her out of Alenor, desperate to wake her without the High Elves.

I kicked the wheel of the cart, helpless and defiant, and a hundred eyes turned at the sound. An unpleasant buzzing filled my ears but faded as the High Elves went back about their business. I trudged onward.

It wasn't that there was *nothing* I could do, though my options were limited. It was that I didn't know what I *wanted*. When my father had started us on the quest to obtain the Mother's Blessing, I was more than happy to go with him. The ten years of his vigil after my mother died had left me stir-crazy. He wasn't the only one who'd lost someone dear to him. But I would have taken up any cause to leave that life behind. I hadn't truly believed in his mission. Then I'd met Elliah, and I'd connected with a kindred spirit, and that had grown into something more. Then came Zoras, with his vast knowledge, and his mansion full of books. He'd let me take a couple, with the promise I would return them. I looked sourly at his corpse and wondered whether my obligation to return his books continued after his death.

What did *I* want? My father wanted to recruit the Alluvium to his cause. I wouldn't abandon my father. Elliah and Illiara wanted freedom, and I didn't want to be separated from Elliah. Illiara walked them into the stomach of the beast in hopes that coming out the other end undigested would set them free. That was crazy. But the books—the knowledge which had sung to me—sat *inside the belly*. It was unfair that the treasure I craved sat locked in a vault that made my skin crawl.

I looked around, trying to find something redeeming in Alenor. A masterfully-built aqueduct looked down upon us from the north, but before we neared it, our procession turned east, onto a wider avenue, and the stone silvervein, previously only glimpsed between buildings, blocked our passage a few minutes' walk down the road.

"It's so... symmetrical," I observed, when I realized Trentius watched for my reaction.

"Isn't it though," Trentius said with pride, as though he himself had been involved in the planning or construction of their governing house.

The symmetry bothered me. Trees weren't symmetrical. Yes, it looked like a silvervein, only with gray stone for leaves and darker stone for the trunk. That took craftsmanship. And the leaves gleamed in color from light bouncing off jewels or metal embedded in the structure.

But that isn't what trees look like!

I looked over the cart at my father, who shook his head and grimaced at the stone tree. Illiara didn't give the building a second glance. Her eyes searched the crowd that lined the street.

They did not look pleased. Grim faces lined the street all the way to the tree. Even the children stared at us. But, more unnerving than the stony glares, was the utter quiet. That many people should have made noise. A baby crying. Children whining. Adults conversing about the weather as they waited.

"Go through your exercises," Illiara said, not loudly. Yet, in the relative silence, I heard her plainly. "They won't throw stones... but you might wish that's what they'd done."

Slate and shards!

Calming my mind was not the easiest thing under the stoic glares of hundreds of pairs of golden eyes. I didn't think I'd ever seen that many people together at once, much less had them all focus their attention on me. Not entirely on me, I realized. Rather, on our group. But some were locked on me. Why?

Filthy half-breed! An image formed in my mind of a slug with feet, then a bird with arms instead of wings. The otherness of the images helped me focus, and I quickly erected barriers like laying bricks around my mind. Me, in. Nightmares, out.

Illiara had trained us for weeks, and though she'd couched the exercises as lessons for calming and clearing one's mind, I'd recognized them from things I'd read—defenses against mind magic. Warders were believed to have a natural resistance, though not an immunity. I'd heard plenty of complaints from Warders who'd fought under the command of High Elves on the front. Though I'd never said it aloud, I wondered how many of their complaints were couched in wanting to blame someone else for their actions. Still, even if Warders had resistance, I was only half-Warder. My Salt half would be fully exposed.

We marched forward, and because I wasn't skilled enough to block out the incoming thoughts, the monsters spilled into the crowd. To my left, an elf had the head of a golden bull with horns. To my right, one had long claws instead of hands. Over the silence, I heard gibbering whispers and hisses that weren't there. The fake sounds I couldn't stop. My bricks only limited the visions. *Get out of our city, half-breed.* No one's lips moved. *You bring a curse upon us. She should never have lived.*

"She is the Mother's creation," my father declared loudly, and my head experienced something like the release of pressure as when one returns from deep water to the surface.

"Don't respond," Illiara said. "They'll just intensify their efforts."

My father looked at Illiara, then grinned. He pointed to a man on the left. "Good one!" Then he nodded to a woman farther down the line. "I killed something like that once along the Contentious. Only it was much bigger." Looking to his right, he said. "Now how would that actually eat? It's got no mouth." He chuckled as we continued down the road, providing feedback to the crowd on their mental creations.

My own burden grew lighter. The crowd had shifted their magic to focus on my father. Likely that was his intent. He appeared none the worse for it; he grinned and laughed. But the pinch in his eyes told a different story. Still, he took the brunt of the attack.

The occasional defamation or threat still slipped through, and I glimpsed non-elf body parts here and there, but not like that first minute. I scanned the crowd for Wood Elves. My father said he'd seen some on his trip. But if they were there, they kept themselves hidden.

I'd been looking behind the main line, and almost missed a step when I realized a woman to my left was half-naked, her golden breasts gleaming in the sun. I couldn't help but look, and without moving her lips, she said, *Filthy half-breed.* Only, it sounded less like a threat and more like… an invitation?

I looked over at my father, wondering why he hadn't said anything. *Just for you, half-breed.* I looked back at her, and she bit on her lower lip. *Just for you. Find me. Ithronel.* Her clothes faded into existence, but she continued biting her lip. Did she wink?

Slate and shards, High Elves are a mess!

We continued up the street, my father calling out encouragingly to the crowd, who, to my perception, had shifted in some way. Their stoic demeanors had cracked. Faces bore hints of smiles. Others looked eager, ready for their turn. Unfortunately, many looked genuinely angry. Not that their anger changed my father's approach. Fortunately, there were no more incidents like that crazy woman whose spell I couldn't quite shake. I looked back for her, but she had melted into the crowd. Yet I heard a laugh like water trickling over rocks.

As we approached the uncomfortably symmetric stone tree, the passageway between onlookers widened, and a complete gap appeared before a group of High Elves in formal robes who blocked our further passage. One, two, three… twelve. Twelve High Elves, with no emotion across any of their faces. They looked taller than the crowd, and I wondered if that was real, perspective, or magic. Or tall boots under the fancy robes?

The thirteenth member of their council rode with us, next to Elliah, and even the preservation spells we'd bathed Zoras in had not kept him looking fresh. The captain of our guard led the cart wide and rolled it to a stop so that Zoras lay stretched before the council. Since that was the side I'd been on, I fell back through the turn and circled behind, as did most of the guards, including Trentius. We formed two rows behind Elliah, the guard behind me, Illiara, and my father. Though we weren't technically prisoners, they made it clear that walking away was not an option.

The pressure in my head, already diminished compared to when we started down the road, disappeared altogether. The populace was not pushing their spells in front of their leaders. Yet my father's mirth faded. Illiara's eyes were on her daughter, her head down. Was her worry so consuming, or did she hope that not looking at her captors would prevent them from seeing her?

I knew too little to have specific fears. High Elves' strength was mental magic. Yes, that was concerning, even frightening. But which, if any, of them would use that magic without scruples? I'd read enough to understand that morality was relative. Warders prized honesty while High Elves coveted mastery. I couldn't say whether every one of the High Elves along the road had poked into our minds, but many had. Yet they'd done it out of a fierce loyalty to their beliefs, a form of morality that everyone respected in their own community and despised in others. Could I condemn the whole lot? A memory of golden breasts intruded, and I wondered where that fit in their morality. I looked guiltily down at Elliah as though I'd done something wrong, though the High Elf's spell had not been my choice or my fault.

I turned my gaze to the High Council. Half were women, and half men. The cut of the robes for the women differed from the men, but many of their faces were indistinguishable to my eye. Golden-skinned with gold hair and eyes; though it was always difficult to guess age on elves, their stern faces and stillness suggested longevity. They'd left a gap between the first six members and the next, like they'd broken into two camps. Zoras had been their tiebreaker, making the council more men than women, and, knowing Zoras, they were balanced in other ways. Zoras had implied he'd initiated the High Council centuries before. Was the council really any more than a curtain behind which Zoras hid? What would they do with Zoras gone?

"Illiara," said a council member toward the middle, his robe and the timbre of his voice declaring his gender. "Your death, and that of your daughter, was greatly exaggerated. I, for one, am pleased by the surprise."

Illiara kept her head down.

A female spoke up from the other group of six. "She fled to dodge death, but it followed her back."

"Yet not the death we had appointed," retorted the first speaker. "There is much to untangle here, and I suspect the puzzle, when assembled, will tell us who shall replace Zoras on the council."

"For once, we agree," said the woman. "You will be guests of the Luminarium while we sort this out, Illiara Silverheart. You and your companions. Guards, show them to their rooms. We will attend to Zoras." They didn't call us prisoners, but neither were they asking for our input.

Two guards from our escort moved to unstrap Elliah from the cart. Illiara stepped in front of one, blocking his way. When he shifted to the side to go around her, she pivoted to protect Elliah. The other guard worked the straps at Elliah's feet, and my father held up a hand between Illiara and the deflected guard. My father nodded to Illiara, who let him pass and untie the remaining straps. My father took his hammer from between the two bodies on the cart and put it in a harness he still kept on his back. He gently cradled Elliah in his arms, and we followed our escorts into the false silvervein.

They led us up countless stairs and down a hall to a single large room that must have been out on a stony branch of the silvervein, if one had viewed it from below. Across from the entrance lay a balcony that let in light, and the room opened to the right and left. Two large beds sat at opposite ends from each other, windows on the far side of each bed bringing a cross-breeze of fresh air. Well, what passed for fresh air in Alenor—the faint scent of smoke and oil dusted the city. Between the entrance and the balcony nestled chairs and a table that held paper and pen, as well as a tray with wine and cheese.

My father turned to the left and placed Elliah on the bed, then he removed the hammer and set it next to Elliah. Was his melancholic frown for the elf or the hammer?

"Anyone have a hook?" Illiara asked, pouring herself a glass of wine. She plopped into a chair, sipping at her glass then nodding.

"A hook?" I asked. For fishing?

She waved her free hand at her head. "Anything you can't seem to take your mind off of. A recurring thought."

"Glintfish stew," my father answered as golden breasts appeared unbidden in my mind.

Illiara let loose a single bark of laughter.

My father's brows bunched, then headed for the door. "I'll just ask if they have any."

Illiara frowned. "Wait, you really want this… glintfish stew… enough to go ask about it?"

"Yes, I can't get it out of my head." He looked irritated with himself.

"Okay, then. That's a hook. An odd one, but a hook. When we walked through the… gathering… of High Elves, some will have dangled bait before you. They're often quite random, but occasionally," she smiled at my father as she finished, "they catch something."

"Glintfish stew was a dish my mother introduced him to," I supplied.

"Disgusting, pasty stuff," my father said with a frown. "And yet I want some."

"Come, sit by me," Illiara told my father. "I know the spell to remove a hook. Axilya taught it to me early on, even though it is nearly impossible to cast it on yourself."

A topless gold-skinned woman inhaled deeply. "*Find me. Ithronel,*" she breathed out, her name hardly more than a sigh.

I smiled in relief. The image was a hook, and it was removable. I wasn't obsessed.

Illiara put her hands on my father's head, mumbling a spell and moving her fingers lightly. She stilled and quieted, then laughed, "That is… rather disturbing." She removed her hands. "So slimy."

"Isn't it though?" my father said, sighing and leaning back. "Thank you. That's much better.

"Of course. They consider it a harmless game that hones their skills." She rubbed her hands together like she needed to warm them. "You?" Illiara asked, looking at me.

She had seen the content of his hook. She would see mine. It was just a harmless game.

"No," I said quickly. "I guess I got lucky." I didn't want Elliah's mother seeing I'd been hooked by an image of a half-naked elf. If it was just a harmless game, then there was no point in enduring that embarrassment. Tinkling laughter, like water over rocks, echoed in my mind.

"Good. Your father took the brunt of the attacks with his bold," she rolled her eyes, "move." She took another drink of her wine. "Actually, it was inspired. It not only took the heat off the rest of us, but many enjoyed the challenge."

"A few were quite… interesting," my father reported, then grinned.

"I'll bet," Illiara said, shaking her head slightly. They were an unlikely couple, my father and Illiara. I don't think they'd put any conscious thought into their relationship, but from my outside view, their attraction stemmed from a mutual recognition of their individual estrangement. Simply put, because my father appreciated simplicity, they had no other options. She took her glass and the bottle of wine and moved to sit by Elliah on the bed.

"Dangerous things, hooks, if left in," she said. "A game for them, but they're not supposed to play it with other species of elves. Obviously that didn't stop them." She moved her daughter around a bit, to no apparent purpose. "That's probably what messed up that poor Trentius fellow. Someone didn't get a hook out quickly enough."

Tinkling laughter danced in my head.

Slate and shards!

Illiara - 3

The dark wine slowly but diligently worked its magic on my jangling nerves. *Holy Mother of rotting Trees, I'm back in the blasted Luminarium!*

More wine needed.

But when I turned to get the bottle from the nightstand, Elliah's weight shifted because of my movement, and I set my glass down instead. It would be a mistake to lower my guard to the extent that the wine would take it.

But I let Beldroth and Hughelas sort out their packs while I closed my eyes and attempted to tune out my location and our plight. Eighty-plus years of practice helped me clear my mind.

Tap, tap, tap...

I bolted upright at the whisper of our door swinging open. We would need to do something to make that louder, so that no one could sneak in, or I would never sleep.

I settled back as Beldroth walked to the door. He would handle it, send our jailer or attendant packing, perhaps ferociously or maybe with a request for something better than glintfish stew.

"Yes?" Beldroth asked as I admired his muscle-bound arms detailed in blue ink depicting symbols he'd explained as important to his deceased Salt wife.

"I'm here for Elliah," said the last voice I wanted to hear in all the world.

"Felaern..." I heard myself say, the name hitting my ears like it came from someone else entirely. The sharp, tangy smell of expensive ink, so unlike the sooty, smoky smell of the ink within my price range, yanked me back in time eighty years. Confusingly, it was a time of peace and excitement for me, before I was on the run. My senses betrayed me, the familiar taste of wine on my lips and the smells of the High Elves warring with the adrenaline pumping through my veins upon hearing the voice of Elliah's father.

Time jumbled, yet I found myself off the bed, dagger in hand. Felaern, in his youth, had won every mind contest, broken every record. Zoras had picked him up and taught him, then sent him on missions that tested and grew him. Treaties negotiated to the benefit of the High

Elves, battlefields regained, uprisings quelled… secrets stolen. But the trip to the Dragon Lands he'd made on his own. He was supposed to be on the Salt island of Ast Velera. I didn't remember why and possibly I never knew. But he'd returned from that trip changed. Lit by an inner fire that drew me like a moth to a flame. Zoras had warned us—mixed races of elves more often birthed Bereft children. We hadn't listened. When Zoras directed Felaern's flame toward our child, I ran. I knew what a threat he was, how dangerous he could be. My dagger pointed at his neck, held back from my former lover by the powerful arm of the man I'd chosen to replace him. Hughelas shifted around his father, getting behind me and closer to Elliah while I panted like a trapped animal.

"Illiara," Felaern replied with civility. "You need not worry. Our interests are aligned… for now."

His words—"for now"—floated in my mind, suggesting that a temporary alignment, being more believable, ought to be more trusted. I poked at my mental constructs, trying to see where he'd leaked in, wondering whether I would be able to tell. I'd had eighty years of practice. But so had he.

"You'll not go near my daughter," I said, reining in my rage and fear, but failing to keep an audible shake out of my voice.

"*Our* daughter," he corrected. Beldroth raised an eyebrow. Beldroth knew Elliah's father was a High Elf. I blushed. My hesitation in sharing the details with Beldroth would cost me. "And someone will. Go near your daughter, I mean. It's why you're here. Better me than a stranger; I already know your secrets. And I'll be blunt: I need this. Saving… *our*… daughter gets me the votes I need to fill the vacancy on the High Council."

"So that's all this is then?" I asked, covering my embarrassment with accusations. "A play for power? That's all *my* daughter's life means to you?" Anger overcame my shame and flowed over the dam of self-preservation, loosing my tongue further. "You tried to have her killed!"

"Nonsense," Felaern responded, still calm. "On both counts. Joining the council is not a play for power. It's a necessary step to save elves. And I never tried to have Elliah killed. I kept her safe. I tricked the council into thinking she died as a baby. Not everyone believed, so it hasn't been easy, but I've kept her, and you, alive… as best I could."

"Do *not* try to pretend you've been our *benefactor*!" Though I told myself I had to remain calm, the very idea made my skin itch. He needed me to lose my cool, let my guard down. And he thought he knew me well enough to trip me up with my own vines. "Stop talking," I said, as he opened his mouth to speak.

"I've known your whereabouts ever since you left," he said, ignoring my directive. "Celendril, Ylva, Curanne, then disappearing deeper—"

"Make him stop talking," I said to Beldroth.

"—into the Border Woods after I had the nursery burned—"

His hauntingly familiar chronicle of my early days as a fugitive came to an abrupt halt when Beldroth's mighty hand closed around Felaern's throat, lifting him slightly so that Felaern stood on his tippy toes, his long golden fingers pulling without effect at Beldroth's lighter-skinned digits.

It was a dangerous move, but Beldroth didn't know that. I'd meant for Beldroth to hit Felaern, not choke him. I wouldn't have much time. Even a Warder's natural resistance wouldn't hold long.

I squandered the time thinking. Felaern had known where we were. For the entire eighty years? Perhaps not, but he knew where I'd bolted at the start. It had been a dumb move, running home. Anyone might have guessed that. The fire... Elliah could have been killed! Had he truly arranged that? Still...

Beldroth set Felaern down, and the hulking Warder backed up a step, causing me to stumble backwards, barely keeping myself from falling. Hughelas drew his sword, backing closer to Elliah.

"Wait," I said, holding out an arm between Felaern and Hughelas like that would stop them, and to my surprise, everyone did as I asked.

"Where were we recently?" I asked Felaern.

He didn't even grin or acknowledge the thought behind the question.

"Your last home was in E'anashys," Felaern answered.

He *had* known. Eighty years of running from a man who'd known exactly where we were the entire... rotting... time.

That only made me angrier, but not so angry as to lose my senses and lay hands on an elf whose mind magic grew more effective through touch. "Why?" I demanded. "Why let me think you were hunting me, that I had to run?"

"You *were* being hunted," he said, his golden eyes showing a hint of amusement, a break in his cold shell. It reminded me, distressingly enough, of the elf I'd once loved. "Running was prudent."

From his perspective, knowing our whereabouts would also have been prudent. But it didn't mean Elliah's life hadn't been at risk

41

from Felaern. Once everyone believed Elliah dead, it was simply… prudent… to let her live. After all, he could have finished the job at his leisure if he knew where she was.

Would we have made it to Alenor if we hadn't encountered Zoras on the way? What would have been the *prudent* move by Felaern? What would have best advanced his plans?

"Let him go," I said, nodding to Beldroth.

Felaern blinked once, the small motion putting me in mind of a wolf cocking its head in curiosity. "You understand that I have the advantage here?"

"I do," I said. And he *did* have the upper hand. Between his magic and his temporary control over Beldroth, whom neither Hughelas nor I would want to hurt in a fight, Felaern called the shots.

Felaern nodded, and Beldroth took a step back, then shook his head like a mountain lion shaking itself dry.

When he crouched like he intended to pounce, I threw my arms up between the two men. I looked ridiculous, one arm outstretched in each direction, like I desired a truly gargantuan hug.

"Stop!" I urged Beldroth, looking over my shoulder. He raised an eyebrow at me, his veins popping with checked anger. Beldroth might have been able to take Felaern. A quick hit would knock Felaern out before the High Elf mind magic halted the raging Warder.

"Everyone… just… breathe," I said, nodding my head like they had already agreed to my proposal. I slowly lowered my arms.

What in the rotting Mother was I doing? If I wasn't stopping Felaern… was I supporting him?

No, no, no, no, no.

Breathe.

"I don't trust you," I said to Felaern. "You *can't* expect my trust. You know that."

"I know that," Felaern replied. "Our interests are aligned." His repeated statement grabbed my attention, as it was meant to do. *Our* interests. He didn't mean joint interests. He wanted to be on the Council. I wanted Elliah awake and safe. How far did our interests align? Solely waking Elliah?

"I want Elliah to be allowed to leave Alenor," I stated. "Alive," I added with haste. After a second where no one spoke, I put in one more condition. "And of sound mind."

Should I have added anything about Hughelas? Beldroth? Myself? What was I offering in sacrifice? Hughelas kept his sword drawn, but he let the tip drop. I risked a glance over my shoulder to see the mottled red of the Warder's fury fading to white, and his veins looking not quite so ready to burst.

"I can guarantee none of that," Felaern said. He held up a hand to forestall my outburst. "I have no idea what state Elliah is in. She may be gone." I almost didn't hear what he said after that. "But *my* waking Elliah is her best shot at leaving Alenor. Alive."

"She's not gone," Hughelas said, earning an unimpressed raised eyebrow from Felaern. "She was close when I spoke to her on the cart." He put a hand to his heart, looking at his father as if hoping he would understand. "I felt it." Beldroth nodded.

"I heard you were the smart one," Felaern said, his flat tone implying the opposite. "But you speak like a Warder. Truth is not relative. It is not personal."

"There we agree," Beldroth said. "But it doesn't mean my son is wrong."

The thought of Elliah being *gone* rattled me, returning me to a day eighty years before. "You would have killed her, Felaern." I'd been so sure. The Felaern I'd once loved had argued passionately with Zoras about elves and their future. Could I have been wrong? "Would you have killed her?"

But even before Elliah was born, something had dampened Felaern's fire. I'd assumed Zoras.

"You don't understand the forces at play, Illiara," he said. "The loss of *one child's* life will be nothing compared to what's coming."

Eighty years before, I'd caught glimpses of the cold metal beneath his flames; only the metal remained.

"You would have killed her," I concluded.

"I... I tell myself I would not have gone through with it," he said, surprising me with a moment of vulnerability. "That saving the elves from extinction wasn't worth the price."

For just a moment, I caught a glimpse of another man. Not the passionate Felaern I had loved, and not the cold automaton that had barged his way into our room. For just a moment, Felaern's eyes widened, and his golden pupils dilated as though fixed on something far away.

Then his eyes refocused, and his words held the same cold blade. "But that path would have led just as surely to her death."

"What's... changed?" I asked, prying at the fleeting fear that had left his eyes.

"Her utility," he answered. "I need to steer the council. You don't know it yet, but *you* need me to steer the council. Long ago, her death would have served that end. But, thanks to your mad dash, I failed, and Berix took Todley's seat. That's brought us eighty years further down the path of destruction." He closed his eyes and shook his head, then snapped his eyes open. "Now, our daughter's *life* gets me there. Zoras balanced the Utilitarians and the Deontologists. I'm considered a Utilitarian. This move, saving Elliah, would show that I choose ethics over utility."

I barked a disbelieving laugh. "You would save her life, for the utility of it proving you don't embrace utilitarianism?"

He nodded. "I would."

Mother of Trees, how had I ever loved such a man? He may have had powerful magic, but he was bereft of passion, his soul buried under six feet of steely determination. I instinctively turned to Beldroth, needing a connection with more warmth, and his brows were knotted in concentration and confusion.

"Utilitarians," I explained, "believe, essentially, that the end justifies the means. Deontologists believe each action must be chosen upon its own moral merit. The High Elves have argued over these two viewpoints for centuries." In my peripheral vision, Hughelas nodded like he understood, but Beldroth's brows drew even lower.

Sighing, I returned my attention to Felaern. "Why should I trust you over another?" I asked. "If I wait, one of your *Deontologist* friends will heal her just the same." Truth was, I didn't trust another High Elf, but I didn't trust Felaern either.

"Two minutes ago I would not have needed your permission," he answered, pointing out that the entire discussion was a boon he'd granted me. "But this I swear to you: should I be able to heal her, I will not leave any hooks or barbs or suggestions."

There was a lot packed into his words. An admonition that he'd had control and relinquished it, so I had no right to dictate terms. Also a reminder of how he had trained me to defend my mind, building on the principles Axilya had taught me when I'd lived under Zoras's roof. He had never tampered with my mind… except when I'd asked him to. It was that difference from Zoras which had drawn me to him. That and his former zeal. And, to my shame, his power.

"Why should I trust your word?" I asked, though I recognized I'd already lost the argument. That didn't mean he would necessarily regain control if I decided to fight him, but if he'd wanted her—or us—

dead, he could have achieved that goal already.

The right answer would have been something to the effect of, *because I am Elliah's father*. But he didn't say that. He looked at Beldroth and said, "You shouldn't trust anyone's word."

What in the fiery rivers of Cenaedth?

Without saying more, he pushed past me. Beldroth reached for him, and Hughelas raised his sword, but I held my palms out to each of them, shaking my head.

Felaern sat down on the bed next to our daughter, giving the hammer on the far side of her a questioning look, then placed his hands on her head. He cocked his head and jerked his fingers back, surprised.

Feeling slightly cocky that I knew something the great Felaern didn't, I moved the hammer so that it leaned against Elliah, then rested her hand on the hammer's head.

"Try again," I said. "Be gentle. She'll be scared."

Felaern placed his hands back upon Elliah, saying, "She should be."

Elliah ~ 2

"Elliah?"

    No voice should have penetrated my guard. I sent my watcher out while trying to duck deeper into a void that had no more depth.

    "Elliah!"

    The voice, though I knew it to be only in my mind, sounded masculine… familiar. Zoras? Maybe. Had it been closer?

    "Elliah!" The shout came a third time, louder than before. It had to be Zoras! I sent my watcher searching for him.

    "Elliah, where are you?" The voice sounded more distant, like it had turned a different direction. Well, good. That meant my hiding place was secure.

    My watcher, a piece of my mind, passed through wall after wall, many that I didn't recall having created, until finally…

    "Zoras," my watcher said upon seeing the familiar figure searching through a bleak landscape of my creation.

    He spun around.

    Not Zoras.

    I didn't completely freak out. I didn't jerk my watcher away. It wasn't the creature with two flaming red eyes that had raked claws through my mind. The High Elf kept his distance, letting my watcher approach him, giving me space.

    "Elliah," the stranger said, both a greeting and a confirmation. He looked a lot like Zoras—a High Elf with similar features. Zoras had a tendency to be aloof. I'd assumed it was because of his age—living a thousand years built up one's immunity to slight inconveniences and minor joys. Zoras had shown emotion, particularly when my mother had slit his throat, but even then, not to the degree that I would expect. Age had put a damper on him. But the elf before me raised it to a new height—cold calculation lay behind his golden eyes.

    "I don't know you," my watcher said for me.

    "No," he said. "I know you, though." He did? How?

    "This is good," he said, gesturing to the surrounding landscape, then he held out both hands toward me as he examined my watcher. "Your skill must come from your father." The hint of a smile glistened in his eyes. "There is hope for you."

Who are you? Why are you here?

His eyes turned back to cold metal.

"Your mother needs you," he said. My mother? Or my Mother? I pictured her, the Mother of Trees, slumbering with her head on her knees. I had the strongest feeling she did need me. Needed me to understand her... protect her... *wake* her? "She needs you *now*. If you want her to live, you need to come out." Then he flicked his hand and disappeared.

If I want her to live? That clarified things—he meant my biological mother, not my divine Mother. But my mother wouldn't live. None of them would. The goddess had spoken. They were all going to die.

But did I want her to die? No. No, I didn't. And the goddess hadn't said *when*. But the stranger made my mother's demise sound imminent.

Crying, I pulled down walls. Wall after wall after wall. They were terrible, clumsy things, but I'd hoped that having so many would conceal me. The stranger implied they'd worked.

Then I thought of those fearsome eyes, and I stopped. Could I really go back out there? The goddess's memories and thoughts had flooded the embankments of my mind. It hadn't particularly hurt; it had just been too much. But then that creature had shown up, and to get me out, it had clawed through my mind, tearing at the memories from the Mother as though they were strands instead of water. That *had* hurt. And even though it hadn't worked—it hadn't scooped out the Mother's memories—it had severed my connection with her. I'd cowered and buried myself, deeper and deeper. Was I ready to go back out and risk facing that monster?

For my mother, I would. Finally, I sensed my watcher nearby, waiting. One more wall and I would expose my soul. Closing my eyes, bracing for impact, I took it down.

***

Nothing consumed me. Nothing bore into my mind and soul. But everything *hurt*. Physical pain in my joints flared, my mouth dry like a desert, my eyes were gummed up, and even my breathing was labored.

"She's alive," said the voice I'd heard in my head. "Though you would hardly have known it. She'd created a wasteland and buried herself in it. Most would have declared her gone. Be glad I needed her."

"I'm ever so grateful," my mother said with unadulterated sarcasm.

Mom!

I forced my eyes to open, but I closed them again quickly, as the light hurt my head and the shapes made no sense.

"Elliah!" My mother's voice embraced me as her arms did the same. "Oh, Elliah, I was so scared."

I tried to talk, but all I managed was a dry cough. My mother released me and, in seconds, cool water dribbled into my mouth, which I promptly choked on.

"I'll leave you to it," said the unfamiliar voice as my mother began a very familiar Healing spell. "She may be a little confused. I lured her out with suggestions that you were in danger."

My mother's spell stumbled. She wasn't in danger? Why had I come out? The world glared and gonged and overwhelmed and I wished I were back in the dark.

"You hollow-hearted heretic," my mother said. "You wish to convince the council you prize duty over utility?"

"I do," said the voice from my head.

"Then start acting like it," my mother snarled.

"I did," said the other voice. "Would you have let me near Elliah if I had come crawling in with an emotional appeal claiming fatherly love?" Fatherly love? Wait! I tried to speak, to tell him to wait, but I only croaked. My father?!? A grim and unfamiliar laugh drifted away, and I barely heard his final words. "The others would have left her for dead… or buried her."

He was gone. I'd missed him. I tried to remember what I'd seen from my watcher. High Elf. Vaguely like Zoras. Nothing more. I wanted to scream.

After several seconds, my mother resumed casting her spell.

"Do you think he spoke the truth?" *Beldroth!* Beldroth was with us. Then surely, so was Hughelas. Where was Hughelas?

My mother finished her spell, but no magical relief soothed me. The very effort of breathing pained and wearied me. Her spell hadn't taken. I longed to return to living in my head.

"He doesn't outright lie," my mother said. "Or he never used to. But I don't know what to believe." She started back into her spell-casting.

"It might help his agenda *and* be the moral high ground." *Hughelas!* His voice had been right beside me. I cracked open my eyes, letting in the tiniest pinprick of light. It proved pointless—the sticky film covering them blurred everything, and the light hurt.

Groaning, I closed my eyes and tried to slip back away from the overstimulating world of the conscious.

"Less talking, more Healing," my mother snapped. I groaned when a heavy weight pinned down my arm. "It's just the hammer," my mother whispered. "I wanted it closer." She once again tried her spell.

More voices joined her chants, and I began to fade.

A wave of soothing balm washed over me, and I sighed my way into sleep instead of the darker place I'd intended.

Hughelas #2

When my mother died, the familiar cave walls that had always offered comfort and solace had turned harsh and cold, pressing in with the weight of the entire mountain, crushing my spirit. Impossibly, I felt the same way sitting high up in the Luminarium.

I'd hesitated to add my Heals to those of Elliah's mother and my father because I'd considered chasing after Felaern. I needed information about Hooks, most notably how to be free of them without revealing what baited the Hook. Then my Heal had landed, and a wave of excitement had coursed through me. My Heal had landed before Illiara's! When it happened, it momentarily connected me with her in some indefinable way, my magic catching for the first time. The mana drain was familiar, but when the spell landed, there was a sort of return feedback. Not energy or mana, just a sense of rightness, and Elliah had sighed, her eyes less puffy, her face less gaunt. It exhilarated me.

But as I'd gazed down at her peaceful face, another replaced it. Golden lips sighed, suggesting the completion of an entirely different activity.

I shook my head like a wet dog.

"You didn't like the sensation of Healing her," Illiara asked.

I had, but… how might I explain my actions?

"It just…" I worked my jaw but no words spilled from me.

Illiara cocked her head. "The first time can be startling," she offered.

Luckily, a knock at the door interrupted us.

My father's eyes narrowed, and after a quick glance at his hammer next to Elliah, he marched to the door like he intended to teach it a lesson.

"Yes?" he shouted through the door.

Another knock.

My father swung the door inward, opening it wide, revealing that he took up roughly the same space as the door. "Yes?" he inquired again.

"I am Elran," said a High Elf I could only see a part of from my angle. "I was sent by the High Council to restore the girl suffering from stillness of the mind."

"You're too late." My father was curt. I wasn't sure what had him out of sorts, but his usual smile was nowhere to be seen. And his response was misunderstood.

"She's passed on?" the elf enquired with surprise and... concern?

"No, the pompous know-it-all you passed in the hallway already woke her up." My father's tone remained snippy.

"I passed no one in the hall, and your description would eliminate very few people in the Luminarium." His tone was softer than most of the High Elves I had so far encountered, suggesting that he, perhaps, did not belong in that elite group.

"He just left!" my father barked. "You had to have walked right past—Hey! Stay out of my head! I'm not *hiding* anything from you." The High Elf hadn't moved; the spell he'd cast had been quite subtle. "His name was Felaern. He woke Elliah and went on his way. You must be blind to have missed him."

Elran inhaled deeply at the mention of Felaern. "You must be mistaken," he said. For a High Elf, he showed more emotion than I'd so far encountered.

Illiara rose from the bed and attempted to wedge her way past my father. It took him a moment to realize, but then he turned to let her through. I moved closer to get a better view. The High Elf was small-framed, conveying youth, and his cherubic face added to that perception. His eyes flicked to mine then back to Illiara. His sprightly features and uncharacteristic show of emotion made him less distasteful than Felaern.

"Do you think I mistook my child's father, Elran?" My father bristled at Illiara's statement, and it dawned on me why he'd been out of sorts. He loved Illiara, and Elliah's father had bested him. He didn't like losing. Who did?

"Illiara, I was pleased to hear that you live," Elran said, bowing his head slightly to her. "And I'm even more pleased to confirm it with my own eyes."

I couldn't see Illiara's face from my position, but judging from Elran's next words, I imagined her skeptical disbelief.

"Truly, Illiara," Elran continued. When he didn't get the response he hoped, he sighed with sadness. "Fine. Then if you won't believe that I specifically am happy to see you, at least believe that your return will ease tensions with the Wood Elves, who have almost entirely moved out of Alenor proper over the decades since your... sudden departure."

"I can accept that," Illiara said as she spun and returned to the bedside. "Elliah sleeps," she said brusquely. "Come back later."

"It is imperative that we speak," Elran said in a raised voice. He tried to squeeze in through the space Illiara had occupied, but my father closed the gap with a simple pivot, shaking his head no, but keeping his bare skin away from the High Elf's.

Rather than risk another dent in my father's ego, I spoke up. "I can talk with you. Elsewhere. If that helps." Besides, I had questions of my own.

Something nudged my mental defenses, but they held.

"And you are?" Elron asked.

"His name is Hughelas," Illiara said. "We've traveled together and been through enough that I trust him. He was there at the Mother of Trees, and a witness to Zoras's death. But like a blush knows it's been caught, I bet you knew all that."

Elron grinned good-naturedly. "Rumor flies faster than the wind," he said. "But neither one told me he has your trust. Come, Hughelas, let us leave the young princesses and their stony guard."

My father harrumphed, still irritated.

I hesitated despite myself. We needed information. With Elliah awake, the next step was getting out of Alenor. Alive, as Illiara and Felaern both suggested. They'd made that sound a rather daunting task. But I had another goal beyond escaping Alenor. Desire to explore the knowledge of the High Elves and Alenor still pulled at me. If the best treasure was guarded by the fiercest monsters, then the danger around us affirmed that the knowledge I hungered for hid nearby. But Elliah's peril was palpable, and that forced me to make a choice I didn't want to make—stay in Alenor without Elliah, or leave with her. Asking her to stay felt immensely selfish, though that's what I truly wanted. Elliah's excitement in the library of Telloria'ahlia had rivaled my own. I imagined the two of us exploring the wonders of the Luminarium and my heart ached. I looked back at her, sleeping peacefully. Unfortunately, the tinkling laughter of the apparition from the streets danced in my ears.

I closed my eyes to shut out the sound which, for obvious reasons, shouldn't have helped. But the laughter faded. I opened my eyes to a look of concern from my father. I waved away his worry, and my father shifted to let me through as I approached. It was much easier to pass Elran. I walked ahead and his soft footsteps trailed me.

We walked down the hall in silence, the gentle curve of the pretend tree limb we followed back to the trunk allowing occasional glimpses through small windows to nearby gray limbs. The light was dimmer than when we'd entered. I'd lost all sense of time and hadn't realized the evening snuck up on us.

"We can wander the corridors of the Luminarium," said Elran, "and dance around our goals if you wish, hoping to gain more information than we provide. Or you could tell me what you hope for and I can do the same. I'm prepared to do either." Elran's calm voice and his touch of humor relaxed me.

Still, my own inner conflict made me snappy. "I can't imagine what information you need from us, and I doubt I can trust you." All true. "But I need information."

"The dance it is, then," Elran said, not exactly smiling, but something in his eyes suggested mirth. "Let me start by offering information you would learn readily by talking with locals in the shops. There are three candidates running for the opening in the High Council. Felaern, Lady Ithronel, and me." Adrenaline shot through me. Ithronel! The woman who'd cast the Hook. "Whoever receives the most votes from the twelve other members becomes the new member."

"And if there is a tie?" I stalled, knowing only that I was out of my depth. A potential council member had bespelled me! That wasn't a coincidence. I'd held a sword to one, a second had bespelled me, and the third stood before me... wanting something.

"If it is a three-way tie, then we wait a day and vote again. If two tie, and the third is lower, the third is eliminated and they vote again."

"Logical," I said, for some reason thinking about Zoras's death, when the Mother's magic had inadvertently caused a felled tree branch to grow through him, destroying his insides. His body had just arrived in Alenor. Cold was a better word than logical.

"Of course," Elran answered.

I had no reason to think Zoras had strong friendships in Alenor, no reason to think Elran would weep about Zoras's parting. Perhaps they'd even been enemies. Yet I simmered at the sheer coldness I'd thus far encountered among the High Elves, and Elran's slightly warmer personality contrasted sharply.

"Illiara and I," Elran said, "and Felaern as well, were friends before she... left." Before Illiara fled with Elliah. "It was a better time. Wood Elves mixed freely with High Elves in Alenor, and the racial purity laws, though codified a century before, had been relegated to the status of being only laws of nature. Felaern and Illiara intended to disprove them entirely, openly challenging the law and the Council itself. Instead, their child was born Bereft. After that fiasco, the High Council went wild, imposing large financial fines on the parents of half-breed children. Mixed race families fled Alenor." Forming cities like Telloria'ahlia. "Over time, the Wood Elves left Alenor proper, keeping themselves separate on the other side of the Aqueduct."

Prior to the library in Telloria'ahlia, I hadn't heard that the High Elves had inked such a law into reality. The information might have reached Aendolin, the capital of the Warders, but it hadn't clawed its way through the Blasted Lands to Bellon. I'd known racial purity only as a prescription to increase magical strength in one's progeny. Plenty of people didn't care, as evidenced by the population of Telloria'ahlia, and my existence.

Elran continued his lesson. "It was one thing to suggest racial purity strengthened magic, and another thing entirely to codify racial integrity and then uphold those laws. It severed our interactions with the Alluvium, increased tensions on the war front, and created a segregated Alenor. Ironically, though Zoras is credited with the idea of racial purity to increase magical potency, he advocated against codifying those beliefs into laws."

My father and I had heard stories of the tensions on the war front. Bellon was a war front of its own, and we had been part of the training team for the missionaries who fought trolls. But several Warders who joined us from downstream said they'd spent time on the front, fighting alongside Wood Elves and High Elves. Rather, *for* the High Elves. Something had changed as the Alluvium departed and more High Elves gained leadership roles. The tenor had shifted from *inspiring* and *emboldening* the troops… to controlling them. Many Warders and Wood Elves had left the army, fed up with the methods being used, even though they'd proven effective at defending the Border Woods. With fewer troops, the High Elves responded with "drafting" recruits, which infuriated the Wood Elves who were trapped by the need to defend their homeland.

"That leads us to the vacancy Zoras left behind," Elran continued. I braced for the questions coming to me. "Zoras, over time, switched parties. When he was involved in the creation of the High Council, he backed laws for the Utilitarian party. But in recent centuries, he leaned toward Deontologist beliefs. But only in the last century, with the passing of councilwoman Berix, did we truly strike a balance."

"And that's good?" I asked. Zoras had said something about stalling the High Council, making them less effective.

"That depends," he replied, "on what you believe."

"What you believe, or who you believe?" I asked, thinking about the hinted-at dire prophecies of the Mother of Trees and her specific warning while I was there that everyone who had visited her—save for Elliah—would die.

"The Mother's prophecies," Elran said. "Zoras should not have spoken of them with you."

"I received one firsthand," I replied. In truth, Zoras had *not* spoken of any prophecies with me. But he'd built a fortress along the Flawless River meant to withstand troll attacks. In a way, he'd told me without actually speaking the words.

Elran harrumphed. "I've read the reports of the guards. What you heard was a ray of sunshine compared to the last few centuries. We were relieved when she fell into her stupor."

I'd read everything I could get my hands on as a child. Bellon had once housed a great library, and though I was born after its destruction, I'd rescued many books from caves and underground rooms that had kept them whole. Sometimes not entirely whole, but at least partially readable. Regardless, I'd encountered stories where the Mother of Trees personally defended the Border Woods. I hadn't known whether to believe them, but Zoras had confirmed the same on our trip down the Flawless. What had happened that drove her off the battlefield?

A shiver ran through me. If the Mother of Trees had spoken dark premonitions, why had the High Elves kept them hidden? And if they wanted those foretellings to remain a secret, why did Elran speak of it to me? What did he want from me?

Regardless, I knew what I wanted from him. Ultimately, books. Books and knowledge. But I had a shorter-term problem. I shifted from foot to foot. Finally, I said, "Hooks." Elran's eyes opened slightly, his surprise making me hesitate. "I... I think... I need one removed."

He shook his head slightly, declining what I hadn't yet asked. "Illiara knows how to remove Hooks. You go to her for something like that. Someone you *trust*."

"I... can't." I couldn't let her see what was stuck in my head. She would be disgusted. She'd never let me near her daughter. Tinkling laughter called to me, inexplicably alluring. A golden, naked woman, even more alluring.

Elran scowled. "You *cannot* go to someone you don't trust to remove a Hook. You have to let your guard down for that person, and they can do far worse than a Hook once inside. If I do it, you will never be able to trust me." His eyes flashed as big as saucers for a moment, then narrowed. "Promise me you won't go to Felaern."

I froze, because I'd considered following after Felaern. "Promise me!"

Puffing out a breath I hadn't realized I'd been holding, I nodded my head. "I promise." Tinkling laughter drowned out the end of my promise. I hated myself for wanting to hear more of it.

Elran nodded, glaring as though he didn't entirely trust my promise. He slowly took the bite out of his glare. "I'm sure she will be understanding." He smiled reassurance. "It will be one of those things you look back at and laugh about."

Laugh. Tinkling laughter like water running over rocks. Unbidden, the image of Ithronel replaced Elran. *You don't think your friends will like me,* she pouted, biting her lip. My pulse raced with desire.

"She trusts you, after all," Elran said, popping the illusion of Ithronel like a bubble.

But that was the problem. Trust. Once Illiara saw the Hook that had caught me, that knowledge would always be there between us. It would sour everything.

"That leads us to Felaern." Elran's words crawled out, like he chased loose thoughts around his own head between each syllable, completely oblivious to my dilemma. In contrast, his next words spilled out. "He must be stopped!"

I stared, startled by his sudden vehemence and assuming he would say more… but the silence stretched on. I tried to think it through for myself. Felaern had declared himself a Utilitarian who wanted to appear to be a Deontologist. He would do whatever he thought it took to achieve his goals. He'd claimed to want to save the elves. But at what cost?

I slowly nodded my head, and Elran's shoulders loosened. "Was there anything Zoras said?" he asked. "Something that might suggest his wish as for who would be his successor?"

That's what this exchange had been about? He just wanted some way to maneuver? That made sense; Felaern had shown himself to be much more crafty. Elran needed some kind of edge. I thought back on the final events of our venture to speak with the Mother of Trees. I'd been focused on Elliah, who'd touched the Mother, screamed, and passed out. Illiara had tried to Heal Elliah, to no effect, then rushed to find Zoras. She'd found him, impaled by a fallen branch. She was with him at the end, not me. So I hadn't heard his final words, though Illiara had repeated them to the High Elf guards when they'd arrived. "Just what I assume you've already heard about the world needing a catalyst," I said, my eyes drifting back toward our room.

Elran grimaced. "If you remember anything that he might have said… anything that would block Felaern… it would be a great help in ensuring the High Elves don't do anything they will forever regret. Let me know if you need anything, Hughelas."

Elran pivoted and walked away, leaving me to the shadows cast by the lowering sun and the intricate stone branches of the Luminarium, listening to tinkling laughter, like water trickling over rocks.

Hughelas #3

The shadows shifted slowly. Unnaturally. And I watched them, unsure why they were wrong. The wind pushed through the windows and I breathed in the air, a hint of something acrid taking away from the otherwise pleasant scent of the outdoors. I held my breath, grasping what nuance bothered me—the shadows didn't shift with the wind. The stone limbs didn't sway in the way of wood, and so the shadows didn't dance.

I let out my breath slowly, no longer able to divert my own attention.

I jumped at a voice directly across the hall. "He's not completely wrong." Felaern!

He leaned against the wall opposite me, though I hadn't seen him or anyone walk up. He had just... appeared.

"Were you there the whole time?" I asked, calming my breathing. I blushed at how greatly he'd startled me.

Felaern raised an eyebrow in answer, telling me nothing.

"If you have a Hook," he said, closing the space between us, "it really must come out."

He reached a hand up toward my head, and I jerked back, hitting the wall behind me but pushing his arm away using my shirt and his robe to avoid skin contact. I managed to draw my sword in the tight space and get it between us.

He pursed his lips, his long, golden fingers still outstretched as though he intended to put them right through my eye sockets. "It doesn't matter whether you trust me," he said, then slowly lowered his arm. "But you need to trust yourself."

I looked down the hall, wondering whether I should make a run for it, as he reached into his robe.

"Elliah trusts you," he said, stopping me in my tracks. He pulled a tattered brown book from some interior pocket. "She also cares for you." He looked at the book in his hands. Worn, with papers stuck between the pages, it looked like it had seen heavy use. "More relevantly, her memories confirmed the supposition that you are intelligent. Your dad thought the same, but you can't trust a parents' appraisal of their children." His tone regarding parents was thickly coated with irony. He held the book out to me.

My thoughts tripped over themselves.

"And you're half Salt," he continued. I didn't move, still wrangling my thoughts, and he wiggled the book. "Perhaps you'll do better unlocking Salt secrets."

He'd seen me in Elliah's memories. He'd commandeered my father's mind as well. How much did he know about me? What might he have done to their minds beyond learn from them?

"Did you leave a Hook in my father?" I asked. "Or Elliah?"

"No," he answered. "If I had, Illiara would clear them out easily enough." He raised an eyebrow, nodding at me, suggesting I had the same option. "I said I would not. I did leave a little something in Elliah to help her heal. She trusted Zoras far too readily. She'll need to grow out of that. Illiara won't be able to root my sentinel out, but it will fade on its own over time."

Why would he tell me that? Because I was powerless to do anything about it? Or was he trying to gain my trust? No chance of that.

I still didn't take the book. I wasn't sure how it might be a trap, but it made no sense, and I lacked any reason to trust the High Elf offering it. "Zoras read it, if that influences your decision. He thought it was nonsense." Why would Zoras thinking it was nonsense convince me to read it? "But I think it explains..." he looked around, up and down, out the windows on either side of the hall, not as though he searched for the thing the book explained, but rather for the thing the book did not explain. "... everything."

Everything. I wanted knowledge. The Luminarium promised knowledge. Yet all evidence suggested I might not get the chance I hoped for. My father had his mission to pursue. Danger hung over Elliah like a cloud. If an opportunity presented itself for Illiara to get her daughter out of Alenor, she would whisk her away. Taking the offered book was surely better than missing them all. Yet I didn't reach out, for the book represented a betrayal. An admission that I wouldn't stay. That, in taking one coin from a stranger, I ruined my chances at finding a trove of treasure.

"Most importantly," he said, "I think it explains Elliah." My gaze snapped back to Felaern. "I think." A quick smile flickered across his face. "I can follow the math, but I lack the creativity to take it forward. It's been in my possession, off and on, for almost a century. It's time to give someone else a chance. Besides," he said with a shrug, "I've literally made my own copy."

I slowly took the book. Leather-bound, it bore a thin strap that held it shut. A journal?

He turned and started down the hallway, away from our room, taking the path Elran had taken minutes before. "That's it?" I said. "You spied on me to give me a book?"

"It wasn't you I spied on," Felaern replied over his shoulder, then stopped. He turned to face me. "Illiara trusts you. Do you trust yourself?"

Tinkling laughter reached my ears, the grip of its teasing sound not quite as firm as it had been. Was he suggesting a Hook could be overcome?

"Utilitarian... Deontologist. Nothing is that simple. Zoras told me something once that has stuck with me. 'Sometimes you must do what is best, and other times you get to do what is right.'" His eyes took on the same vulnerability they'd shown when speaking of the possibility of killing his own child as a baby. "'There are no days more glorious than when those times collide.'"

Snapping his eyes back to the present, he said, "I don't intend to lose this council seat." Turning, he held a hand in the air, fingers open, swirling it like he stirred a cauldron. "Trust Illiara. Trust yourself. Fate of the world and all." He disappeared down the hall, leaving me to fraudulent shadows.

Elliah ~ 3

Even in my dream, I was paralyzed by indecision. I couldn't go back into hiding—it would hurt my mother if I gave up and succumbed to the darkness. But neither was I ready to face up to that *thing* that had broken into my mind.

"I can't do it," I whispered.

"It's just a broth," Zoras said. "You must be hungry. Why don't you try?"

A flash of anger heated my face. Was he really that clueless? Too irritated to glare, I just flicked my eyes his way. A part of me knew I dreamed, but in the way of dreams, that didn't matter.

"I haven't provided you much, if *any*, wisdom from my absurdly long life," Zoras said with an indulgent smile. He sat on the bed, a respectful distance between us. "This one is important: an impossible task paralyzes you. You cannot dwell on it. Focus on the next step. If you don't know the next step, take one in the right direction. If you've unsure about your bearings? Guess. Your biggest enemy is your own doubt." After a few seconds of contemplative silence, he added with a small smile. "It's just a broth. You must be hungry. Why don't you try?"

I half-grinned at his absurdly small step, even as I shook my head no. It just wasn't that simple. No one would live but me? I couldn't carry the burden the decaying goddess had placed on my back. I hadn't even been capable of defending myself from that creature who'd clawed its way into my head.

Yet, my chest tightened at the thought of being left alone. *Maybe if I eat, he will stay and talk?* I would go back and hide later.

The wooden bowl shook, absurdly heavy in my weakened state, as I sipped the broth. Salty, thick, and warm—it filled my soul as well as my stomach.

I sighed in satisfaction. Still irritable despite the comfort, I pointed out his inconsistencies. "You created a High Council of supposedly the wisest of elves, which you then neutralized, making them incapable of fulfilling any true purpose. So while they remain flaccid and inconsequential, I am to practice… random… action?"

Zoras smiled. "Flaccid. What a spectacularly Wood Elf way to describe the High Council." Waning philosophical, he said, "Would I give soup to an elf with an arrow through her chest? Or cast strength on an elf who drowns? To each, her own medicine."

"Words are your medicine?"

"Words have power, to be sure," he continued in his reflective tone. "Even in our thoughts, we use words to frame ideas. But ideas are the genuine power, and words, mere vessels."

"So says The Mouth."

Zoras frowned humorously. "I regret telling you that moniker."

His response lightened my spirits. I could handle possibly just a little more. Maybe one question. "Where's my mother?"

"Your mother. I'm afraid she is in trouble," Zoras said, the words causing deja vu. My mother was in trouble—that declaration had drawn me out of my hiding place. The world bumped about as I tried to remember who said it. Zoras continued. "She was never tried for her original crime of demiurgul revivification."

The dream-world snapped back into place. "Demi... what?" I asked.

"What better way to hide the fact that it became near-impossible to wake up the Mother of Trees?" he said. "We simply made it illegal. Demiurgul revivification. Waking up the goddess."

"It was such a big problem that you had to create a law against it?" I mouthed the words *demiurgul revivification. Insanity.*

"Oh, yes. Many, many elves pilgrimaged to see the Mother." True enough. The small settlement of Mother's Den had formed in the nooks of the forest. But they weren't allowed to climb the silverleaf and see her. "In order to preserve her image, we prevented access."

"But we broke in," I said, the memory forming around me, and I saw myself slam my hand on her leg and shout. "And I woke her up."

"Yes, they will put you on trial as well." I cringed. "Don't worry," he said, but even as he talked, the world faded around him, replaced by a swirling cloud of images. Worlds of creatures that spent their entire lives in the air. A life spent entirely underwater. Creatures living in fire. Worms boring vast caverns into planets. "Your trial will be short. You're clearly guilty and there are witnesses."

His words sounded teasing, and should have jerked the dream back to our conversation, but they didn't. The cloud swirled faster, and Zoras and I sat amidst it.

"But you will survive, Elliah," Zoras said, as two red flaming eyes burned away everything else. "You will survive."

I screamed.

***

"Elliah!"

My mother's voice was frightened, calling my name like I was about to stumble out of our silvervein.

I gasped for air as the world rebuilt around me. I was sitting up in the same bed I'd lain in moments before. My knee hurt, and my hand quickly found the haft of Beldroth's hammer by my side. I'd clearly hit it with my leg.

Zoras was nowhere to be found.

The knots in my head took their time to unravel while my mother fussed, shifting from where she'd been lying beside me to sitting up and facing me.

The bed shifted as Beldroth sat at the end near me. I hadn't even noticed him.

"Elliah?" My mother asked gently.

My breathing slowed. The dream waned as reality took hold. I hadn't realized magelight bathed the room in its soft glow until a second joined the first, near Beldroth. Behind him, dim light peeked through the windows.

"Where's Hughelas?" I asked, desperate to see the one person who had believed I had worth because of my differences. I shifted the hammer, leaning its head against my hip instead of my sore knee.

My mother nodded across the room to the darkness on the other side of the room. "He had a rough day yesterday," my mother said. Squinting, I spotted a lump atop another bed. Beldroth must have come from there too.

"Is he okay?" I asked.

My mother nodded. "He's fine. Just sleeping. How are you?"

I did a quick inventory. Other than a banged knee, nothing hurt on the outside. They'd Healed me well. On the inside?

I avoided looking down into the yawning chasm of doubts and fears.

A knock at the door drew my attention. When it was quickly followed by the sound of the door opening and then smacking something solid, I swung my legs off the bed. I was farthest from the door and Beldroth had launched himself ahead. The noise and bustle woke Hughelas, his tall frame sitting up groggily. My mother planted herself behind Beldroth faster than I managed to rise.

The world spun violently from my movement and was just beginning to settle when a voice from the hall said, "I brought food."

That voice. It was the same elf who had been there before. My father? A chill ran up my spine and my nerves jangled. My mother had rarely talked about my father, or allowed me to ask about him. For many decades, she'd talked about him like he was dead. I'd come to understand, over time, that she didn't want me to know the story because she didn't want me repeating it. Didn't want whispers of it getting out. I'd only recently learned my father was a High Elf. I looked like a Wood Elf—except for having slightly longer limbs than my mother, and golden freckles that had faded as I'd aged. When he'd left, he'd said something about fatherly love… but I didn't know. Was that a metaphor? Was *he*? I found myself trying to peer around my mother and Beldroth.

Beldroth had wedged a sword between the slightly open door and the short hallway wall, impeding the door from opening further.

"You're not welcome here, Felaern Keawynn." My mother's tone left no room for doubt, Felaern. Felaern Keawynn. Elves' second names changed over time, something like titles or reflections of their behavior or decisions. Keawynn meant something like 'betrayer,' and from my mother's tone, it was probably just her name for him. Which only suggested to me further that he might be my father.

"When the sun rises," Felaern said, "you will be summoned to the High Council. If you wish to depart from the Luminarium, still breathing, you should listen. You can make whatever choices you like with the information," Felaern said. My mother quietly growled. "And, as I mentioned, I brought food."

Snarling, my mother snapped, "Let him in."

Beldroth pushed the door closed, retrieved his sword, then opened the door. He did *not* sheath his weapon.

A High Elf walked in, not as tall as Zoras, though similarly featured. His nose and cheeks were thin, like Zoras's, though Felaern's bone structures suggested skeletal where Zoras had been merely lean. His eyes locked with mine. I expected to see some hint of… well, something… that would tell me whether he was my father. But the chill in Felaern's golden eyes made Zoras seem warm in comparison. His eyes moved away as quickly as they'd landed.

"Venison pastries for the Wood Elves," he said, holding a tray with covered metal dishes. "Mutton stew," he said with a nod to Beldroth, who licked his lips. "Pike chowder." His eyes lingered on Hughelas. "And broth, in case Elliah isn't ready for meat."

I didn't know when I had last eaten properly, but those dishes sounded like too much. Facing the day was too much. What if I just focused on the next step? Broth... broth was manageable. Why did I feel deja vu over broth? For reasons I couldn't explain, I suspected the broth was Felaern's way of showing he cared more than he let on. He juggled setting the tray on a bedside table while no one offered to help, then put his back to the windows, waving for anyone to eat.

Beldroth was the first to take him up on the offer. Picking the bowl Felaern had indicated was mutton stew, he spooned up a mouthful and sighed. "This tastes like bullhorn ram. I didn't know you had those in Alenor."

"It's not," Felaern answered. "It's just sheep from the Heartland. Puny, almost-domesticated creatures. Nothing like your magnificent bullhorns."

"You've seen them?" Beldroth asked, while the rest of us picked up our food. I shot my mother a questioning look while Beldroth and Felaern talked. I wanted to convey the question: *is Felaern my father?* But judging by the way she sniffed the food and nodded her head, I think all she got from my look was: *is it okay to eat the food?*

"I have," Felaern answered while my mother and I exchanged nonverbal misinformation. "I spent quite some time with a Warder named Tassarion. Tassarion Balceran when I knew him."

Beldroth's eyes widened slightly. Someone important to Beldroth?

"You'll not win our loyalty with good food," my mother said, though she started eating. "Or your name dropping."

I slurped down a few mouthfuls of broth, and it settled well enough that I decided to nab a bite of the venison pastry before it disappeared down my mother's throat. Still, the food couldn't distract me from my question—was Felaern my father? If I asked, and he wasn't, how awkward would that make the room? My mother carried Beldroth's *child*. Pointing out that I didn't know who my father was in front of Beldroth might not endear my mother to him. Though it killed me, I would have to wait.

"Our fates are intertwined, Illiara." Felaern finally said. "Ithronel is no longer a contender," he said to himself. "Overnight, she became utterly convinced that the role wasn't for her. It's as if a whisper in the wind told her to bow out, and who am I to question such... persuasive instincts?"

"What did you do?" my mother asked, dripping scorn.

"Nothing," he said. "I had no hand in it. I had every intent in winning the council seat despite her. Regardless, there are now only two of us competing. Elran wants the council seat." My mother's eyes widened slightly at that, and she looked over at Hughelas. "He achieves that by discrediting both you and Elliah, and by association, me. He takes you down, takes Elliah down, gains the council seat, and we *lose*."

"How?" I barked, seeing my opportunity. "How does it take you down by association?"

Felaern looked to my mother, and I knew. I knew! *This is the man we've been running from all my life!* This man, who tricked me back from my mental hidey-hole, who brought me broth and fed my mother and friends.

"You got your long fingers from him," my mother said. "True fatherhood," she said, nodding to Beldroth, "requires more than a fluid donation."

"So what if we lose," my mother said to Felaern. "High Elves don't believe in capital punishment. I can wait out a sentence."

Wait! So that was it? We weren't going to talk about Felaern being my father?

"Conscription," he replied. "You'll find yourself on the war front, unable to disobey a command. It may not be capital punishment, but it's a death sentence nonetheless."

"That's against the law!" my mother protested.

"It *is* the law. Things have changed while you were away. Maybe they can't Coerce Elliah. Her natural resistance might protect her." Of course he knew about my *natural resistance*. He knew I was Bereft from birth. But really? We're not going to talk about it? "They definitely couldn't keep me bespelled. But," he said with a nod of his head, "there are many ways to die."

"Seriously?" I blurted. "'You got your long fingers from him,'" I said in my mother's voice. "That's all there is to say?" Hughelas weaved his way through the people and dishes to sit by my side. He looked worse than I felt, like he hadn't slept at all.

"Felaern fathered you," my mother said, scowling. "He's also the one we hid from for eighty years."

"I'm the one you *thought* you hid from for eighty years," Felaern corrected.

My mother turned red. "He's the elf we hid from."

Felaern shrugged, like there was no convincing some people. "Then you should have tried harder. *I* knew where you were, most of the time."

The sound of my mother's teeth grinding reminded me of years of my creating the same response in her. Finding that oddly comforting, I drank more of the broth, enjoying its warmth.

"You were safer when you were hiding," Felaern said, holding his arms out to display our current surroundings and their inherent danger.

"Let's get to it," my mother said. "You want us to back you for the High Council, and you'll get us out of Alenor. I don't understand how we can help, but if we did, how can we trust you to uphold your end of the bargain?"

"Our interests are aligned," Felaern said, his tone that of a parent teaching a lesson to a child for the millionth time.

"Enough of our interests being aligned!" my mother shouted. She took three breaths, each slower than the previous, before continuing. "When we were... eighty years ago, you came back from the Contentious," Beldroth raised his eyebrows at that, "convinced there was a way to save the elves. Magic, you said, was bent and broken." *What?* "You'd colluded with a *dragon*." *What? What?* "Don't push me away with nonsense about our interests being *aligned*."

Felaern cocked his head, seemingly gathering his thoughts. "You won't believe me," he finally said, straightening his head.

"Try me," my mother replied.

My broth was almost gone, my interest piqued, and my energy rising.

"Zoras sent me to the Contentious to find him a connection with the Warders. I hoped for learning and wisdom. What I found was ... Tassarion Balceran. Who told me every bit of sheeplore imaginable." Beldroth stood straighter, and while I saw no real change in Felaern's eyes, I had the strongest feeling he was laughing. "I traveled to As Velera to find Zoras a similarly worthy liaison among the Salts." He turned his gaze to Hughelas, who tensed at the attention. "And found way more than I bargained for. The Salts are explorers, and they'd explored magic in ways the High Elves had never dreamed. But they also knew geography, and they had maps that... supposedly... predated the Breaking." He paused, but not getting the reaction he hoped for, he shrugged and continued on. "I went looking for the place marked by a statue that had caught my attention in Aendolin."

"I remember," my mother said. "You told Zoras the statue was of elves feeding a dragon."

"I've seen that," Beldroth said. "Jenat's Lament. There's a mural of the same… half a mural… in Bellon."

Felaern cocked his head at Beldroth. "I wish I'd known that." Pursing his lips for a moment, he continued on. "Clues from the Salt maps led me to the Dragon Fangs, and yes, an encounter with a dragon. What I found there was the epitaph on the tombstone of elves. And, yes, I struck a bargain. Don't—" he held up his hands again to forestall my mother. "I know you think you want to know, but you don't. And it isn't relevant to why you should believe I will get our daughter out of Alenor." *Our* daughter. I shivered, unable to digest the thought that I had a living, breathing father. "The thing that you won't believe is this— there were numerous, consistent reports of what the Mother of Trees said. To paraphrase, 'a remnant shall survive what's coming.' That's what I've worked for, what I've bargained for, what I've *shed blood* for. It finally made sense out of the nonsense that the Warders went on and on about." Beldroth bristled, but Felaern looked him square in the eyes and said. "I have hope."

"You egotistical monster. Don't…" my mother said, but trailed off without finishing.

The door swung open without a knock, and a tall male High Elf in purple robes glided in. My mother and Beldroth spun, and I set my empty bowl on the ground without looking away.

"You shouldn't be here," the newcomer said to Felaern.

"On the contrary, there is no place more vital for me to be," Felaern replied.

"Perhaps," replied the newcomer, "but you should have found it impossible to get here." With a light sigh he continued. "I am High Counselor Iolas," he said to everyone but Felaern. "I am here to escort you to a meeting of the High Council."

"For…?" my mother asked, as Beldroth planted himself slightly in front of him, causing the visitor to take a half step back and ultimately resulting in two more High Elves entering from the hall with swords drawn to flank Iolas.

"Your trial," Iolas answered with a raised eyebrow as he looked far down his nose at my mother.

Felaern moved to my mother's side, and Iolas told him, curtly, "*You* will be staying here."

"You intend to try the mother of my child for a crime I *forced* her to commit, and you don't want me there?" Felaern sounded incredulous, oozing wide-eyed innocence.

Iolas blinked. Then he donned the smile of a vulture who had spotted a bloody wolf collapsing from exhaustion. "You will *all* be going."

***

The trip from our room to the council chamber took a long time. I tired quickly, and my mother insisted we take breaks every few floors we descended. I had plenty of opportunities to look out the open-shuttered windows to see the dawning day. We were never without our High Elf escort, and conversation was mostly limited to subdued questions of weariness.

"Are we in a stone silvervein?" I finally asked at one landing, when the rising sun clarified enough for a guess at what I was seeing.

"We are," my mother said, pursing her lips in distaste.

"And is that an… aqueduct?" I asked, pointing at the structure beginning to appear to the north. To this side of the aqueduct, buildings dotted the ground, some with early fires already pumping forth smoke. Treetops poked above the far side of the tall barrier.

"It is," Felaern said. *My father* said.

My mother frowned even more, but I found the structure and organization of the city oddly appealing—the engineering and artistry required to build a stone silvervein, the ability to transport fresh water over long distances, all the buildings full of elves designing and creating. Alenor promised potential and change. It was a sentiment hugely at odds with the city's dark promise of trials and death.

We neared the ground by the time we arrived at our destination. The High Council met in a chamber in the center of the trunk that formed the Luminarium, a high-ceilinged room that accommodated the council members, a small audience, and a space between the two where they brought us.

Twelve purple-robed dignitaries sat behind a dark, wooden table which curved slightly to match the contour of the room. Behind me, the audience consisted of about thirty High Elves.

Our escort halted at the door, but a High Elf waited for us in the center of the room. He attempted to introduce himself. "I am—"

"Your services won't be needed," Felaern said.

"Services?" I asked, as the High Elf nodded, looking relieved, and walked past me.

"He was appointed by the council to represent us," my mother said. She reached out to him, then yanked her hand back, letting him go.

We were about to be tried, for crimes we had most certainly committed. I repeatedly clenched and loosened my fists, acknowledging my apprehension, letting it go, then having it sneak right back up and pounce on me. The quiet of the filled room only made it worse.

I tried to turn my attention to *anything* else. I pored over the details of the room, wondering why the High Elves chose to have a wooden table in a tree made of stone. Wood Elves would have grown such a table, making it a natural extension of the tree. While it was alien to my senses, I found its clean cut held a certain elegance. I glanced over at Felaern, my High Elf father, and wondered if that appeal came from the parent I never knew. Had Varitan, my High Elf teacher in E'anashys, disliked me because he saw in me the things he'd left behind? It was an odd thought to sneak in, but it was a day for odd thoughts. Dragons, the eradication of elves… demiurgul revivification.

When the council members stood, I breathed out a huff of air. *Finally!*

But the High Elves, maybe in particular the High Council, took formality to an excruciating extreme. After a litany of introductions, performed by Iolas, procedural statements regarding details such as who they'd appointed to administer their processes and announce their decisions—Iolas, it turned out—and the review of the minutes from their last meeting, "for accuracy and completeness," my attention waned. How it was possible to be simultaneously anxious and bored, I didn't know, but I shifted focus to my mental exercises to pass the time and calm my nerves. Even if they hadn't stopped the creature with the fiery eyes, they calmed me. Plus, my father, who clearly was a mage of some ability, had looked around the place I'd hidden myself and said it was good. Maybe there was hope for me.

I didn't even realize the actual trial had begun until Felaern rose to his feet.

"Your Eminences," Felaern said. I dropped my mental exercises instantly. "This trial cannot proceed." The trial had begun? My mother blinked rapidly, eyes assessing the situation. If love of procedure was a High Elf quality, I'd inherited the lack thereof from my Wood Elf mother. "The 'Council Chamber Protocol for Judicial Proceedings' states, and I quote, 'Any trial or judicial proceeding within the realm must have the presence of a *full* council to ensure fairness, impartiality, and the proper dispensation of justice. In the absence of a full council, any trial or judicial action shall be deemed null and void, and proceedings shall be postponed until such time as a full council can be convened.'"

Okay, finally! Not that I'd completely followed his argument. He was saying they shouldn't have a trial without a full council? Replace Zoras first?

Murmurs of uncertainty filled the chamber, but the members of the High Council didn't speak. They exchanged glances and raised eyebrows, frowns and nods of agreement, but they uttered no words. Did the High Elf love of procedure dictate that our trial had to be postponed? Angry scowls from several members suggested they were *not* interested in entertaining a postponement. But instead of someone from the council speaking up, a response came from the audience.

"Esteemed council members, we find ourselves at a crossroads of uncertainty and intrigue." I turned to find a High Elf standing, his voice smooth, his demeanor composed.

"Elran," my mother growled in a whisper. "What are you *doing?*"

If he heard, he ignored her completely. "The allegations against the accused demand your immediate attention, for they strike at the very heart of our realm's security and stability. To delay the trial is to risk further discord and unrest among our people."

"We cannot ignore the weight of the accusations leveled against the accused. The crime of awakening the sleeping goddess is not one to be taken lightly, and your duty as custodians of justice demands swift and decisive action. To prioritize an election over this trial is to betray the principles upon which the High Council stands. Moreover, there is abundant precedent in trials which occurred while former High Council member Zoras was absent!"

Many heads on the council nodded their agreement. My mother looked like she was chewing sticks. Beldroth, fascinated but confused. My father, listening but cold and detached, like it didn't concern him. Hughelas had his head down in his hands, fighting off weariness—or despair?

"It is your solemn duty," Elran continued, "to ensure that justice is served without delay or hesitation. By holding the trial first, you demonstrate your unwavering commitment to upholding the rule of law and holding all accountable for their actions, regardless of station or circumstance."

To my surprise, Beldroth was nodding his agreement. Did he not understand the result of conducting the trial first? If my father pushed for the election first, he must have believed the council to be stacked against us.

"Furthermore, the accusations against the accused threaten to tarnish the reputation and integrity of the High Council." Gasps sprinkled the audience. "The evidence against them is overwhelming. To allow the specter of suspicion to linger unchecked would be to invite scorn and derision upon your governance. Only by swiftly addressing these allegations can you restore faith in our institutions and reaffirm your commitment to our people."

Great! Elran had called them a bunch of dull axes trying to chop down a silvervein if they didn't put us on trial immediately.

"Do not falter in the face of adversity. Rather, stand united in your resolve to seek truth and deliver justice to those who have wronged us. The eyes of our realm are upon you, and it is your duty to show them that the High Council remains steadfast, unwavering, and just."

Murmurs of tension rippled through the chamber, and the air crackled with anticipation. Elran's persuasive rhetoric had cast a shadow of doubt over the council, his words resonating with many of them.

But, "the eyes of the realm?" What, the thirty pairs of eyes in the room? Plus another ten or twelve guards around the doors? But prompted by the declaration, I looked closer at the elves at the highest part of the back of the room. They all held crystals. Communication crystal, like Zoras had used on the ship. The proceedings *were* being watched by more than I realized.

Felaern had remained standing as Elran made his speech, and Felaern's voice rang out with authority as he responded.

"Esteemed council members, I beseech you to consider the order of proceedings with the utmost care. In our time-honored traditions, the election of a new council member has always taken precedence over key matters of trial and judgment. To deviate from this established order would not only undermine our laws but also cast doubt upon the integrity of our governance."

Felaern sounded different from when he had spoken with us. Passion infused his words but never reached his eyes.

"In the interest of fairness and justice, we must prioritize the election of a new council member to ensure that our deliberations remain untainted by external influence. The appointment of a new council member is paramount to upholding the balance of power within our realm and safeguarding the welfare of our people."

Felaern wasn't going to give up on postponing the trial. But his words fell on deaf ears—the council members remained quiet.

"Moreover, the *integrity* of the trial itself hinges upon the *composition* of this esteemed council." Council members squirmed at that. "By electing a new member first, we reaffirm our commitment to impartiality and transparency in our proceedings, ensuring that the trial receives the full scrutiny and diligence it deserves." Elran bristled every time Felaern used the words "we" and "our," as though my father were already a member of the High Council. "Furthermore, the High Council has *never* voted without input from the *full* Council. Councilman Zoras *chose* not to weigh in. Abstention is a *choice*. Absence is not."

His words found purchase. Council members exchanged glances. Furtive nods and subtle shakes of the head took place among a whispering murmur from the audience. My mother grinned like a cat who'd cornered a mouse. Beldroth nodded his head slowly, as much in agreement with Felaern as he had been with Elran. Hughelas's head sank lower into hands. I didn't understand what had gotten into him. Why, instead of applying his sharp mind to our predicament, did he instead dwell in some world all his own?

"In these tumultuous times," Felaern continued more loudly, "unity and cohesion are more vital than ever. By swiftly electing a new council member, we send a message of strength and solidarity to our people, assuring them that their interests are *our* foremost concern."

"Let us not allow discord," Felaern said, turning briefly to face an angry Elran, "to sow division among us. Instead, let us stand united in our resolve to uphold the principles of justice, fairness, and integrity that define our High Council and our people. Together, we shall navigate the challenges that lie ahead and emerge stronger, more resilient, and more united than ever before."

Felaern's impassioned plea resonated with many council members, and more nods of agreement than shaking of heads decorated the High Council. Iolas scowled, but if I understood correctly, he was only their voice—he could only echo what he saw from his fellow council members. He stood, slowly, and the room grew quiet. It seemed we at least had a stay of execution.

To my surprise, Hughelas shot up from the seat beside me. He blurted into the silence, "In order to open up a seat on the High Council, Felaern paid my father to ensure Zoras did not survive his trip to the Mother's Den."

Beldroth : 2

I stood. Whatever my son was up to, or whatever trouble he'd gotten himself into, he wouldn't have to face it alone. I wasn't into one of the most cherished pastimes of Warders, but I'd often heard a phrase from missionaries under my care. "It isn't a question of whether sheep will wander; it's a question of when and where they'll go."

Where has my boy gone?

There was a momentary pause in the bedlam from the audience when I stretched. Loosening up before a fight might make the difference between survival and death by cramped muscles. One typically did not get the luxury, but I wasn't one to inspect the wool on a gifted lamb.

"What do you need me to do, son?" I asked during a side bend in his direction.

When he didn't respond, I studied him more closely. Sweat dripped from him, and he practically shook, like one sick with fever.

Ah, that! Illiara had warned me.

"Order," Iolas shouted. "I will have order." Before the din had completely died, he continued. "Given this dire and incriminating testimony, we will proceed with the trial, adding the charges of murder and hierarchic disintegration."

And things had been going so well. I'd quite enjoyed the minutes from the previous meeting—superior note taking! The Lithos Sinod, those who governed the Warders, could learn a great deal. I'd intended to find and ask Trentius about their methods after the meeting. I'd spotted him at the far door to the main audience seating when we'd entered, and he'd returned my wave.

Then the speeches from Elran and Felaern had been so passionate! I wasn't sure for whom to root. Yes, there was value in following rules and precedents, but electing a council member surely wasn't as important as trying criminals!

Even though I didn't trust Felaern, who needed to keep his distance from Illiara, he had obviously swayed the council to elect a new council member before Illiara and Elliah went on trial. I didn't see how it mattered, one way or the other—the Mother of Trees had Blessed my mission, after all. I was destined to succeed.

Still... the Mother *had also* declared that everyone would die except for Elliah. I'd spent ten years mourning my wife. My own death didn't concern me, but a familiar emptiness tugged at me when I thought of my companions leaving the physical plane before me.

Illiara concentrated, marching through a spell-casting, while Felaern divided his attention, eyes darting between Hughelas, Illiara, Elliah, Iolas... and Elran. Elliah had shriveled in on herself. That poor girl. It broke my heart—I knew how it felt to want to hide from the world, having spent a decade in that state myself.

Hughelas twitched, and I wrapped an arm around him to keep him steady. Illiara had told me he'd return to his normal self within a few days, and I trusted her.

It didn't mean she was right, though.

"Hold on, son," I told him, loudly enough for him to hear me over the rising din. I grimaced, wishing for a role that allowed me to act instead of wait.

"Guards!" Iolas shouted, pointing at Illiara. "She's casting! Stop her!"

Oh, good! Something to do.

Guards moved in from either side and I launched myself to incapacitate the two nearest me so I could get back in time to stop the other two. I was careful not to allow skin contact for more than a moment. Only a fool stepped twice on the same crumbling cliff.

In seconds, I returned, though more guards would arrive from that direction to replace the two I'd downed. To my surprise, Felaern held off the two from the other side, somehow intimidating them with just raised hands with fingers in a strange gesture like he posed on the edge of a spell. Maybe he had, and they knew it.

Before my eyes, Illiara completed her spell, and I wrapped her in one arm and Hughelas in the other as each sagged in exhaustion. Hughelas's light-blond hair grew brighter, then a yellow light lit his head like a flame. The room grew quieter as a snake of light crawled from my son, climbing into the high-ceilinged room, stretching farther and farther in a sinuous dance.

"No one leaves!" I shouted when I realized that, while the guards had charged into our section—and much of the audience had stayed to watch the drama—some had chosen the safer path of finding the nearest exit. Illiara had told me the snakelike light would need its target nearby.

Trentius blocked the door, raising a spear in salute. What a level-headed fellow! Unfortunately, the crowd didn't see it the same way, and holding his ground took grit, especially when the light crawled their way.

His job became easier when the small group scattered before the light, but not quickly enough for one of them to avoid the serpent strike. Like a python digesting its food, a lump of light traveled the path back to my son, and I held him there as the audience left their fallen member lying prone under the magical spell.

In the absolute quiet of the council room, Felaern boomed. "Given the illegal use of a Hook spell to force false testimony, I believe there is now only one contender for the Council Seat. I accept the appointment."

Iolas, already standing, slammed his fist on the table. "As you contended, Elran has not yet been tried, and so cannot be disqualified from a Council Seat."

"I'm pleased to find our interests aligned. Shall we get on with the vote then?" His grin was downright ravenous.

***

The snake-light dissipated, and I set Illiara, who hadn't completely passed out, back in her chair, then I picked my sleeping child up and cradled him like I hadn't done since he was a baby. Illiara had warned us that the spell to trace the Hook back to its creator would exhaust Hughelas. Even setting the trap on the Hook had taken its toll on them both, though Illiara had recovered quickly.

The High Elves continued their debate, but my focus was on my son. I wasn't in a panic, but it would have been nice to be excused to a place where I could let Hughelas sleep in a bed.

"Is he okay?" Elliah asked me softly. I had turned my back on the audience and the bedlam going on around Elran, but it meant I cradled my son facing the High Council. Elliah had checked on her mother, then put her back to the council to speak with me.

"A little worse than just sleeping, I'm afraid," I whispered back. "But Illiara assured me that, with as short a time as the Hook had been in him, the damage would be small."

Elliah looked confused and worried.

"Elran used a High Elf spell called a Hook on him. We didn't know it was Elran who had done it. But she said it was, 'a most insidious Hook,' laced with embarrassment and guilt that made it difficult for him to admit something was wrong. Removing it was possible, but she said there was also a way to trace the Hook back to the one holding the line, if the one who had cast it were activating the Hook."

Elliah leaned around my shoulder to see Elran being held up by guards, while Felaern shredded the arguments made by the High Council. She cocked her head, then shifted back, so that we were once again face to face.

"And that didn't hurt him?" she asked, looking down and putting a hand on his cheek.

Such a strong but sweet girl, like her mother.

"It *did* hurt him," I answered, and Elliah's brows knit. "But Illiara assured me that the damage would be temporary because the Hook hadn't had time to catch onto 'anything truly integral to his being.' He will struggle with recent memories, which she said might be a 'thorn that conceals a rare bloom.' That's a good thing, right? She meant it might be for the best if he doesn't remember?"

She nodded her head. I was glad I hadn't misinterpreted.

A sudden silence made me look around—the High Council *must* have been communicating through their minds, because they hardly said anything. Or else they managed to communicate an awful lot through small facial changes. But Iolas managed to conceal his distaste as he announced, "So be it. Welcome to the High Council, Felaern. I'm sure your contributions will be… truly unforgettable."

"Wonderful," Felaern said, taking two steps forward and, in a most uncharacteristic display of emotion, put one hand on the railing that separated us from the High Council and leaped over it. "Now let's dive into the validity of punishing people for breaking a law that should never have existed in the first place."

Shaythyl the Red

I was not patient. Particularly when *everything* was at stake.
Fire lies.
I knew that, but I had no other source.
My other schemes were falling apart. Fire hadn't lied about that. Which, of course, was the trickiest thing about Fire. Despite the simple phrase, Fire never outright lied. It deceived. True Sight was confusing enough, not that I'd ever experienced it directly. Arsyli had gone insane in the end, after the Breaking.

The Breaking. When the Mother ripped our future to shreds, irrevocably altering… everything. Arsyli hadn't Seen that. It wasn't supposed to have happened. Ironically, Fire had shown me. But… Fire lies.

Far below, one of the hulking trolls appeared from their cave, lugging a boulder that would have crushed multiple Warders at once. They'd gotten bigger over the centuries, and I found myself, as always, looking for signs of Him. But the troll simply carried the boulder away around the south side of the Tarn, never looking my way, intent on adding to the wall between the Border Woods and the Tarn.

I was not patient, but my contingency plans had burned away, and I had no choice but to wait. And fret. And grow more bitter and angry. I looked over at my daughter, sleeping, almost of age to take over. But unable. Because of the Mother. The future we lived wasn't supposed to have happened. The unfairness gnawed at me.

Suddenly, my heir's head shot up. I climbed slowly to all fours, whereas Cyrli practically launched into the air, wings outstretched. By the stars, she was a beauty. We would have been amazing. Had the Mother not stolen our future.

The one thing that hadn't diminished with age was my eyesight, but I could not see what she stared at to the west. I stretched, creating a small avalanche that would never make it all the way down the Dragon's Fang, as the elves called it. The snow-capped mountain kept me from burning up, but I still remembered my younger days on the same mountain, and how the cold chilled me when not nestled near my mother, the magical furnace.

"He's gained power," Cyrli explained.
I'd almost given up. After all, Fire lies.
I failed to contain a rumble of satisfaction that caused another

tiny fall of snow down the mountain.

"Do you know more, my most beautiful queen? He will do as he promised?"

"He says the plan is already in motion." She still stared off to the west, her ears perked like she heard a distant sound. In a way, she did, though not with her ears. "A... Warder?" She didn't know the word. Arsyli's wards, once upon a time. We'd lost so much. "A... Warder... arrived whose mission can be used to achieve our purpose. The Warder claims the Mother's Blessing." A shiver went through me, dislodging another cascade. The Mother's Blessing? She would not Bless what we intended. Everything was broken. Ever since the Breaking. Still, Fire had hinted. Even though Fire lied, it would speak where Water kept silent.

"Ask him," I said. "Does the Warder carry the bone of a dragon?"

Such an unexpected oddity, the shine of our magic, not quite Ancient, but old. It had to have been from Jenat. We'd argued, even fought. Had she perished? Or, like my daughter, had she given a tooth freely?

"He says... he says they have a dragon bone." My daughter cocked her head sideways. "I'm sorry, I don't understand what he's saying. Elves don't think clearly. I don't know who 'they' are."

I'd sent lackeys, and then nieces, to retrieve the bone I'd glimpsed. *We collect our dead.* They'd failed. Then the bone had disappeared. *Bones don't vanish.* Yet it had. Still, the ward of Lairras claimed "they" had it. If so, why couldn't my nieces see it?

Jenat, as a white, had the ability to See. If that bone were hers...

"I want that bone back," I said.

Cyrli stared off to the west. "He says they need it," she informed me.

"I. Want. It. Back!" I said, stomping a foot that caused the mountain to tremble. *We would have our dead!*

I looked down the Dragon's Fang to find the troll had returned. The troll's sight would never be able to pick us out atop the mountain, but I saw it just fine. So I didn't miss the flare of red in its eyes.

"We are not done," I said. It was a struggle to lift my bulk off the mountainside, but it would be even harder to fly back up. The mere thought drained me. But my commotion had stirred the Father, and getting on his bad side was the last thing I wanted. "Tell him to hurry," I said wearily. "Our time is almost at an end."

Hughelas #4

I had only vague, dreamlike memories of departing Alenor. I'd been exhausted, mentally wracked by the Hook and then the Trace. But over the next few days, walking through the woods and glades, my energy returned, and my mind unscrambled.

"Where are we going again?" I asked my father, quite sure I had asked before, but knowing he would indulge me. A troop of High Elves marched in front of us. Then Elliah. I looked behind, not recognizing anything, but finding Illiara jogging to catch up, carrying a bundle of small, white flowers.

"Cenaedth," he answered. The familiar-sounding answer settled in like it had found a home. I didn't think I would have to ask again.

"Cenaedth," I echoed. "Alluvium," I continued. "We're going to see the Alluvium."

My father smiled brightly as we climbed a small hill which concealed our view. A quick scan of the sparse trees and the sun made it clear we headed north and slightly east.

"I'm sorry," I said. "I know I've asked before. Why?" I thought I knew. The puzzle pieces lay about, but I still struggled to keep them in place.

The Alluvium practiced fire magic. I'd read they used to lead the war against the trolls. But I recalled discussions back in Bellon about how my father had never encountered a single Alluvium in the Blasted Lands, despite their role in its creation. In recent history, they'd exited the war. They'd become reclusive. Insular. One only found half-breeds, like me, but composed of different races, outside their mountain home. Which meant, logically, some pure-breed parents had settled outside their mountains. I hadn't considered it before, but I would surely have found some in the half-breed towns we'd passed. Telloria'ahlia. Faellon. I'd definitely spotted Alluvium bloodlines in Faellon.

"Not supposed to say, exactly," my father said, frowning and nodding toward Elliah.

"I wish you would stop asking," Elliah said over her shoulder. "So I wouldn't have to be reminded that I'm not allowed to know."

My heart quickened at the sight of her. Slate and shards, she was attractive! A memory of tinkling laughter quickly faded before I placed where I'd heard it, but with it came a wave of embarrassment and a desire to withdraw.

"You're not allowed to know?" I asked stupidly. Did *I* know? Like a name on the tip of my tongue, I couldn't come up with it. Ice. Fire. Water. My thoughts were like a boulder cascading down a mountainside, hitting other rocks and changing directions without choice and losing bits along the way.

"Apparently *my father*—" she said with irritation, and I tripped. My brain wouldn't kick into gear, but Elliah talking about her father sounded foreign. I caught myself and carried on. "—told *your father* that he shouldn't let me in on the plan. And your father bought into it." She stood straighter and spoke in a deep, monotonic voice. "'Her mind isn't strong enough to guard the information yet.'" She must have been imitating *her* father, because I couldn't fathom mine saying that.

"The Father of Stones doesn't have a pathway to *my* mind," my father said.

That statement, however, was perfectly on point for my father.

"You have *got* to be kidding me," I exclaimed. I turned on my father. "You don't *actually* think that the Father of Stones, if he even *exists*, can see into Elliah's mind, do you?"

My father froze, sucking in a breath, eyes expanding like saucers, yet he held in whatever retort he wanted to spew.

I jerked my arm away when someone put their hand on it. When I realized it was Elliah, I was utterly mortified by my actions, and my anger fled.

"She's not the only one who doesn't know," said a High Elf whose name escaped me. He beamed though, proud of his declaration. "'Whispers in the Woods: the Secret Quest to Save the Elves.'"

"Trentius!" I blurted, my brain connecting the dots despite me.

"You remember!" he exclaimed with excitement, and Elliah raised an eyebrow.

Another hand on my arm—I didn't jerk away—made me look backward into the eyes of Illiara. "It's good you're remembering," she said. "What's your last clear memory?"

I believed Illiara hoped to distract me, but between embarrassment and my thoughts darting off like finches, I let her steer me and tried to think about my memories.

I remembered Alenor, but with all the stability of a dream. A tree made of stone. A trial. A parade? Fog and disconnected pieces jumbled in my head. Even distant memories, though clear, were jumbled: reading in the caves of Bellon, scouting trolls at the Witless Tarn, watching my mother die. There was a more recent death. "Zoras," I said. "Dying. Dying before the Mother of Trees. While She just *sat* there." The memory pained me.

"What better place to meet one's maker?" my father said solemnly.

I shot him a look, my fists tightening as my shoulders bunched and eyes pinched.

"He's literally there, *with his maker*," my father insisted. When I continued to glare, he added, "I hope I'm so lucky."

My mouth dropped open.

"Perhaps we should move on," Illiara said, eyebrows raised in concern, though I wasn't sure for whom she was concerned, my father or me. "So you remember the time before Alenor. Do you remember the burned out building we passed as we entered the city?"

Burned out building… I'd been talking with Trentius! I nodded my head.

"Then the walk to the Luminarium?" she asked.

The Luminarium… the stone tree? Again an image of a parade rattled through my mind. Zoras on a cart next to Elliah. High Elves lined the street. But the memory vanished as quickly as it came. I waggled my hand in the air to show I didn't entirely remember.

"Okay," my mother said. "The memories of your time in Alenor might clear up over time, but they might not. Let me lay it out for you. When we marched into Alenor proper, a couple of folks landed Hooks in you and in your father. The one in your father, I removed trivially. Yours was more insidious. If you ever remember it, you should not feel guilt over it. The Hook was deep, and cleverly done to snag things you care about…" She glanced over at Elliah. "… and things that drive you." *That drive me?* "Your deeper Hook would have been harder to remove, and, in fact, we chose not to. Instead, we used the fact that it was deeply embedded to snag the one who created it. We went on trial, and a spell cast at the right time literally saved us, turning the tables between Elran and Felaern."

Elran and Felaern. I couldn't put faces with the names, but I recognized them in a foggy mush of High Elf. I shook my head.

"After that," my father said, taking up the narrative, "Felaern was elected to the council and got Illiara and Elliah's trials dismissed under the 'Sanctified Mandate.'" My father puffed up like a High Elf in full lecture mode. "'The Invocation of the goddess's will supersedes all other jurisdictional law.'" He blew out air in harrumph of frustration. "Zoras put that mandate in place in order to convince Warders to let the Mother be taken off the battlefield." In a whisper, he said, "Though I suspect they lied about the Mother wanting to rest." Our High Elf escort, except for Trentius, hadn't stopped with us. If they heard and cared about my father's claim, they didn't show it. My father continued in a normal voice. "Felaern explained it to me after the fact. He basically got us out of there as quickly as possible. As promised." He said the last to Illiara with a nod of respect.

Illiara grunted in response. "I don't know what to believe," she said. "Yes, he did what he said he would, and that saved our pretty asses to be sure. But now he's throwing our cute butts into the lava pits!"

"The deal was to get us out of Alenor if we backed him for the council," my father said to me as much as Illiara. "You did your part. He did his. We're done. Cenaedth, I *wanted* to go to. The Mother Blessed my plan. We couldn't have asked for a better outcome."

Illiara grunted again, unconvinced. "And if we chose to go our own way, you think our *escorts* would support that?"

My father's eyes followed the High Elves who continued walking away. "It doesn't matter. I want to go to Cenaedth. They merely keep us safer."

"It matters," Illiara said softly.

The High Elves eased to a stop at the crest of the hill, waiting for us.

"So," Illiara asked. "Do you remember where we are going?"

We had just talked about it, yet I still struggled to pull the memory. "Cenaedth," I finally answered, and Illiara smiled encouragingly.

Cenaedth. Home of the Alluvium, dark-skinned elves that lived underground and worked Fire magic. We needed them. "We need an army," I murmured, more drawing a conclusion than remembering.

"Careful," my father said, nodding to Elliah.

"The Father of Stones isn't targeting Elliah!" I barked. My emotions, as stable as an earthquake, jumped from embarrassment to anger and back to chagrin.

"He might be," Elliah said softly. "Something got in my head... something other than the Mother of Trees."

My father backed her up. "Felaern said it might have been the Father of Stones."

I was stunned. Yes, there was a time when I wasn't sure the

Mother of Trees was real, and yet I'd met her, as disappointing as that had turned out to be. But the Father of Stones? There were not even valid sightings of him in records of old battles. Just rumors. Hints. A belief that *something* other than cunning Warlords drove the trolls into war frenzies. Origin stories for the elves and the trolls. But despite my disbelief, it was clear that Elliah had been frightened. I hadn't talked to Elliah since the Mother of Trees. Images flashed through my head that denied the truth of that, but I couldn't *remember*.

I let out the breath I hadn't realized I was holding.

"Okay," I said. "We won't talk about the ultimate goal," even as images of the ice-covered peaks of the Dragon's Fangs popped into my mind. Fire, ice, water. "But why are you going along with my father? This is his mission, not yours."

I was looking at Elliah when I asked, but her mother answered first. "Elliah wants to help the Mother of Trees." A blush crept into her cheeks as I stared. Was she serious? Was she trying to lift my father's spirits? That would be… insane! Not just fanatical, but deadly. My father followed a mission he believed a dying being would divinely influence in his favor.

"She needs me," Elliah eked out.

She looked down at her feet, unable to meet my eyes any longer. That convinced me. She meant it.

Okay. Elliah intended to go with my father. Illiara wouldn't abandon her daughter. "I guess we're going to Cenaedth," I said, a little numb to my own words.

"Excellent!" my father declared, pounding me on the back and marching forward toward the High Elves. Illiara and Trentius followed him, leaving me with Elliah.

She looked up at me with a shy attempt at a smile. I didn't understand what she was thinking, nor could I connect my own shattered memories and feelings. My insides, both guts and mind, clashed like striated metamorphic rock after a tectonic shift. *Yes, I definitely feel like schist.*

Without saying more, Elliah and I slowly gathered with the rest. There were eight High Elves in all, most roughly my height or a little taller. Stern and aloof, save for Trentius, they scouted the land ahead like it held vipers instead of tallish grass and a caravan of wagons heading from east to west at the bottom of the hill.

"What luck we found a caravan," my father said. "The Mother smiles upon our journey."

I cringed.

"They park there in the spring," said a High Elf, his tone distant. "The heavy rains create moving rivers."

"Moving rivers?" Elliah asked. When she cocked her head and her tongue peeked out of the side of her mouth, my heart beat faster. Shame I didn't understand cascaded over me like a rockfall, and I studied my boots rather than stare at Elliah.

"The grasslands are flat," Illiara said, "with little rock. Mud shifts. The rivers shift. A small change upstream can cause a rapid swing downstream. Moving rivers. The caravans park to the north and south of the grasslands. Here in these hills on the south side. In the foothills of the Witless Mountains to the north. The rest of the year, these *Wood Elves* travel."

Elliah cocked her head at her mother. Still cute, and still inexplicably embarrassing. "Wood Elves?" she asked. "But there are no trees."

"Indeed," Illiara answered.

"Well," my father said, bright and full of cheer. "Let's cross those *moving rivers* and get to Cenaedth!" Without waiting, he tromped down the hill toward the unmoving caravan below.

Illiara - 4

The way Beldroth's eyes squinted in suspicion made me squirm like I sat in a bath filled with leeches.

"When we get to Cenaedth, should I expect to find another cadre from your reverse harem?"

His words stung. But when he grinned, my worry melted away. Did he really have no concerns about our relationship? He didn't need to, but it took self-confidence—

I halted my train of thought, suddenly realizing how every man who'd played a significant role in my life oozed self-confidence. Yet Beldroth... he tempered confidence with empathy. And his confidence stemmed not from an internal fire, but rather a belief in something greater than himself. Even if the object of his belief didn't deserve it.

"So let's meet this fiancé of yours," Beldroth said with a thunderous clap of his large hands.

He strode toward the waiting party of Wood Elves like he went to greet old friends. Behind them stood squat trees curved from the ground, the first non-grassy growth we'd seen in days. They rimmed the outskirts of the swamps, their swirls a response to battling winds between the ocean and the mountains, their roots clutching onto a vein of rock that jutted all the way from our destination, the Druinheim Mountains. They stood like a withered army, thrashed by winds, pounded by the shifting floods from the grasslands, clinging to their position to thwart all attackers.

The days traveling through the grasslands had gone a good way toward healing Elliah and Hughelas, at least separately. Hughelas recovered more rapidly, his mind rebuilding as his energy returned. Elliah? Elliah had been scared almost to death. Her road back would not be a stroll down a forest trail to a scenic waterfall. But the peaceful travel in a mucker caravan with Wood Elves from the grasslands had been a warm broth for her soul.

"Okay," I sighed, my smile strained as I kept my back to the Wood Elves from Fael Themar. Elliah cocked her head at me curiously, and Hughelas's eyes followed Elliah. He blushed and looked away. I'd seen his Hook, knew why he was embarrassed, but I didn't know how to help. I hoped it was just a matter of time. *Because time heals all wounds, right?*

"Okay," I said again, then spun around before Elliah asked anything more.

I wished there was a way to avoid Fael Themar. More specifically, to avoid Taegen, the fiancé I'd left for Felaern, the Wood Elf determined to find a city lost during the Breaking and who founded the city around Fael Themar through grit and charisma. But with the spring floods, the safest passage to Cenaedth took us through the nascent city.

I'd convinced myself we might not encounter him. He might have been too busy, after all, overseeing the birth of a city. Or traveling. Or dead.

But, somehow, news of our party, a group of High Elves, a Warder, a mixed-breed Salt, and Wood Elves, had beat us to Fael Themar, and I'd quickly fessed up to Beldroth… when no other choice remained. Taegen sat astride a mucker, as majestic as one could be atop a flightless feathered beast that waddled on four webbed feet.

With a sigh, I jogged to catch up with the long-strided Warder, casting a quick glance back to be sure Elliah still walked with Hughelas. They walked with Hughelas holding a book open between them as Hughelas pointed at it and spoke, his words carried away by the winds before they reached my ears. He still didn't remember the exact details of how he'd come by the book, but I'd recognized it immediately. Regrettably, I hadn't snatched it away and thrown it in the fire. That was the book Felaern had returned with on the trip that had changed him. He'd argued endlessly with Zoras about its contents. The trip had lit a fire in him, and the book had convinced him that breeding across races would create children with more powerful magic. He'd convinced me. Elliah wouldn't exist without that book. Yet he'd been wrong. Elliah had been born Bereft, just as Zoras had warned. Fire or mud—I should have thrown it in one of them.

But it had given them something to do, other than the thing kids their age were prone to do. I put a hand to my belly, a slight flush of hormones or hypocrisy heating my cheeks.

Taegen dismounted his rare, black mucker as we approached, but the two Wood Elves he brought with him remained atop theirs. Their mottled green and brown feathers blended so well with the landscape that the elves almost appeared to be floating in the air. Their leader's eyes stayed locked onto me, until Beldroth's hulking form prevented it.

"You must be Taegen," Beldroth sang, and I caught up just as

Beldroth grabbed Taegen by the shoulders, smiling. Taegen's escorts tensed, but didn't overreact. "I've heard so much about you."

A welcoming smile bloomed on Taegen's lips. His perfect lips. Under deep green eyes that glistened as he peered into the soul of whoever they landed upon. Heat crept up my cheeks. *Sodding trees, but that man is attractive!*

I'd hoped that, over eighty years, he would have gained a scar or two. I certainly had. But no. He looked like he could outrun a cheetah, or throw it into a tree... or take it in his arms and pull it close until their hearts beat as one, their breath intermingled, their...

Rotting fungi! Get it together, woman!

"I'm afraid you have the better of me," Taegen said, his smile somehow becoming even more welcoming. "I merely heard we had visitors from Alenor." Beldroth released Taegen, stepping back a half step. "As though that wasn't wonder enough, I'm honored with the visit of an old friend and, perhaps, some new ones?"

The High Elves and our muckers still lagged behind, Beldroth's rapid stride providing several seconds without them. Taegen's smile became... wistful... as his eyes again fixed on me. "Welcome back to Fael Themar, Illiara. I'd always hoped the stories of your demise were just... stories. I have much to share with you."

Heat rose at his final words, innocent as they might have been. *Rotting fungi!* I blushed when Beldroth turned to me with a raised eyebrow and a smirk.

But our conversation halted as the High Elves approached, lining up in a semicircle before Taegen. My daughter and Hughelas trailed behind, but caught up as we all stood quietly. Finally, Skaljian spoke. "Taegen, founder of Themopolis. The High Council sends greetings and requests safe passage through your lands."

What Taegen should have said was something to the effect of, "Might I show my people's hospitality to the emissaries of the distinguished High Council?"

Instead, his eyes locked on Elliah, and he said, "She looks so much like you."

Something in the way he cocked his head, and Elliah's slow blush under his stare, chilled my blood like a dive in icy water. I nearly slapped him, restraining myself with barely a twitch. He didn't bother looking at me, but he grinned, and my anger boiled.

I placed myself to block his vision of my daughter, coincidentally putting me closer to Beldroth, who I wrapped an arm around. To drive home the situation, I put my other hand on my belly. I doubted most of the rest of the world could tell I bore a child, but my little clue would clear it up. His gaze indeed drifted to my stomach.

That's right, stud! Not yours. Again.

Petty? Yeah, well, he could shove it up a sappy knothole. It was rumored that Taegen no longer tried to draw followers to Themopolis… he simply populated it with his offspring.

"Come," Taegen said to our entire group. "Let the delegates of the High Council experience the wonders of Themopolis." His smile, a thin veil revealing genuine mirth, remained in place as he turned and climbed his mucker. "See to their comfort," he said to his aides. "They will *all* see that which we have discovered."

What had they discovered? *I have much to share with you.* Taegen's words shifted meaning, and I managed to keep my eyes from rolling or emitting any kind of disbelieving grunt. Taegen always had something new. A smokescreen of sensational evidence that led to his continued pursuit of a fabled lost city. I managed to contain myself until Taegen disappeared amidst the shriveled guardian trees along the ridge.

Then… I sighed, my soul making a desperate bid for escape, only to realize there was no way out.

Elliah ~ 4

"I said, 'Lower your weapons!'" Skaljian, the leader of our High Elf escort, barked the order at his squad for the second time. But would they listen?

And the day had begun with such promise. Well, moderate promise.

Starting with Taegen...

***

My mother had left *him* for Felaern? Taegen was nine kinds of beautiful! The longer his gaze had lingered, the more... exposed... I'd felt. From time to time, Hughelas looked at me the way Taegen had, like I was a mouthwatering slice of meat fresh off the fire.

I shivered the thought away, grabbing Hughelas's hand as we navigated the rocky ground along a path between the twisted trees.

"You should walk them," my mother said to the Wood Elf guides atop their muckers. "Their feet aren't made for rocks." She'd had us pull our packs from our muckers. Trentius had done the same—for a High Elf, he knew a surprising amount about them and even had a surprising affinity for muckers and other animals. I hadn't seen them before the grasslands, though Trentius told me a mucker pulled the cart that brought me from the Mother's Den to Alenor.

"Feathered deer with webbed feet and bills," Trentius had said in his matter-of-fact way when I'd first seen them. The description wasn't quite right. The muckers' legs and necks were shorter and thicker than a deer's, they lacked horns of any kind, and they weren't nearly so skittish. Plus, they liked to be around elves. Tamed. "Domesticated" was the more accurate word. Trentius claimed herds of wild muckers wandered the tall grasses of the plains, but apparently no one saw them because of their natural camouflage. While unfindable herds sounded far-fetched, the muckers had come from *somewhere*.

My mother grumbled when our hosts ignored her, remaining astride their muckers. Truthfully, though the ground to the sides displayed jagged rocks, the path we traveled was relatively smooth, a well-worn trail that sat on lower ground. The elves of Themopolis had worked hard to create such a passage.

Upon clearing the twisted trees, I got my first look—and smell—

of Themopolis, the city built on the edge of Fael Themar, also known as the Faelian Swamps. The land sloped down at an almost cliff-like steepness to a wonder below.

Either the land had stretched fingers into the murky water, knuckle islands protruding without connection, or the water had attempted to swallow the land and bit off more than it could handle. Every meandering shoreline hosted knobby trees that interconnected at their roots, like one giant organism held the land and water in place. The smell was musty and earthy, but a sweet overtone drew my eyes to the white and purple flowers that peeked through the trees. Stone and wood buildings dotted the shore closest to the grasslands, stretching in a line rather than sprawling out into the swamp islands, though buildings had grown like warts even in the swamp. To the north, a river spilled water from the grasslands, cascading off the hill we stood upon and tumbling in a series of waterfalls down to the town, where an elf-made barrier collected the water in a pond, and the swamp swallowed the spillover like it was nothing. Buildings hugged that pond the same way they embraced the shore. Empty pools dotted the strip of land between the hill and the swamp, pockmarks on the scar that defined the elf toehold.

"I… don't understand what I'm seeing," I said to my mother, waving vaguely toward the empty pools. While my tone relayed confusion, for the first time since my encounter with the Mother of Trees, wonder gripped me. It was like nothing I'd ever seen, and the reality was so much more grand than the childhood stories from Telana Talonforged.

"Remember what I told you," my mother said. "The river shifts. Sometimes it comes through where you see it, sometimes where we are standing now. There are more openings farther north." I looked behind us to be sure a wall of water hadn't snuck up. My mother smiled. "The shifts *can* be quite sudden." That explained the smooth passageway; it wasn't the work of elves, but of water.

"Fascinating!" Trentius exclaimed. "And the buildings *in* the swamp?"

I studied the swamp more closely. Trentius was right—not all the buildings sat above water.

"The ground here isn't firm," my mother answered. "Buildings sink, and, oddly, sometimes they rise again." She pointed, and I found a stone building on one of the knuckle islands covered in green-brown algae.

"Lost Landmarks Loom Large as Swamp Slowly Surrenders Secrets," Trentius mumbled to no one in particular.

"Come," my mother said, starting forward. "It is not wise to linger here." Indeed, our mucker escort had disappeared while I'd stared at Themopolis. The route, if one wasn't liquid, climbed out of the ravine to the right and then down a zig-zagging trail carved into the steep slope.

We caught up with our guides and trailed them to the rim of a half-empty pond surrounded by quiet buildings.

"Many of the businesses shift operations to whichever pond the grasslands fill," my mother explained. "Themopolis... Taegen, specifically... came up with the original idea of the waterwheel and aqueducts in Alenor. But Themopolis's physical problems are more challenging. Each pond would have to distribute to the ones on either side, because they never know which will get water." She scanned the cliff wall as best she could to the north. "Has any progress been made?" she asked our guides.

They completely ignored her and continued on their way. My mother's lip twitched in a snarl, but she didn't press the issue. Very unlike her. Growing up, she'd always had us lie low. Oh, sure, I saw her anger. But showing it to others was unsafe. Was this her true nature, dampened down my whole life to keep me hidden?

"More importantly," Trentius said, "they don't have the magic to make it effective."

Hughelas cocked his head. "What do you mean?"

"Water magic," Trentius said. "The hydro-powered scoop wheel in Alenor can lift water without magic, but it wouldn't work on the scale of what's needed for Alenor. No sir. That whole aqueduct system wouldn't be effective without the aid of spell-casters."

"So can the High Elves teach the Wood Elves?" I asked.

"High Elves can't work it," Trentius said with a scoff, earning him a glare from his High Elf comrades. "Well, it's true. It's a closely held secret in Alenor, who keeps the water flowing."

Curious, I asked. "Who?"

"Mixed-breed Salts," Trentius said. "Not like Hughelas here, but part Wood Elf, part Salt. Despite what is popularly believed, the whole city would have stagnated without the aid of Wood Elves and, Mother forgive them, mixed-breeds."

"Trentius, that's enough," commanded Skaljian, their leader, who spent more time reigning in Trentius than he did all the rest of his squad combined. I sympathized with him—taking care of Trentius was a bit like caring for a child. But I pitied Trentius too, because he was an adult who endured the constant criticism of his commanding officer.

"You'll be staying here," one of the Wood Elf escorts said, stopping before an inn by the half-drained pond. They finally dismounted their muckers. "We will be here in case you need anything." Like the buildings around it, quiet and stillness suggested it lay dormant.

"We won't be staying more than a night," Skaljian replied. "We journey on to Cenaedth."

Our Wood Elf escorts exchanged a look, something dark... brooding.

"As far as I'm concerned, the sooner you're gone the better," said their speaker, earning scowls from the High Elves. "But Taegen still thinks there might be benefits in being... neighborly."

"The High Council has always encouraged Taegen's... enterprise," Skaljian said with his nose in the air, matching the Wood Elf's pause. "Zoras, the Mother keep his soul—"

Beldroth's eyes flew wide, his shock apparent at Skaljian's reference to the Mother.

"—sent his daughter to marry your... *Taegen.*"

"Fortunately," said the Wood Elf, "our *Taegen* came to his senses."

No one missed the scrape of Beldroth's sword leaving its scabbard. Even without a weapon, Beldroth was an intimidating hulk of a man. And while I could have let the insult to my mother go unanswered, I pulled my hammer from its sling. Not only did the Wood Elves answer with swords of their own, but several more melted out of the building, nocking arrows to bows. Several of the closest High Elves responded by drawing swords or raising their hands as though they intended to cast spells.

***

Even if the High Elves lowered their weapons, I doubted Beldroth would, and I wasn't going to stand by and let him deal with the situation alone.

"Let me handle this," said an unexpected voice. Trentius, no weapon drawn, pushed between Beldroth and the closest Wood Elves. "I know it looks easy, but Wood Elves are *masters* at staring contests." He arched an eyebrow dramatically and opened his eyes wide. "But I can take them."

A Wood Elf at the back, arrow trained on Trentius, snickered. Trentius had picked one of the two Wood Elves with swords to square off against, and the other chuckled, his sword lowering slightly. The High Elves lowered theirs, even sheathing them, obeying their commanding officer with a show.

Beldroth looked over at my mother.

"It's okay," she said. "I know I insulted Taegen, and by association, three quarters of the population of the Faelian Swamps." Fortunately, that drew a chuckle from the Wood Elves. "We will stay to see what Taegen wishes to show us." The Wood Elves smiled at that, perhaps appreciating the solidarity.

"My orders," Skaljian said, "are to get you to Cenaedth with 'all due haste.'"

"And you shall," my mother answered. "*After* we see what Taegen wishes to show us. Surely," my mother said with a wry grin, "the Mother's plan cannot be thwarted by so simple a courtesy." That got a bright smile from Beldroth, who sheathed his sword, but it earned a grunt of irritation from Skaljian.

"High Elf's Hypnotic Stare Stuns Sylvan Sentinel in Showdown," Trentius said with a bow and a hasty retreat, leaving everyone but Skaljian with a puzzled smile.

Beldroth : 3

Thwack!

I brushed sweat from my brow with the back of my hand, the cool air threatening me with its chill if I let the pace of my efforts slow. I picked up another stone the size of my head, spun in a circle twice to get momentum while I cast a spell, and I flung it out of the pool with a touch of magic.

Crack!

I act like I didn't notice his eye rolls, his clenched fists, the grinding of his teeth. I act like it doesn't bother me.

Thwack!

But my son's newfound disrespect for the Mother of Trees frustrates *me!*

Thwack!

Days of wandering the grasslands, whether on foot or on the muckers, had worn away my edge, so I'd left the others to their meditations and taken up much-needed physical exertion. Large rocks dotted the trails we'd hiked down, and I'd applied myself by clearing them from the path.

Thwack!

Upon completing that task, I climbed into the near-dry pool bed and emptied out the large debris. I stayed clear of the bit of water—for all I knew, that was the source of our drinking water—but I'd pulled out everything I could reach without getting wet. I'd hauled or tossed the obstructions over the side, using magic where needed.

Thwack-crack!

I stood straighter and rolled my shoulders, enjoying the sound of the rock breaking on impact. It reminded me of fighting trolls. A simpler time. When the Mother was good, the Father was evil, and the fight was clear. A time before *children*.

I stretched my arms, thinking. It was that search for a simple fight that had taken me into the mountains, the trolls having more or less abandoned the Blasted Lands. Over the years of my vigil after my wife's death, fewer and fewer Warders came to train under me. There was less need because the trolls attacked less frequently. Miserable trolls.

Miserable children. Why was Hughelas being so disrespectful? He'd seen the goddess with his own eyes! Witnessed her power, the whispered covenant of rebirth and renewal her magic called forth, reconnecting severed limbs to the silvervein and bringing them new life. Did he not see the metaphor? Not feel the promise of a new life like a caterpillar metamorphosing into a butterfly?

And why was Illiara humoring that pretty-boy, Taegen? We had the Mother's work to do. The whole point of traveling to Fael Themar was to increase our pace—travel along the edge of the swamp was quicker than the grasslands and avoided the moving rivers. One look at Taegen and suddenly we needed to stay?

I searched for another head-sized rock to hurl at the massive stone that sat outside the pool. Wanting to get out of my head, needing to *break* something. A candidate slightly bigger than my fist offered itself up, and I chucked it out of the pool with a little underhanded spin.

Thwack! Thwack!

It danced away from the first rock and hit another. Very satisfying, even if it was a tad on the light side.

A giggle drew my eyes up to the back of the pool. Across the water, atop the wall, two children sat on the edge and watched me, and not far away, a young woman Wood Elf with uncharacteristically light-blond hair waved tentatively. *Pretty.* She pointed to my left, and I followed her direction. The pool had stone teeth set in it. All I could figure was that the teeth slowed the rushing water when the river flooded in. A nice, head-sized rock had hidden behind the tooth. I walked over and scooped it up, and, just for fun, jumped atop the stone tooth. Its flat surface barely had room for me, but that made it perfect for the exercise. I cast a spell that stitched one foot firmly to the ground, using the anchor to my advantage.

Thwack!

The woman clapped lightly, and I looked back at her smiling face. The blush creeping up her cheeks drew my awareness to the fact that I'd left my tunic at the top of the pool. I frowned, suddenly self-conscious about the blue etchings on my back, wondering whether anyone who lived so far west knew how to read them. Some of the symbols had been youthful... mistakes. She pointed to my left again, and from atop the tooth, it wasn't hard to see what she indicated: a rock the size of my arm. I looked back up at her, and she flexed her muscles humorously and pointed at the rock again.

Why not?

I hopped down and approached the rock. Realistically, carrying it out would have been the right move. I squatted and picked it up, straining to set it atop the tooth. I quickly worked my spells. There wasn't time in battle for anything fancy. Shield and strength. Warders understood how intimately those two were connected. Shield wasn't just for taking a punch from a troll. I found a solid rock and anchored my feet to the stone beneath me, lining the muscles I would need, tying them to tendons and bones, then lifted the rock, bringing it behind my head. Using my legs, arms, my whole body, and my magic, I hurled the stone.

Crack!

That was how Warders fought trolls.

The magic fled, and I sucked in air like I'd run a race. That had challenged me. I turned to thank the woman for her encouragement, but she stared, mouth hanging open, at the target. Shrugging, I trudged up the sloping edge to the shortest end of the pool to climb out. It was time to leave my frustrations behind. Time to plant my smile back on my face and be what everyone needed me to be. To my surprise, the woman stood there, breathing hard from a quick jog around the pool. She reached down to help me out, like her tiny arm would do anything but come out of the socket if I grabbed it.

I waved for her to step back, and when she did, I once again used a spell to boost my jump, leaping to the ledge which sat slightly higher than my head. Many decades of practice, and training so many missionaries for battle, enabled me to cast the spells with hardly any mnemonics at all. I'd seen older Warders who, to all appearances, worked their magic from pure thought. I knew better—they were just very subtle, and very good.

The way she stared up at me, out of breath, flushed, I worried that I'd misconstrued her attention, and I walked over to retrieve my tunic. She was a pretty little woman, no question. But I had chosen Illiara. I slid my tunic on and turned.

I almost jumped. She was right there, staring up at me with big, blue eyes. Pleading eyes.

"I…" I stammered.

"Teach me," she begged.

Eyes wide, I blushed about having misunderstood her intent. I'd attributed Illiara's direct approach to sex to be a part of her Wood Elf culture, and I'd assumed too much. Still, I wasn't sure what to say; one couldn't teach a Wood Elf to use Warder magic. "I..."

She scooped a fist-sized rock—her tiny fist—and held it out before me. She stared at it, and stared some more, grinding her teeth. Sweat beaded on her brow. With veins popping, she screamed, and the rock cracked.

"Teach me," she said, panting.

A Wood Elf with Warder magic. I thought her blond hair was unusual.

She didn't have the ageless look of an elf who had seen centuries. Warder magic was dangerous. She was young and pretty... perhaps even more dangerous. "Have you had... relations... with men?"

She looked down. Shy? Sad? Because she hadn't had any relations or because she had and I'd hit the nail on the head? She nodded her head.

Gently, I raised her head up and, with a soft voice, asked. "Did he survive?"

"Yes! Broken bones..." She sucked in a half-sob. "No one comes near me. They think I'm cursed."

"Cursed? Ha!" I put an arm around her and hugged her, pulling her close. "Blessed by the Mother," I said, and she truly cried then. How marvelous—a Wood Elf with Warder magic. A change was coming. Even Zoras's dying words had mentioned a catalyst.

Illiara, Elliah, Hughelas, and Trentius appeared suddenly, out of breath, but slowed when they saw us together. Illiara squinted suspiciously at the woman in my arms.

"Someone screamed," Elliah said. "Is there trouble?"

"No," I said, as the woman in my arms extracted herself, turning her head the other way to wipe away her tears. "Everything is fine." I smiled.

The woman choked back a sob that snuck up on her the way they do once you've humored them. Ah, of course she was still sad. I hadn't said I would help.

"What's your name?" I asked her.

"Marinna," she said.

I shouted to Illiara, beaming, "I'm going to teach Marinna how to have sex!"

Hughelas #5

Creatures slid off the banks into the still water almost without sound. Scaly heads appeared near the boats, and occasionally we bumped things, or things bumped us. Though it unnerved me, nothing showed violent interest. I imagined a garonaut, like the one we'd seen in Anysa whose rider said it had come from the Fealian Swamps. If one of those hulking creatures were under our boat, it could easily topple us. I shivered, thinking of the things I *couldn't* see under the murky, algae-covered water.

"So, who in your family is a Warder?" I asked Marinna, more to listen to something other than Illiara yelling at my father than out of genuine interest. We were all stuck in the boat together, and Illiara continued to chew a hole in my father's ear despite the lack of privacy. Marinna stared out the front of the boat, looking at nothing, and Elliah and I had joined her. The yelling spilled from the back of the boat, but found no home in the still, brackish waters. Trentius rode in the middle, alternating between attempts to talk to the Wood Elf oarsman and to Taegen, who had taken up the other oar, and failing to engage either of them.

Taegen focused on some internal debate, looking occasionally at either our arguing parents or the boat full of High Elves that trailed us. A ship like the Knoll, the craft we'd taken down the Flawless River, would have held us all, but would never have been able to navigate the swamps. It was too big, and some of the passages too narrow, or too shallow. Instead, we occupied two flat boats, which Taegen had shown up with that morning. He had even charmed the High Elves into indulging him… sort of. He'd actually shown a reluctance to include them, despite having arrived with transportation sufficient to carry everyone. His hesitancy drew the High Elves in more than I think an invitation would have done. I couldn't tell whether Taegen's reluctance was genuine or a calculated ploy.

"My great-grandfather, I assume," Marinna answered. "My great-grandmother came here from the Border Woods, pregnant. Her daughter, my grandmother, looks like a Wood Elf. Perhaps a little taller and more broad of shoulder than most Wood Elves, but… normal. My mother doesn't even have the girth." She shrugged. "Great-grandmother never talked about the war, or my great-grandfather. She was one of the founders of Themopolis, alongside Taegen, though I suspect her motivations were not so adventurous as Taegen's, but rather an exit plan from the war."

Marinna stared off into the distance. She had not hesitated to tell my father she would join us, even upon learning that we intended to leave Fael Themar as quickly as possible. In fact, after an initial hesitancy that seemed all about the poor word choice of my father, she'd seemed eager. She'd vanished and reappeared with a pack in time to accompany us on our trek into the swamp proper.

"I hate to pry," Elliah said. "But..." Elliah paused, squinting. "Actually, I can ask this without prying into *your* business." She turned to me. "Hughelas, why is your father making this about sex?"

Chagrined, I regretted my attempt to drown out our arguing parents.

"I'm here, growing your *child* inside me, and you can't keep your gaze where it belongs?" Illiara shouted. "What kind of mate are you?"

Weirdly, I found their worldly argument less discomforting than the copious thinly veiled references to my father's *Blessed* mission. But I still wasn't exactly *enjoying* their private argument performed in public, so I plowed ahead with the conversation I'd started. Instead of answering directly, I said to Marinna, "You broke things as a young woman. Not normal things, like plates, or tools. You broke tables, beds... bones."

Marinna bit her lip and nodded her head.

"It's normal," I explained. "Among Warders."

"You had that?" Elliah asked.

"Even I," I said with a slight, albeit sarcastic, bow. "Father made me practice every form of magic, but basic Earth, Water, and Air spells came the most naturally. You've seen me try to Heal," I said, catching Elliah's eyes. "I'm rubbish. I'm even worse at Fire."

"You can work every kind of magic?" Elliah asked, her eyes widening.

I grimaced. For the entire time we'd traveled together, I'd purposefully avoided saying that. I hadn't wanted to point out how different we were. More and more of late, I'd found my tongue getting ahead of my thoughts. Perhaps some latent effect from the spells cast on my mind in Alenor. My empathy grew for Trentius and his talkative nature.

"Earth magic is about bindings," I said, avoiding Elliah's question except for a sheepish glance her way, and directing the topic to Marinna's interest.

"Bindings? Then why do I *break* things?" Marinna sounded frustrated. I found it hard to relate to how little she knew about Warder magic. It was totally understandable that she hadn't had anyone to train her, but... well, in Bellon, I'd had books, and two parents who understood completely different types of racial magic. Between all of that, I hadn't lacked for information.

"Creating too much pressure on the wrong things," I said. "Earth magic works best through touch and focused emotion, so things around you tend to break when you get worked up."

Marinna nodded, her brow furrowing.

"Then you worry and get more worked up," I continued. "And more things break. People start to think—"

"I'm bad luck," Marinna finished.

"I know from experience," I said. "All *those things* are expected among Warder youths, but they didn't expect the sudden gusts of wind or slippery rocks that came from my mother's magic. 'Hard-luck Hughelas,' the missionaries called me."

Marinna nodded absently, undoubtedly reliving past blunders.

"I still don't understand why your father said what he did," Elliah said, glancing back at our arguing parents.

"He didn't mean anything by it," I answered. "He's not... simple. But sometimes he sees things very simply. Earth magic works through touch. Without training, it can appear with high emotion, anxiety, stress... exertion."

I looked at Elliah meaningfully with the last word.

She formed an "O" with her mouth as realization dawned.

"He's not intending to be involved in sexual relations," I said. I tried not to look at Marinna, but even from the corner of my eye, her blush was apparent. "He intends to teach you control."

"So why are our parents still fighting?" Elliah asked, looking back at the couple who hadn't quieted down.

"Frankly, I think they both enjoy fighting," I said, turning to look at them myself. As if on cue, my father pulled Illiara close for a kiss, reminding me of the time I'd done the same with Elliah. The swamp felt suddenly warmer, and I turned quickly back around to study the shore.

We rode in relative silence for a few minutes, my father having more or less calmed Elliah's mother. I envied him. Direct. Simple. He got what and who he wanted. We all followed him on *his* mission. What about what *I* wanted? What about *who* I wanted?

I tried to refocus my thoughts on the topic with Marinna. The idea of controlling magic made me want to look something up in the book I'd taken from Alenor. I still didn't remember how I'd come by it, but Illiara assured me multiple times that, if I had it, Felaern had meant for me to have it. She didn't say that like it was an entirely *good* thing, but I was glad I hadn't stolen it. Regardless, I'd left it in my bag, in the small room Taegen had provided at the inn.

Sensing I was being watched, I turned to find Taegen still rowing, but studying me.

"Is it far?" I asked, wondering if I might get back in time to read more of the book. The author introduced a form of math new to me, representing cyclical behaviors very simply, then using that to express stable versus unstable feedback.

He took a hand off the oar and let it drift, to point ahead as we rounded a corner in the canal. "That's where we're headed."

A set of islands appeared before us that didn't fit in. Black rock rose out of the swamp like a grove of giant charred tree stumps in an otherwise verdant forest. The vegetation on the dark stone differed from that which sprouted from the boggy islands around it. A few trees climbed straight out of the rock, red flowers on the tips of their sinuous limbs reaching for the sun. Small grasses and dark green plants clung tightly to the black, porous island in patches. Upon close examination, the swamp had managed to coat the lower rocks in moss.

"Is that volcanic?" I asked, surprised and confused. I'd never seen volcanic rock before, but I'd read about Cenaedth before we left Bellon, and I expected that, at the Alluvium capital, I would see not just volcanic rock, but magma as well.

"Yes," Marinna said. "Nothing active, but it must once have been. We've always called them, imaginatively enough, the Black Rock Islands."

"Very creative," Elliah said, her eyes sparkling with humor.

We floated closer, Taegen resuming his effort to get us there.

"You've shown me these before," Illiara said from the back of the boat. "You claimed even then that they were evidence of a lost city. Please tell me you're not wasting our time." Taegen quietly clenched his jaw, or he chewed on second guesses.

"Could *you* teach me then?" Marinna asked. I'd become so preoccupied with the volcanic islands and Taegen's mysterious discovery that I didn't know what she was talking about. "I mean, can you teach me theory? You two seem to have learned enough control not to break bones."

Once I understood, it was my turn to blush. Elliah and I hadn't actually done that particular bone-threatening activity. My attention shifted completely away from the approaching islands.

Marinna misunderstood my blush, thinking I was just shy, not knowing that Elliah and I had intentionally slowed down, and that I regretted it… and hadn't yet told Elliah. She pushed ahead, saying, "I'm sorry. I'm not trying to pry. I just can't believe I'm suffering from a problem whose solution is… common knowledge… among the right people. Would any Warder be able to teach me?"

"Many would," I said. "Not all. My father is a particularly good teacher. He ran a mission in the Blasted Lands." Marinna cocked her head in question. The Faelian Swamp was halfway around the world from my home—I shouldn't have been surprised she wasn't familiar with the Blasted Lands. "He taught fighting, using weapons and magic. Earth magic is all about control. He taught that. It's a place where his simplicity pays off."

I faced out toward the Black Rock Islands, noting that Elliah watched our parents. Marinna looked down at the water.

"Is that why you want me, mixed-breed?" Elliah said. "You know your magic won't break my bones?" She sounded serious, and I whipped my head toward her. Marinna gasped. But Elliah wore a mischievous grin.

Truth be told, the thought had crossed my mind. I'd never mentioned it… the inherent presumption tripped me up.

"Watch who you're calling mixed-breed, mixed-breed," I retorted, earning another gasp from Marinna.

"You're…" she stammered to Elliah. "You have mixed blood too?" But she had already moved her hand closer to Elliah's, noticing her longer fingers, then looking over the rest of her. Elliah turned and held up her hand, inviting Marinna to do the same with a nod of her head.

Marinna placed her open hand opposite Elliah's, and I couldn't see Marinna's face, but she sniffled. I didn't understand her level of emotion, but suddenly Marinna sobbed and pulled Elliah into a hug.

Just as abruptly, she stepped back, mumbling, "No touching," like she repeated a message she'd heard countless times.

"It's okay," Elliah said slowly. I knew from her own story that Elliah wasn't a hugger. She'd had her own demons that kept elves at bay. But she wanted to comfort Marinna. "It's okay. You're not going to hurt me with your magic." Elliah stepped forward, wrapping Marinna in her arms, and Marinna cried.

Out of curiosity, I cast the spell to let me see magic. The hammer was on Elliah's back, almost hidden by the inky darkness that was Elliah. Marinna's magic sizzled like hot grease on a frying pan. *Wow, she's got a lot!* It was no wonder she had trouble controlling it. Still, it wasn't focused, and it popped harmlessly into the abyss of Elliah through their touch.

I returned my attention to the Black Rock Islands. We angled toward a relatively flat section of the otherwise jutting rock. Taegen wanted Illiara to see it, or he wanted the High Elves to see it and he used his past relationship with Illiara as an excuse. I couldn't tell which. Why were we there?

Crack!

I jumped, looking down for the source of the noise, as did everyone else. Marinna's magic coursed harmlessly into Elliah. But at Marinna's feet, the boat hadn't fared as well.

Elliah ~ 5

Hughelas dropped to his knees and cast a spell, placing his hands on the boat. Marinna responded by pulling away from me like our hug had broken the boat, sobbing, and the creaking of wood grew louder, like a mighty limb about to snap in a gale.

"Carry her, Elliah!" Hughelas spat.

I froze. *What?*

"Carry her!" he shouted again, then he cast another spell and returned his hands to the boat.

I glanced quickly behind me—Beldroth would have no trouble carrying Marinna. But he knelt on the floor at the back of the boat, working magic.

The rowers paddled madly as reptilian heads broke the water, paying homage to the bounteous gift they were poised to receive. I did as I was told, squaring and shifting my arms around to get one under Marinna's knees. She didn't resist, as startled and confused as I, but recognizing the danger and willing to try anything. Fortunately, she was small-boned and tiny, but I wasn't exactly large for a Wood Elf myself. With the hammer already on my back, cradling Marinna wasn't easy.

The creaking, groaning wood quieted. Swamp creatures splashed their disappointment, nudging the boat just to be sure it wasn't ready to release its bounty.

Sweat dripped from my brow and my arms shook by the time the boat bumped the rocks, causing me to stumble a step deeper into the boat. But I didn't drop my precious cargo.

"Get her off the boat," Hughelas hissed.

I turned in a series of small shuffles, trying not to lose my balance, until my toes hit the front of the boat. Taegen himself somehow leapt off and held out his arms to me.

"No," Marinna growled, and Taegen moved out of the way, holding the lip of the boat against the rocks.

I didn't think I could get my leg over the edge, balanced on one foot, carrying all the weight I had on me. I leaned forward, setting Marinna's feet down as best I was able, then tumbled as her feet hit the rock.

Taegen kept me from hitting the ground, pulling me to land on him instead of the rock. I panted into his beautiful face as he lay on his back, one arm under me and the other still clutching the boat.

Someone helped me rise, and I scrambled up the rock to make way for others, trying to avoid thinking about the awkwardness and discomfort I'd experienced near Taegen. Marinna sat on the stone, her misery slowing to a steady trickle of tears. Whatever her magic had done with the wood of the boat, the Black Rock Islands didn't buckle.

Shortly afterwards, the second boat unloaded, and three groups formed. The High Elves clustered together, our ragtag crew assembled around me and Marinna, and the Wood Elves pulled the boats out of the water. Then Taegen walked up the rock between the two groups on shore and waved for us to gather.

"They will stay with the boats. Come." He walked deeper into the island, climbing up the incline. The island was not wide; I'd seen as much as we'd approached. But the far side stood much higher out of the bog than the side we'd landed on.

"Caves dot these islands," Marinna said. "We used to explore them as kids. Dare each other. I imagine that still happens. They stopped inviting me after… after a time when I got scared."

I could imagine.

"Don't worry," Beldroth said, putting an arm on her shoulder. "I will teach you control. First, you will learn how to breathe. I will teach you as we walk."

He began coaching her immediately. "Breathe in through your nose for four counts." He demonstrated. "Now," he squeaked, trying to let out as little air as possible, "hold it for seven counts." He ticked off five counts, then squeezed out the conclusion. "Then exhale through your mouth for eight counts."

After his slow exhale, he explained. "Do it repeatedly when you're anxious. It calms the mind and the body. It works with anger too. While it isn't a natural thing to think of in either situation, it is harder to remember when angry."

Breathing exercises were part of what my mother had taught me. I'd only in the last month learned that she'd acquired those exercises from High Elves, as part of a routine to build up mental defenses. I'd assumed all elves did them, as I had nothing to compare against. Apparently, Wood Elves did not. Had we no magic that intrinsically caused harm? We. I still thought of myself as a Wood Elf. Odd, that. Healing and growing things were the dominant spells that Wood Elves mastered. I'd never heard of a Wood Elf choked off by vines from a temper tantrum. We… they… didn't need to lock down control to the same degree as Warders or High Elves. In fact, Wood Elves encouraged passions.

"Why are we here, Taegen?" my mother asked as we neared the summit. "We've indulged you long enough."

The peak of the rock revealed a hole. A rope, secured at the top, dangled into the opening. I stepped past the hole to the calf-high ledge beyond it. Continuing past the ledge, one would tumble down a steep rock into the swamp below.

"Recently, we had a pair of visitors," Taegen said. He looked meaningfully at Beldroth. "Two Alluvium… from Cenaedth." He let that sink in, then grabbed the rope and lowered his body into the hole.

"If you'll follow me," Taegen said, an inviting smile plastered on his face. Yet his eyes pinched, the smile never reaching them.

"Wait," Skaljian said, his exasperation clear. "We've indulged you, followed you out into this putrid swamp when we should have been traveling north to Cenaedth. Now you want us to descend into a hole in the ground? What could possibly be down there to warrant this madness?"

"Only one way to find out," Taegen said with a wink and dropping out of sight, the taut rope gone slack after several seconds. The descent wasn't long.

"Dramatic as ever," my mother mumbled under her breath, moving toward the hole, which lit up slightly from below.

"You're not seriously considering going down there?" the commander asked.

"He's overly dramatic. But," she sighed, "if you've never heard the story of why he came *here*, to the swamps… well, whatever he's found might be worth seeing."

"I take it that visits from the Alluvium are not a common occurrence?" Beldroth asked Marinna.

Marinna shook her head. "Not common, no, but occasionally at the north end of the swamps. I've never heard of one coming this far in."

My mother nodded and opened her hands in a gesture to the High Elf captain conveying that the matter was out of her control. She cast a magelight then started down the rope.

Beldroth didn't hesitate. Technically, he hesitated slightly, casting a spell on the rope. It reminded me of when I first met him—he'd fought those drawgs on the ground, then he'd been in our silvervein, helping my mother Heal me. There was no way the flimsy ladder that led into our home would have supported his weight without magic.

"It's safer if I stay up here," Marinna said. "Safer for you, I mean."

"Nonsense," Beldroth shouted from below. "It's the perfect chance to practice your breathing. I'll wait here for you."

He started counting. Marinna stood there as Beldroth marched through four, seven, eight, and I waved her over when Beldroth began again. "Better just go," I said. I had no doubt, especially from the exasperated look on Hughelas's face, that his father would keep counting for a loooong time.

Trentius spoke up. "I want to see this. 'Alluvium Adepts Ascertain Ancient Anomaly.'"

"Ascertain?" Hughelas asked skeptically.

"It needs work," Trentius agreed. "Captain," he said, "we can't just let them go unprotected into a dangerous situation. It's our duty to get them safely to Cenaedth."

Skaljian jutted out his jaw, clearly frustrated, but he nodded. "The rest of you stay," he told his men, whose hard faces betrayed their relief. "Trentius has volunteered."

Trentius leaned over and, in a conspiratorial whisper to Hughelas, said, "High Elves aren't crazy about caves. That's one thing we have in common with our Wood Elf cousins."

Numbers continued to float up from below—a liturgy of soothing math.

Marinna grimaced, but she followed Beldroth's orders, breathing as she'd been instructed, hesitantly taking the rope, then nodding at me and lowering herself down.

I gave Marinna the count of a full four plus seven plus eight, then decided it was safe to follow her down. I caught Hughelas's eye, then raised an eyebrow at the rope. He half-grinned, then cast a spell on the rope as I lowered myself down it.

The hole tilted slightly, slanting back toward the center of the island, though it was nearly vertical. It was less wide than I was tall. Should the rope break, Beldroth would be able to wedge his body across the gap and climb out. Plus, there were Wood Elves and High Elves who had stayed out. They could bring more rope. We wouldn't be trapped. Yet I didn't discount Trentius's words—neither side of my heritage was crazy about caves.

As I descended, the light from below overtook the light from above, casting big shadows on black rock as I lowered myself. The hole dropped into a horizontal cave several of my body-lengths down. Were we deeper than the swamp water? It was hard to judge. But the weight of the stone squeezed down on me, and the thought of the swamp water and the creatures it contained suddenly flooding in the chamber compelled me to hurry over to stand beside Beldroth. He looked not just unafraid, but like his soul had taken a bath in a hot spring. It appeared that all three of us—my mother, Marinna, and I—hoped that proximity to contentment encouraged it.

Beldroth talked quietly with Marinna, smiling encouragement. The tunnel was wide enough that Taegen stood apart from the rest of us. If he looked concerned about the cave, it didn't show. Three magelights floated in the corridor, which stretched off in either direction, each way curving so that vision was limited. However, the direction in which Taegen stood had a smooth floor, while the other direction looked rough. We waited for Hughelas, Trentius, and Skaljian, then gathered closer to Taegen, who turned and started down the corridor.

The cave fit two people side by side, and since Beldroth was talking with Marinna, my mother scooted up beside Taegen. Hughelas and I walked together, and Trentius took the rear guard with Skaljian, mumbling his fascination in short phrases. The passage sloped down almost as steeply as a staircase.

"It's been a very long time," my mother said, "but I don't remember this passage." The tunnel curved this way and that, but continued to descend lower and lower underground.

"The Alluvium carved out this corridor," he answered. "It has not seen many feet. Yet."

"Is he still here?" my mother asked. She looked suddenly concerned. Talena Talenforged traveled to the Alluvium, where ghosts stalked caves with pools of burning lava. I often skipped over that section, because it had scared me as a child, even though a friendly ghost helped Talena escape the maze of tunnels.

"No. There were two Alluvium. A man and a woman. The man died. The woman returned to Cenaedth." He grimaced. "Angry. Angry about her companion's death. Her parting words? 'Fire lies.'"

"But they found something?" my mother asked. "Something of Stellaris?"

"Stellaris?" Hughelas and I both blurted, then looked at each other strangely. All other thoughts fled my mind as I wondered if the mythical city might have been real.

Taegen smiled. "I told you there was something you needed to see. Honestly, I need the Alluvium and their fire magic more than I need the High Elves, but the High Council is going to insist on inclusion once they hear what I've found." He waved a dismissive hand back the way we'd come. "I'd rather they have only themselves to blame for not participating."

That explained the odd reluctance Taegen showed toward bringing the High Elves along.

"Um, I'm a High Elf," Trentius said from the back, raising his hand, then jerking it down after banging his knuckles on the rock above. "I'm participating," he said over a mouth full of knuckles. Skaljian scowled equally at Trentius and Taegen.

"And I appreciate you and your spirit," Taegen answered smoothly. "I've burned too many candles waiting on the High Elves, and suffered through their broken promises." He eyed my mother sideways.

"Zoras is dead," my mother said, looking ahead.

Taegen stopped, and all of us behind him stumbled to a halt. He looked at his feet, sighed, and started forward again. "I am sorry for your loss," he said, his voice gravelly with emotion that cracked through his diplomacy.

"How do *you* know Stellaris?" I asked Hughelas.

"There's a poem in the ancient tomes of Bellan. It was called something like 'Before the Breaking.' I can't remember it exactly, but it referred to Stellaris as the City of Schools. The idea sounded beautiful to me. You?"

While I'd enjoyed books, schools had not had the same appeal. Schools had too many people, and my life of hiding had never meshed well with crowds. The idea of a city of schools sounded far from beautiful to me. "The Tales of Talena Talonforged," I said. "Talena visits a city on the bottom of the ocean, but it is populated by creatures that are half-elf, half-fish. It was a grand story." I shrugged.

"Unbroken," my mother said, smiling. "The poem's name was 'Unbroken.'"

Taegen began chanting, his voice as pretty as he was.
"In the depths where currents sigh,
Lies Stellaris 'neath the sky,
City of Schools, once proud and wise,
Now sleeps beneath the ocean's guise.
Amidst the waves, its spires gleam,
Where scholars chased their lofty dream,

*Knowledge flowed like ocean's tide,
In Stellaris, where great minds collide.
But fate's cruel hand, a watery veil,
Took Stellaris, its secrets pale,
Now whispers haunt the ocean's deep,
Of wisdom lost, forever to keep.
Yet on distant shores, where flames ignite,
Fumaro stood with fiery might,
City of Magic, its power untold,
By the volcano's fiery hold.
In Fumaro's streets, spells danced bright,
Bathed in the volcano's fiery light,
Mages weaved their arcane art,
As lava coursed through the city's heart.
But the mountain roared with fiery wrath,
Consuming Fumaro in its fiery path,
The city's magic, now lost to flame,
A memory etched with sorrow and shame.
Stellaris and Fumaro, once proud and bold,
Now lie silent, their stories untold,
Yet in their ruins, whispers remain,
Of the cities lost, but never in vain."*

He finished as the tunnel ended, stopping at another hole in the ground. A large rope clung to a metal stake pushed into the wall. The hole differed from the one that led into the tunnels, a crack that bisected the hallway. The crack also rose above us, but my mother sent her magelight up, and the crack ended a few yards above, nowhere near the surface after how far we'd descended.

Otherwise, we would be swimming among toothy reptiles, I thought.

"That's right," Hughelas said, nodding his head. "And I'd forgotten about Fumaro. City of Magic. This is volcanic rock. So you found Fumaro?"

He shook his head no. "A Warder taught me that poem," Taegen said, nodding to Beldroth. "Several centuries ago, on the war front. Back when the Faeltic Forest still lived." Beldroth nodded back grimly, standing straighter before a fellow soldier? Taegen, despite his beauty, was quite old. "Come, see for yourselves." Taking his magelight with him, he lowered himself down the next hole.

When it was my turn, I found the hole only went about my height before opening up into something much larger. I paused on the rope to look around. Magelight caused glimmered reflections from the stone below—granite? One magelight shone from directly below, but another, my mother's I suspected, raced around the chamber. The walls and ceiling were volcanic rock like that which we had climbed through, forming almost a perfect dome slashed by a crack. Ancient bones and rocks lay near the center of the floor, along with a statue that had more or less endured whatever tests time had thrown its way. The air smelled ancient, like a forgotten tomb—before the Alluvium had carved the passage, the dome would have been sealed off, for a very long time.

The crack through which we descended lay toward an edge of the dome, and I realized as I continued to shimmy down the rope, that my first impression of the cavern's size had been incorrect. After having let myself go down several body-lengths, I still hadn't reached the height of the top of the statue, and I looked down to find my mother still on the rope. My legs had grown accustomed to the extra weight of the hammer, but I grimaced at the thought of climbing back up. Even the descent proved taxing. I gave up on looking around and focused on clinging to the rope and looking down at my target.

Dropping gratefully to the floor, I rolled my shoulders and pondered how I would get back out. I couldn't help but think that if Marinna panicked and broke the rope, we would all be trapped. How long would it take the elves up top to investigate, then go find a new rope long enough? My mother's magelight continued to dance around the statue and bones, but Taegen kept his at the base of the rope.

He eyed me while I stretched, raising an eyebrow at the heavy war hammer. Answers to his unspoken question danced through my head. Family heirloom? But he knew my family, possibly better than I did. I wished to become a Warder? No. Because the Warder needed a break? Ha! For protection? True, and honest enough.

"Why don't you bring up a magelight?" he asked.

My mouth hung open, the answer to a different question readied on my lips. My eyes zipped to my mother.

Thud!

Beldroth slowly straightened beside me. He had to have used magic not to have broken any bones after dropping so far. Earth magic.

"She is under my training," Beldroth said. His not-a-lie fit as well as mine, like a baggy tunic that covered all it was meant to. "Breathe," he said to me, mouthing a four-count of inhalation.

"Control," Beldroth said to Taegen.

"I'm familiar with Warder training," Taegen said. "Unless I am quite poorly informed," he said, his eyes indicating he wasn't, "her blood is half High Elf, not Warder. While High Elves also teach control, it isn't for the same reasons nor toward the same goal. They encourage an effluence of magic in their mental exercises, where Warders emphasize restraint."

I looked at my mother. Was that true? Were the mental exercises she'd taught me meant to be laced with magic? Wait! Was that why my defenses had proven ineffective against that flame-eyed monstrosity?

"Leave her be, Taegen," my mother said. "As you pointed out, her blood is only half High Elf. We must look beyond traditional training."

More ill-fitting lies. I would have a wardrobe full of deception if Taegen kept asking questions. But beyond one last long look, he let it go, turning toward the relics and thus allowing me to do the same.

Unfortunately, my mother's magelight no longer explored the middle of the cavern, but instead raced around the base of the dome.

The skeleton loomed larger than I realized from my last look on the rope, even though we stood a stone's throw away. A stone thrown by me, not Beldroth. The bones and statue created huge shadow-fingers on the dome ceiling opposite the magelight.

The granite beneath us was more jagged than I'd realized from above. Large chunks had buckled and tilted at small angles against one another. The moving light exaggerated the broken landscape.

Beldroth sent a light toward the bones.

"Is that—" I began.

"Dragon," Beldroth said. After several seconds of stunned silence, he murmured, "Dragons collect their dead."

Marinna appeared by my side. "We don't have dragons in the swamps." Clearly untrue. "But I've heard tales. They breathe fire."

"Only the reds," Hughelas said, dropping down with less impact than his father. "Only the reds breathe fire."

"Those are the bones of a white," Beldroth said, clearly uncomfortable.

Marinna made an *oh* face. "What does it mean," she asked, "that they collect their dead?"

"Exactly that," Hughelas said. "Dragons rarely do anything alone. But even when they do, if one dies, another will find the carcass and cart it off."

"Why?"

Hughelas shrugged. "Respect, most think. No one has ever seen where a dragon takes the body of a fallen comrade. At least not seen it and lived to tell the tale."

"Yet there it is," my mother said.

"As I said," Taegen said, "A pair of Alluvium showed up in Themopolis several weeks ago. One called himself a Red Prophet. He spouted all kinds of nonsense. 'The Mother stirs,' he said. 'Elandra calls. The end is near.' And similar catastrophes. The woman with him appeared to accompany him purely to prove him wrong. They argued like an old married couple. He claimed Fire had called him to Themopolis. That's Fire with a capital F, mind you. Like the magic?" He shrugged. "Every time he would rant, she'd tell him, 'Fire lies.'"

"They asked about volcanic activity in the swamp, and I brought them to these islands. These islands have been here as long as I can remember. To my knowledge, they've never been active. The Alluvium couple spent days in the tunnels. Finally, the woman emerged. Just the woman. She said her companion had died. That a crack had opened," Taegen pointed above us, "and he fell in. We've cleaned up the mess." I scanned the ground around us and imagined a stain in every shadow caused by the broken granite. "With disdain, she told us, 'He was right. His end *was* near. Fire lies.' And she left."

We waited only for Skaljian to finish his descent.

"Once I saw what they'd discovered, I sent to Cenaedth to request more Alluvium. What was the Red Prophet looking for? What more might be down here? What knowledge might we uncover? But my envoy never returned."

As soon as Skaljian climbed down, Taegen wasted no more time. He turned and headed to the bones and monument. We only had to walk a short distance before it was clear the giant reptilian head faced us. Like it watched and waited. It took longer to recognize that the bony tail wrapped most of the way around the monument, leaving a small path between head and tail that Taegen homed in on. The dragon's empty eye sockets stared at us, the magelight and shadows tricking me into seeing the giant skull turn our way. And it *was* giant. Even the Warder would have easily fit inside its mouth without bumping his head. I imagined the hammer on my back pulling toward its brethren, calling it to wake, to free it from its captivity. Dragons collect their dead.

I exhaled a breath I hadn't realized I held once I passed the skull. The dragon hadn't stirred. We marched on next to the arching tunnel created by the dragon's ribs.

"Trolls," Beldroth said, squatting. He stared at a pile of fist-sized rocks, then picked one up and stood. He brightened his magelight and nodded his head at several small piles. "Several trolls."

"And elves," Taegen said. He pointed at a collection of yellowed, desiccated bones in a pile near the start of the dragon's tail, close to the statue. They hadn't fared as well as the dragon, whose bone looked pure enough that its death had been in the last decade. The elf bones lay partly in and partly out of a pile of sand that traced the length of the dragon. I cringed when I realized the dirt between my toes had once been dragon organs.

"A final battle," Beldroth said, "in this… cage."

"But the cage itself?" Taegen asked. "Imagine, if this had once been a city. And this spot, out in the open air."

Beldroth sent his magelight high, and my mothers' light chased it. Together, they still didn't illuminate the vast dome. "A shield," Beldroth said. "A shield that held back a mountain of lava." He whistled. "Who could have possibly created a shield that big?" Taegen raised his eyebrows, like the answer was obvious.

And, of course, it was. "The dragon," I said. "The dragon held the lava at bay, only to die inside it."

Taegen nodded, agreeing.

"But why?" I asked. "It makes no sense. It had the power to hold off the lava, but not to escape?"

Taegen nodded again, but said, "I don't know. Perhaps it hoped for rescue. Maybe it hoped to rescue someone. Possibly, it had no hope at all, but could not both cast a shield *and* fly out." The magelights settled back amongst us as Taegen theorized.

"'Wings of Sacrifice: Courage Amidst Tragedy.'" Trentius mumbled. "What about the statue?"

Taegen cocked his head at Trentius's odd declaration, but then turned to the statue. "Yes, the statue. Another mystery."

Up close, the statue was an unexpectedly amorphous blob. From a distance, I'd thought it might be a person sitting, but that had just been the angle. Its stone base stopped a little above my waist, and the outer rim was decorated with gems. Gold and silver lines connected the various colors of embedded gems in swirls. It reminded me vaguely of the outside of the Luminarium, where the High Elves had decorated their stone tree with gems. On top of the base rested two smooth hills of stone, one bigger than the other. I'd imagined the bigger one being a torso and the smaller knees, but they were just two lumps, one thinner and taller than the other.

"What in the world," my mother said, her eyes roaming the gems.

"The High Elves are going to go crazy over this when they learn of it," Taegen said, nodding his head in a sort of apology to Trentius.

"I'll say," Trentius agreed. "They'll want to know whether there's more of these to discover too."

"In fact," Taegen said, "we found other piles of rock and gems in this cavern. Like there used to be more of these. But this is the only one that survived the cataclysm that created the cavern."

Trentius whistled, looking around the cavern again. "Wow, you sure lucked out."

"Luck had nothing to do with it," Beldroth said.

"Yes, yes," my mother said with a sigh and a small eye-roll. "The Mother willed it."

Beldroth smiled, as though he didn't detect the sarcasm.

"It's Stellaris, Illiara," Taegen said, smiling. "It's the lost city I set out to find centuries ago."

"You gave up that quest," my mother said, her mouth set in a line.

"I never gave it up," he said. "I followed the tales here, to the swamps, but I got no farther. Themopolis grew around me. But it has to mean *something* that I've found it, right on the edge of the city I've spent generations establishing." He waved at Beldroth. "Without Themopolis, would the Alluvium have come? Would they have found this cavern? Would you be here? Now?" He kept turning between Beldroth and my mother.

Beldroth grinned, "I think we have a new believer."

Uh huh.

I shared a look with Hughelas. While I had his eye, I reached back and tapped the hammer, then nodded to the dragon skeleton sprawled out around us. He cocked his head in question and I wiggled my fingers, then looked around with wide eyes, hoping he'd get the hint. I wanted to know what his magic-seeing spell would reveal. After a moment's thought, he nodded.

He turned his back to the rest of us, who still marveled at the gem-studded, metal-laced platform. The patterns of metal looked similar to motifs I'd seen in books on magic; I'd flipped through some, even though I couldn't wield magic. Most tomes on magic established understanding through practice, then built upon it. My mother had tried to teach me, but I'd found it very difficult to understand spell progressions because I could never practice the simpler ones. We'd halted those lessons in mutual frustration decades before.

It didn't matter though. If there were clues in the patterns, one of the others would see them. So I secretly watched Hughelas, who put a hand over his eye to block out the presumably intense light from the bones of the dragon. He shambled back to the pedestal like a man trying not to collide with a tree in the fog. When he reached me, he cocked his head in curiosity at the platform. Did he see something different under the power of the spell?

"Rot!" my mother barked, covering her eyes with her hands. Hughelas had cast the spell so often, I'd forgotten that my mother *invented* it! She must have cast it as well.

"What's wrong?" Taegen asked, looking more suspicious than concerned.

"Sudden headache," my mother said, looking down. "Comes with pregnancy." Taegen narrowed his eyes at the reminder. She paid him no attention, but looked at the platform, covering the sides of her eyes.

Hughelas's eyes finally stopped on a green gem about the size of a thumb. He reached a hand out, holding it over the gem, and glanced at my mother. She nodded, and he placed his hand on the gem.

He jerked his hand back with a hiss, and I braced myself for whatever foul magic he'd triggered. Everyone tensed, but Hughelas put his hand to his mouth and muttered, "Sorry, I cut myself."

Sure enough, several drops of blood traced the platform, starting from the gem. He looked over at my mother, who nodded her head, like she'd seen *something*.

They both scoured the platform again, my mother pointing at an amber gem the same size as the green. Taegen watched with curiosity. "I do you the honor of showing you my treasure, and you keep secrets," he said, his face masking any feelings he had on the matter. It reminded me of Zoras, and I again wondered if centuries of life caused a certain disconnect, like emotions were layers of clothing, and sometimes became too heavy or warm to be worn.

"You showed us your secret so that we would send Alluvium back from Cenaedth," my mother responded. "And to spread word back to the High Elves in Alenor so that they would know of your prize. What value has a treasure that is kept buried?"

"And creating a bloody mess of it will increase its worth?" he asked, a drop of venom lacing his words.

"Understanding its purpose will," my mother responded. "Scrolls and gems, Taegen. Scrolls and gems."

"My lady?" Taegen asked, his brow scrunching, and I was sure I looked no different.

"Ink and paper hold a spell," my mother said while scouring the base of the statue. "The better the ink?"

"The more likely the scroll will work," Taegen said. "And the more powerful its effect."

My mother nodded, still spending half of her attention on her search. "I assume you know of communication crystals?"

"Zoras taught you how to make them?" Taegen's eyes narrowed. "Name your price for their secret and it is yours."

Skaljian moved toward my mother as though his physical presence might halt the conversation, but Beldroth blocked him with a frown.

"He did not," my mother said. "Though I do not believe the secret died with Zoras. I suspect Felaern was trusted. But that doesn't matter right now. What matters is that it's possible. Scrolls and gems, Taegen. They can hold magic."

She stopped her search.

"Elliah, would you mind dusting off *that* gem?" She pointed at the amber one.

I scooted over a step and reached forward, leaning over the platform to do as she asked. She squinted at the gem.

My mind flipped back to our quest to see the Mother of Trees. A spell set upon the arched entrance of the wall guarding her silvervein had put the others to sleep. It hadn't worked on me because I was Bereft. If we had searched, would we have found a gem embedded in the stones of the entryway?

"Let me take the hammer," Hughelas said. "That looks… awkward."

In fact, it was not physically awkward, but I knew he was looking with bespelled vision.

I did as I was asked, wondering what they were getting at, but knowing the spell was providing information I could not see.

"I think there's still a bit of dust on the gem," my mother said.

Taegen harrumphed in irritation, but I once again followed her direction.

My mother sucked in her breath when my fingers touched the gem. Had I imagined a spark? Hughelas put his hand back on the other gem, though with a bit more care than before. When he touched the gem, a surge of energy coursed up my arm, then vanished.

"So close," my mother said.

So close to what?

She leaned over and whispered to Beldroth.

Beldroth walked a few steps over to a rib of the dragon, then reached up and wrapped his hands around it as though he intended to climb it like a tree trunk.

"What are you doing?" Taegen asked in almost a panic. No more muted emotions!

While Taegen was distracted, my mother quickly sidled up to me, holding out her dagger. She whispered, "Cut your finger. I can't see properly."

Even though I sensed time wasn't on our side, I hesitated. Cut myself?

"Do it!" she hissed.

Ignoring my doubts and trusting my mother, I took her dagger and sliced the tip of a finger. I shoved the blade back into my mother's hand as dark blood pooled and dripped. It reminded me of when my mother had spilled blood into her inkpot while writing scrolls on the Knoll.

I'd missed whatever words were exchanged between Taegen and Beldroth, but the debate finished with Taegen's irritated declaration: "Time for everybody to leave."

I looked at my mother one more time for confirmation, and at her nod, held my bloody hand to the gem. Just as before, energy pulsed through my arm, only… it wasn't energy going in. It flowed out.

Illiara - 5

When Elliah's eyes glazed over, I panicked. I reached to shove her away from the platform, but her arm was like a tree limb, her open-palmed touch rooted to the gem as though she clutched it—or it clutched her. I tried Hughelas, who was similarly transfixed, but when I grabbed his arm, my mana drained from me through the connection. Placing a hand on Elliah did not have the same effect.

The platform slurped up Hughelas's magic, and through our contact, mine. I didn't know what it was doing to my daughter, but the gem she'd touched "devoured the light," just as she did. Was there an equivalent to mana for negating magic? Anti-mana? How much could Elliah produce? Because the platform was parched.

When Hughelas sliced his finger, the light from Hughelas had jumped across to the tiny glow from the gem, and I *knew*. Blood in the ink. Blood on the gem. Blood was the key. But was I happy that I'd confirmed blood was important for imbuing spells?

Not with my daughter stuck to the gem, getting sucked dry. But realistically, once her mana ran out, the gem would lose its hold. Right? But I'd heard stories of elves overextending themselves, particularly during war, bleeding their mana and pushing on. Death by Thaumic Rupture, they called it.

The draw on me faded, and Hughelas released the gem, looking dazed. A mana drain would do that. But Elliah remained affixed to the pedestal. I couldn't hide the situation from Taegen. He looked both worried and excited—no matter the outcome to us, he had witnesses to a magic that surely predated the Breaking.

Time ticked on, and still Elliah pushed energy into the pedestal. She grew pale, and her breathing shortened. I told myself I witnessed only normal symptoms of rapid mana depletion. It happened all the time in children. Everyone in the room had seen it. Had lived it. Except I'd never seen it with Elliah. She'd never used magic. And it scared me.

I grabbed her arm again, but still, no sympathetic draw of magic occurred. I grabbed her cheeks, forced her to look at me. "Elliah!" I shouted, but she had neither eyes to see nor ears to hear. I pulled out my dagger. If I severed her hand, could I reattach and Heal it?

I doubted it.

Massive arms wrapped around me, one grabbing my wrist with the dagger and holding it. "She'll be okay," my mighty warrior whispered.

I strained against him, but more because I had to do *something* than because I had a plan. She would be okay. Please, she had to be okay… it was my fault she had cut herself, my fault she was stuck in some magic or anti-magic lock, my fault she never had magic…

When she pulled her hand back and sucked in air, all my energy fled. Beldroth's arms weren't holding me back, they were holding me up. Of all people, Trentius caught Elliah. I was so caught up in watching Elliah's eyes, waiting for them to open, that I took a few heartbeats to realize the rock on the platform was moving.

As important as I knew that had to be, I couldn't look away from my pale, exhausted daughter. Was she breathing? When her eyes fluttered, opening like she'd been called forth from deep sleep after a day of hard work, my own breath returned. I got my feet under me, leaning back into the comfort of Beldroth for just a moment before pulling away. With a hand on my belly, I wondered how mothers who'd lived long enough to have multiple children survived the stress of watching their children tackle life, with all of its frighteningly easy exits.

I reached my other hand out to Elliah, casting a Heal that didn't land as I pulled her to her feet. Her tired eyes remained fixed on what was happening upon the platform.

The rock in the middle, the gray formless blobs, moved. Not like rock should, but rather like a fluid, a bubbling gel. It didn't glow red, like lava, but it moved like it. Both lumps grew, taking on the shapes of two people standing upright, one much taller than the other. The smaller became a woman in a robe, the gray stone making her race difficult to discern. The larger one wasn't an elf… it was a troll!

"Why," said the troll, "did the elf bring a ladder to the pub?"

Almost no one moved. Marinna reached out a hand, not near enough to touch the statue, but with eyes as big as saucers. I'd never seen magic that animated rocks. Was the troll real? It was a Warlord. At least if the proportion of size to the elf was correct, it was a Warlord. It stood further away from us than the elf, who turned back to the troll with a look of exasperation clear even in its grainy form.

"Really? We'll be *dead* soon. The world is *breaking*, and the last message you want to save for future generations is a *joke*?"

The troll shrugged. "She didn't tell us what to say."

"Of course she did," the elf replied. "She said magic is broken, and the future along with it."

"But that will be *obvious* to anyone who someday sees this, Elandra," the troll responded. Elandra? I'd just heard that name. Taegen had mentioned it in regard to the Alluvium. *The Mother stirs. Elandra calls me. The end is near.* The troll continued, not giving me time to pursue the thought. "That's hardly news to *them*," he said, throwing out an arm toward us.

What was this? They argued, the troll and the elf, but they argued as two who knew each other, who had worked together. A troll and an elf? We were mortal enemies!

"Are you alive?" Trentius asked them.

They didn't turn or respond, but carried on like we weren't there.

The elf bent her head and put her hands over her ears, pacing in a tight line. "What else did she say? Something about the way magic was broken. Bent! That's the word she used. Magic had been *bent*. It formed a loop... no, that wasn't it."

"A five-dimensional spherical cage," the troll said calmly. "If it helps, that's what she said."

"Of course it helps, you moron!" the elf shouted.

"Moron? I'm not the one who called a five-dimensional spherical cage a *loop*." The troll hadn't moved while the elf paced.

"Mother of Dragons! You are so exasperating. Of all creatures to be stuck with. My visions, my fears... they all come to pass."

"Ah, yes," the troll said. "The bit Jenat conveyed regarding the Mother sounded important."

"The bit?" the elf practically shouted. "You mean her crazy ranting about the Mother having to die? And don't forget that the message comes from a dragon who has caged herself in, keeping her own children from collecting her? I'm not entirely sure she hasn't lost her mind!"

"Well, she is a Seer, and both magic and time just took a smack to the noggin,'" the troll said, imitating hitting himself in the head. "She might be rattled."

"But she thought it important enough," the elf statue said, "to sacrifice herself to record this message. Look around—the other recorders are demolished. Stellaris is covered in molten lava. Our schools are destroyed, our knowledge wiped out. This is the one message we get to send to the future. Surely there was something specific we were meant to convey."

"Hmm," the troll rumbled, "perhaps a recap would be helpful? I mean, if Stellaris is destroyed, no one will know how close we were."

The elf waved impatiently for him to get on with it while she continued to think.

"Well," the troll Warlord said with a hand to his chin, "we're fairly sure we've worked out how to leave this planet. Jenat Saw that we would explore new worlds within our lifetime. So everyone's been pretty excited about that." He spoke calmly, matter-of-factly, about the prospect of *leaving the planet!* "Then the meteor hit, causing earthquakes, typhoons, clouds of ash… and magic went sideways." He leaned and took a step to the side. "Cities crumble as we speak, elves and trolls dying by the tens of thousands. The trolls near the meteor have gone insane, killing their former allies. Dragons got walloped too. Jenat says leaving the world is now impossible… and, if I understood correctly, that was the Mother's *point* in breaking the world. She created a cage. A 'five-dimensional spherical cage.'" The troll smiled at the contemplative elf. "She broke magic, irrevocably altered the future, and pretty much destroyed the world."

After several long seconds of silence, the troll shrugged and said, "Jenat says our only way out is to kill the Mother of Dragons. 'Mother of Trees now,' she said." The troll cocked his head like an idea dawned on him. "Possibly she meant *your* now and not *my* now. Talking to a Seer is confusing." He shrugged. "Jenat is holding back a mountain of lava, so we're alive for the moment, but I don't foresee any god-slaying in my future. So that message must have been meant for you," he said, gesturing toward us.

I looked at Beldroth out of the corner of my eye. His eyes were as big as saucers, and his mouth hung open like it had come unhinged. Maybe Beldroth had come unhinged. Kill the Mother of Trees?

After several more seconds of silence, the troll Warlord asked the elf, "You haven't thought of a better message?"

She held out a hand to stop him from talking. The troll waited patiently and quietly, wasting precious time, then asked, "Why did the elf bring a ladder to the pub?"

The elf shot him a viscous glare, then the rock melted back into amorphous blobs, the troll's larger than the elf's, stopping more or less the way they looked when we'd entered the chamber.

"What in the fiery pits of…" I muttered.

"Do it again!" Taegen shouted. His eagerness waned when he looked at my daughter, who barely held her eyes open. "Everybody's going to want to see this. Everybody! Show me what you did."

Beldroth : 4

"No," Illiara said as she spun around the room, "no more bogwater for the Warder."

"That's right," I said. "Not one, but two!"

At least that's what I tried to say. Everyone looked puzzled, and I knew my words had tripped on their way out, but I couldn't quite spot the stumbling block. I focused on Illiara, and she stopped spinning, only to be outdone as the room elected to dance around her.

I closed my eyes hard, wondering if she might be right. But I wanted another bogwater anyway. I hoped to drown out the monsters rummaging through my brain. Dead dragons. Talking stone. Mother of Dragons. Mother of Trees.

My eyes flew open when someone slapped my back. "But we are celebrating, Illiara!" said a voice just behind me. I recognized the voice, and while his name danced swiftly out of reach, I knew I didn't like him. "Stellaris, Illiara! Ancient wonders unearthed!"

"Ancient Artifacts Arise," said a more familiar voice. "Astonishing Archaeological Adventures Await."

Taegen—the pretty-boy's name was Taegan—frowned, but Trentius smiled, impervious to disappointment.

Marinna, who sat next to my Salt wife, downed another shot of an amber liquid that burned even more than bogwater.

Wait... something's not right.

"Trim the sails tight when the winds blow free," my Lyrei said, "lest ye be lost to the depths of the sea!"

I chuckled, as I always had when Lyrei let loose one of her pearls of wisdom, a metaphor reminding me to get my thoughts under control. But... that wasn't right. Lyrei was buried back in Bellon, near the bones of a dragon as big as the one we'd found under the swamps.

Lyrei's white hair darkened to brown, Illiara replacing my long-dead wife. How apropos, that advice on dealing with the knowledge from those buried in ancient Stellaris had come from one similarly deceased.

"Come on, big guy," Illiara said. "You need to go to bed."

I had to admit, she was right. Slurring my speech. Seeing my dead wife. I had gone deeper into my drink than I realized. But I had reason to drown my sorrows! The Mother of Trees was *our* name for the goddess who created us. But in ancient times, She had other names... Mother of Life, Mother of Elves... Mother of Dragons. It was unthinkable, killing the Mother of Trees. Yet She had directed my steps, so She had brought us that message of doom, preserved though magic.

Marinna slapped down another empty glass, grabbing my attention. How could she possibly continue drinking?

Illiara's face suddenly dominated my view. "Not with her, idiot."

What? Oh, bed. I calmly and rationally reminded Illiara that we had resolved our misunderstanding regarding Marinna, and that I had no intention of actually bedding said elf: "Mephglplx grunklip."

"Exactly," Illiara said, getting under my arm and trying to force me to stand. "Idiot."

I played along and let her think her little form would support me. When the room spun, I moved on instinct, slapping my hand on the table and lacing the connection with magic, creating a bond that kept me upright despite myself.

"Okay, mighty warrior," my Salt wife said. "Time to let go."

Lyrei's white-skinned, white-haired face once more faded to Illiara's darker tones. "Come on," she said. "Let go."

"I'm trying," I said, intentionally speaking slowly, and the words came out the way I intended, but I still wandered the perilous pathways of strong memories and self-doubt. Losing Lyrei had devastated me. I'd become so lost, so alone. Unexplainably, the process of training missionaries, and even raising my son, only isolated me further. Hughelas was smart like Lyrei, but he didn't appreciate simplicity the way she did. I spent ten years mourning, but I hadn't truly let go. "I've tried for over a decade."

Illiara squinted. Then she wiggled out from under my arm and silently slipped away.

I plopped back down onto a creaking barstool, releasing the spell and covering my face with my hands. Had I just chased away Illiara?

What is wrong with me?

Why was I seeing Lyrei? Hearing her? Smelling...

I inhaled deeply. The tavern smelled of sweat, dirt, and mold. Not Lyrei. At least I still had a toehold on reality.

"Why did she leave you?" Lyrei asked.

I rubbed my eyes, the stool groaning dangerously beneath me with my motions. and when I opened them, I found Marinna across from me, not Lyrei.

"Why did she leave you?" Marinna asked. Was Marinna asking about Lyrei or Illiara?

I tried to get my words together to ask, but they'd once again scattered to the winds. Daughter of the Nine Winds. That was Lyrei's title. She'd told me it was a secret, but that if I was ever desperate, using it would get me passage on a Salt ship. "Probably," she'd said. "But possibly," she'd said with a laugh, "a long walk off a short plank."

"Fine, don't answer," Marinna said. "I'll go talk to her." Taegen started to follow her, but she spun on him. "No," she said, and he held up his hands and turned back to the table.

I hadn't meant not to answer. Fantastic. The only thing worse than having one woman angry with you was having two. I looked to the side to find Elliah scowling. Three. Hughelas sat next to her, but he had his nose in that book. I doubted he'd caught any of the exchange.

I stood. Though unsure *exactly* why old memories were digging themselves up, I knew my state of mind was very dark. Very much like the days after Lyrei's death. I let the room stabilize. Trolls were evil, intent on destroying elves. But the message from ancient history suggested that wasn't true—the troll and elf had worked together. The troll had said the Mother of Trees had to die, and the elf hadn't disagreed. It had been looking right at me. That was no coincidence. We were in the right place, with the right people to activate the message. A white dragon had preserved it, given its life to be sure the message was delivered, knowing no dragon would be able to collect its corpse, entombed under tons of rock and water. The entire room had only recently been discovered. It wasn't a coincidence: I was meant to hear that message.

I took a step and the room spun, but someone quickly moved to one side of me, putting an arm on my back. Simmering with inner turmoil, knowing Illiara was gone, Hughelas was oblivious, and Elliah was angry, the physical contact felt too personal for the possible people left. I flung what I assumed was Taegan away with a shove of my arm and a grunt.

I turned to square off against my enemy, only to find Skaljian, the High Watch squad commander, down on the ground between tables.

Wrong again, Warder, I thought.

I sagged, uncharacteristically amorphous… like the underground statue.

As the High Elf picked himself up, I offered a hand, wondering if he would take a swing at me, and purposefully not defending myself from such an attack. But he didn't. He took my hand and put it over his head, getting his arm around me. But instead of some move meant to flatten me, he held me up. "Let's get you out," he said gruffly.

Another arm wrapped around my back, and I discovered Trentius on my other side. "We've got you," he said.

I put an arm around each of their shoulders, growling with irritation, but not at them. At my situation. What did the Mother expect of me? She'd Blessed my mission, which would destroy the trolls. But she'd sent me a message too. A much older message which required much more foresight and planning. True vision. Which one was right?

Stepping outside, breathing the musty fragrance of the swamp flowers on the night air, cleared my head a bit. I stood there and soaked it in, the High Elves caught by my reluctant mass.

We'd entered the swamps in a "sleeping" camp, but after leaving the volcanic island, they delivered us to a camp that was "awake," meaning the water from the grasslands poured in. Silver Falls, they called it.

The tavern was a short walk from the place Taegen housed us. Wooden planks in various states of decay covered the ground in front of the shops, and a muddy road traveled north to south, connecting the towns and the families that didn't follow the fickle water. A few buildings sat on the swamp side of the road, more disheveled than their partners near the freshwater lake.

Back at Zoras's mansion, I'd had a heart-to-heart with my son about the dragon I'd buried in the deep caves of Bellon. "When this is done," Hughelas had said, "we can go dig her out. Then they can collect her." My son's words, which had meant so much to me when he'd uttered them, had haunted me in the cave under Themopolis. With every glimpse of the skeletal remains, I'd seen a white dragon, still covered in flesh and scales, but dead all the same. The one in Bellon had died with its tail curled around my dead wife, just as the skeleton dragon's had curled protectively around the pedestal. My life had presented brief opportunities to examine dragons' skeletons—dragons collect their dead—but I'd seen reds, greens, blues, and whites, and I was sure the skeleton belonged to a white. Just like the one I'd killed.

It was all too much. If fate pulled my strings, was I to blame when it yanked on a knot?

I wouldn't blame Illiara if she didn't forgive me. After all, I'd told her I'd moved on. I believed I had. She'd seemed amazed by my explanation of the Vigil, the time I'd spent letting go of my deceased wife. It was a mistake to offer to teach Marinna. I clearly wasn't ready for anything.

We found Illiara leaning against a post that held up an awning over the walkway in front of the building where we slept. Marinna talked with her, but they both grew quiet as we neared, Marinna finally ducking into the building. We meant to move on in the morning. To recruit the Alluvium... for *my* mission... Blessed by the Mother... who had to be *killed*?

"Don't even," she said when I was close enough. "We're not talking until you sober up."

From the scornful purse of her lips, her expectations of an intelligible, much less an intelligent, response were low. "I'm sober enough," I said.

She raised an eyebrow. Skaljian and Trentius disengaged and disappeared into the building. We stood in silence as a mucker waddled by, its feet squelching in the mud, carrying a saddle with stuffed leather pockets, an elf trodding through the mud less loudly alongside it. I took the opportunity to bind myself to the ground and the same post Illiara leaned against, just in case the world decided to get wobbly on me again.

"I'm really sorry," I said when the noise from the slurping muck subsided.

"For chasing after the pretty little girl or missing your dead wife? Or are you sorry for getting me pregnant?"

"Mother of Trees, woman," I grunted, rubbing my head. It hurt already. It would be terrible in the morning. "I'm not chasing Marinna. I never was. And, yes, I miss my dead wife at times. But I'm not sorry you're having *our* baby."

"Tch," she snarled, still angry.

"Illiara Silverheart, you are the perfect woman for me. I'm sorry I'm seeing my dead wife. I don't know why—"

"Wait, you're what? *Seeing* your dead wife?"

"Um," I said, realizing how overloaded that word was in our vocabulary. "Yes, I keep thinking I see her. Like she's talking to me. That happened a lot right after she died. But I performed the Vigil, and it stopped, pretty quickly really. Within a few months. I don't know why it's happening again." Not completely true… the dragons had done it, somehow. "But it isn't a reflection of my feelings for you."

"It's not?" she asked, scornful disbelief clear in her voice.

"No! When she died, I was just so angry." I stood there, struggling to proceed, and Illiara raised both eyebrows.

"I have something I have to confess," I said.

Illiara closed her eyes, rubbed her head like I had done moments before. "Go on. Let's hear it."

"After my wife died, and I killed the dragon, I… I collapsed the cave on its corpse."

Illiara froze.

"I was so angry. I wanted to hurt the dragon the way it hurt me, but it was already dead. 'Dragons collect their dead.' They do, you know. Always. Only I wanted it to be hard for them. I thought perhaps I would pick off a few more. I…"

As the seconds ticked on, I wondered what she was thinking. What she thought about me as a person.

"That's it?" she asked, still not looking at me. "That's your whole story?"

"Well, the dragon bones in the buried city dug up old memories. It made me think of the dragon I killed and buried, and my wife that *it* killed."

"So all this drama is because you feel *guilty* about keeping dragons from collecting the dead body of the dragon you killed after it murdered your wife?"

"Well it's not *drama*, but yes." What I had done in my anger wasn't right.

"Okay," she said, finally looking at me. "Okay, Warder." She took a breath and exhaled loudly, like she pushed out foul air. "Okay… Beldroth." She spoke more gently. "We can go back to our room now. But there's to be no more flirting with Marinna."

"There hasn't been any yet. I shan't start."

"Tch," she replied, but her noise didn't sound as irritated as it had before.

"In fact, we should leave her here," I said. "It was a mistake to invite her." I inched closer to Illiara.

To my surprise, she scowled. "We will do no such thing. Your instinct was right. She needs to leave with us."

"But—"

"No," she said, glaring. "She's going. You'll train her. Just keep your hands off her."

I nodded, but I had my doubts. Negative thoughts gnawed hungrily at my beliefs. I'd trained missionaries during my dark days of my vigil after Lyrei's death. I had the skill and experience to do it. The loss of Lyrei was deep and personal, but I got through it by leaning on my faith in the Mother. If that faith were unfounded, if the Mother's power could be *extinguished*, then any comfort I'd found was... meaningless.

Hughelas #6

"The strength of the forest lies in its many trees, not the lone branch."

I cringed at Taegen's words. Fortunately, I wasn't the only one who recognized them for what they were. Illiara, shorter than Taegen, planted herself inches away from him and mustered a taut ferocity that threatened to topple the cold distance of Taegen's long years. "You had little use for those words when the High Elves applied them to recruit Wood Elves into the war." Spittle flew from the intensity of her words. "You will *not* use them to keep my daughter captive!"

I'd been the last one to leave the inn, having stared at the book from Felaern, at explanations of mathematical transformations, and wishing I'd had a quill and ink while I absent-mindedly ate breakfast. After Eliiah had banged on the table and grabbed my attention—the others were walking out the door—I'd stuffed the book into my pack.

I'd had a moment, just a moment, of wondering what would happen if I just… stayed. But, while I didn't believe in my father's mission, that Elliah had embraced, I had no interest in the swamp either. The magical statue from a past civilization was fascinating, but I was more interested in *how* it had worked than *why* it had survived, and that knowledge would be in books and studies, which one wouldn't find in the swamps.

Taegen had been busy—he had an armed guard of thirty in a semicircle around the door of the inn, and less militant elves had rallied behind them, filling the streets in either direction.

"We can't let her go," Taegen said. "She's the only one who can activate the magic. We need her."

Beldroth stood to the right and a little behind Illiara, his sword drawn but kept low. The High Elves had flanked him, swords also drawn to match the readiness of the Wood Elves.

"Remarkable," my father said to no one in particular. "I've fought side by side with Wood Elves before. Never against them, except in practice." He sounded so resigned that he might have been bored by the prospect. "But I've seen many Wood Elves, and I can't help noticing how much this group looks alike."

He was right. Muted variations of Taegen's beauty decorated the crowd. That woman had his eyes. The man next to her, his chin.

Green and brown eyes, common to all Wood Elves, added to the similarities.

"Our gene pool runs as shallow as the swamps," Marinna said beside me, her bright yellow hair and bright green eyes a stark contrast to her statement. But even her features otherwise resembled those of her community.

"We're on a mission from the Mother of Trees," my father said into the disconcerted crowd, his usual overbearing smile when he spoke of the Mother absent. His smile, not as pretty as Taegen's, had the strange power to disarm people, and might have gotten us out of town without trouble. "Trying to stop us…"

He trailed off, and Illiara throttled her anger enough to put a hand on his shoulder, which he didn't appear to notice or take comfort in.

"Technically," I said, "there are others who can activate that magical message." Maybe we could still talk our way out of town.

"I don't have access to Bereft," Taegen said.

After the message had played in the cave, Illiara had cast the spell again to see magic auras. I'd depleted my magic too much, but she regained mana remarkably quickly. She said magic, and its antithesis, remained in the pedestal. She predicted that it would not be as difficult to activate again. But she'd shared that information with me quietly, and we hadn't attempted to reactivate the magic. I doubted Elliah had the… anti-mana… to spare.

Nevertheless, Taegen had worked out what happened. He had enough clues from the stories about Illiara to make good guesses.

"Do trolls ever make it this far west?" I asked.

Taegen turned his gaze on me, his eyes pinched. He took in the implications of my question, looking at Elliah, then Illiara, then back at me. "They do not," he said. "It is one of the benefits of life in the swamps."

"But you are not without options," I said, keeping his attention on me. "You've tackled more difficult problems," I said, appealing to his ego. "Without resorting to impinging on the freedoms of the people who followed you to escape the shackles of war."

Taegen was ancient. Like Zoras, that made him difficult to read. Calling him out in public was a poor choice, but I saw no other path.

Seconds ticked by with the shifting of the crowd and the buzzing of insects the only noise.

Taegen studied Elliah, who had set the hammer down in front of her, close to my father. Smart. He would be able to use the hammer while she protected us from magic.

"Stay," Taegen said to her. "While we retrieve a troll."

"No," she answered. "The Mother needs me."

I cringed, her response too similar to my father's fixation for me. He would never have used those words, as they implied a weakness he refused to see. I comforted myself with the knowledge that her zealotry had more grounding in reality than his.

Taegan considered her answer, then said. "Please do us the honor of accepting our hospitality for a time."

"She said no," Illiara snarled.

My father switched his sword to his left hand. Like he knew where it was, my father reached back and picked up the hammer with his right. He wore a grim determination I hadn't seen in some time— one that, to date, he reserved for trolls.

Taegan hadn't missed it, but his ageless mettle matched my father's darkness and Illiara's anger. "I really must insist," he said.

I drew my own sword, wincing as my father said, "I hoped that would be your answer."

Marinna 1

"Now hold it there," Beldroth said in the tone of someone distracted—someone operating by rote memory—while my arms and shoulders burned with strain. "I will be extremely sore with you if you break my sword." After a few seconds, he added, "And don't alter it either!"

Hughelas sparred with Elliah nearby, also under the tutelage of the Warder. He glanced at them occasionally, barking some instructions or criticism or correction. It was apparently a regular part of their days.

Beldroth's sword was long and heavy, despite appearing feather-like in his grasp. I held it straight out with two hands, using no magic, just controlling it. The early parts of the endurance exercises Beldroth assigned me always gave me time to think. To remember.

And all too often, my memories returned to the night Taegan had found me. He was an absentee father… to an unknown but legendary number of children. So the fact that he'd sought me after the disaster with Nesterin, whose Healed bones hadn't knit cleanly and would result in a lifelong limp, had scared me.

But he'd very quickly calmed my fears, telling me he wasn't upset, that he just wanted to talk, and I'd let him in my room. But I'd kept the door open, not entirely believing that he wasn't there to punish me.

I remember running my fingers over the rough wood frame of the door as he paced the room, his hands clasped behind his back. He spoke in the tone of someone explaining something grand and important, something only he seemed to understand.

"Our people have grown weak," he'd said, his voice low but intense. "We've only ever had a trickle of new elves arriving from the front, but even that has dried up. But you… you have the potential to restore what we've lost. You're special, Marinna."

I had shifted uncomfortably, furrowing my brow, wanting to feel excited for being special, but not sure that being known as a walking health hazard was the kind of special I desired. "What do you mean?"

He'd stopped pacing and turned to me, his eyes shining with a fervor that made my chest tighten. "It's in your blood. In our blood. Together, we could—" He paused, his gaze lingering on me in a way that made her skin prickle. "We could be the beginning of something powerful."

I'd stepped back, unease rising in my throat. "I'm your daughter," I'd said, but the words had caught in my throat. Surely, I'd misunderstood his look.

His expression had softened, and for a moment, he'd looked almost hurt. "You don't understand yet," he murmured, taking a slow step toward me. "But you will. This is about something greater than either of us."

My heart pounding, I'd bolted through the doorway, my feet carrying me far from the words I couldn't quite make sense of and hoped I was wrong about.

"Breathe," Beldroth said, and the realization that I *wasn't* breathing caused me not only to gasp, but to drop my arms, unable to even maintain my grip on the sword as my arms flopped to my sides.

I bent over double, hands on my hips, and panted as the world spun and darkened around the edges.

"Slow your breathing," Beldroth said, unconcerned for my dismay. When I didn't obey, but continued to suck wind, he said, "You can lie down and raise your legs, or sit with your head between your knees. Most Warders prefer to clench their fists."

No way was I sitting or lying down. As I focused on my breathing, clenching and unclenching my fists, the blackness slowly receded. Everyone's assurance that Beldroth's quick temper was unusual provided scant comfort. "Something's eating at him," Illiara had said. "But he's locked it up tighter than a squirrel's ass in a lightning storm."

Luckily, he had me as a target for his frustration.

"At least you didn't break it," he snipped, picking his sword up and running a hand lightly over the flat of the blade, the dirt it had acquired from its spill magically jumping off the edge in front of his fingers. "But never drop your blade."

I curled my lip, though he couldn't see it from his angle. His companions told me that Beldroth was normally all smiles and epithets, and they urged me to be patient. Honestly, though his cynicism evoked negative responses, I didn't entirely mind his attitude. It made it easier, in a way—I was learning enough to control my magic, and when I learned enough, I would disengage, no guilt and no strings attached.

Plus, he didn't *have to* help me, after all. He received nothing from his generosity, and his irritability was a cousin of my father's aloofness, making it familiar and comfortable in its own peculiar way. It was hard to stay angry at that.

Over the days of travel, the training had moved from mental exercises and breathing to physical efforts that rapidly tested and exhausted me. The muscle work had started with heavy branches. "Warder magic is weaker in wood than stone," Beldroth had explained. "It will be harder for you to break wood by accident with chaotic magic, and so a good place to start."

And I'd broken the wood. I'd broken several pieces. A lot, in fact. But eventually I'd exhausted my body without snapping the weighty tree limbs.

Several days into the physical training, with my arms, shoulders, legs, and core all slightly more defined than when we'd exited the swamps, he moved me to rocks. "Rocks like these break easily," he said, though I didn't understand what he meant. Round rocks? Head-sized rocks? Limestone? "Just so you understand, some don't. Crystals, with their aligned bondings, will split along flaws, and a perfect jewel is difficult to break with magic. Rocks like these have no particular inner structure, and shatter more easily than wood. They're what our magic was made to destroy. Now, hold that one out."

We'd spent several days working with rocks in the mornings or when we'd camped at night... and even while hiking during the day. Our trek had climbed up from the swamps into the western edge of the grasslands, then marched steadily north, heading slightly inland. My arms became lean cords laced with purple veins. My abs flattened. Unexpectedly, my legs muscled up even more quickly. And the rocks stopped breaking.

During training, I wasn't allowed to use magic. The point was to gain control. But in the evening, I got out my chisels and used the same rocks as canvases. I would leave them behind the next day, creating a breadcrumb trail of faces, flowers, and whatever else called out to me from the stones I'd hefted for our exercises... once I'd stopped breaking them.

"That's really good!" Illiara said one night, the upper body of a young elf carved into the stone before me. Holding the rocks for the exercises provided a lot of time to see the art inside. It made the chiseling swift.

And her comment had excited me—it gave me hope. I would get my magic under control. Then, my art would be safe from me. I would be okay.

"Sculpting is a common pastime among Warders," Hughelas told Elliah another night. "We had many statues, albeit most of them damaged, in the ruins of Bellon. I'm told Aendolin has many marvelous pieces of work, some quite ancient. Supposedly from before the Breaking."

"I would like to see that," she responded, smiling at him. It was obvious the two liked each other, but they didn't act on it. It wasn't my business why.

"Me too," he said with a laugh. "It's ironic how much of the world I've seen now, but missed my own backyard. I've read that some of the artists learned to manipulate the stone using magic."

That idea had parked itself in my heart like the eggs of a mireburrower planted under one's skin. I hoped it didn't itch as much making its way out.

"You're ready for my sword," Beldroth had informed me that very morning. We'd entered the foothills of the mountains, and the clear morning had allowed us a view of the distant ocean… clear of any swamps. My soul had sighed with relief and homesickness both. "This should be easy. Metal is harder to break than stone."

"Then why do it?" I'd asked. Why spend time on something simpler? Why prolong our efforts?

"It has joints," he'd answered. "Weaknesses that your magic, uncontrolled, will exploit. Having the blade or guard fall off the hilt, in the midst of a battle, is deadly. Managing forged weapons is easier than stones, but much more vital, and stress can influence your control."

So, at the end of the day, after we'd hiked deeper into the foothills, he'd had me hold his sword straight out, with its ponderous weight, until one of us broke. Deep down, deeper than my exhaustion, I was proud it was I who broke and not the sword.

"Now," Beldroth said with a bright smile—was it the smile everyone missed?—that quickly crumpled into something more resigned, "we make some things easier and others more difficult." I'd liked his bright, encouraging smile, but I related more to the resigned one. Did I smile brightly when I sculpted? I probably stuck my tongue out and squinted, but I think I wore that smile inside. I liked thinking that it might be possible to live a life that brought out such a smile.

"How so?" I asked, straightening and relaxing my hands, my breathing approaching normal. I needed to understand what he intended, so that I could decide how much I cared.

"Easier, because I'm going to start teaching you spells that will bind you to the ground and to your weapon. It won't be as hard to hold things." With a ghost of his bigger smile, he said. "You won't drop my sword."

I'd anticipated breaking off from the expedition when we reached the towns or villages in the mountains along the Witless. Illiara knew what I needed from Beldroth. I needed control over my magic, which he'd taught me as we'd journeyed, and which I would be able to continue to practice on my own. Plus, I needed to get out of Fael Themar. I'd thought lying low in Runt, the southernmost and rarely used pool of Fael Themar, would be enough. But Taegen had found me there too. Maybe it was a coincidence, but... maybe not.

I'd told Illiara I wanted to put as much distance as possible between me and my father... that I suspected he had... inappropriate intentions.

"Well," I said, rubbing life back into my shoulders, "that would have been nice to know."

"If you learn the spells first, then learning control is harder," he responded. "I've seen many warriors suffer for it. The spells are alluring, but control is key."

But did I *care*? I wasn't trying to become a warrior. I didn't plan to fight trolls. All I wanted was a quiet place where I could sculpt in peace, without dark looks from neighbors who thought my light hair meant I was cursed. Without shattering my hard work with an all-too-frequent emotional outburst. Without unwanted amorous attention from my father.

Still, the way Beldroth had torn through my former townspeople... Being able to protect myself would make *any* place more habitable. I did wonder how Beldroth planned to get the army he intended to recruit back through Fael Themar. Taegen would be ready for him. But Beldroth had fared well enough with his small crew against three times as many Wood Elves, and Illiara had Healed what injuries they'd sustained. With an Alluvium army backing him up, passing through Taegen's swamps wouldn't worry Beldroth.

"After that, I'll teach you how to manipulate structure," he said. "And then how to do the same over a distance, so that you can cast shields and project sound."

"Project sound?" I asked. What in the world?

"Sound is just vibrations," Beldroth's *sword* said, in more or less his voice. "The spell is fairly simple to cast on things you're touching."

Illiara, who happened to be bringing Beldroth some meat from a catch she'd made hunting that evening, ran a hand up his arm, saying, "Better not teach her how you use that vibration spell, or she'll never bother finding another mate."

I didn't know what she meant, but it was clearly something saucy. Yet, he merely sighed resignedly. Illiara grimaced, handed him the knife with meat spitted on it, and said, "If you're going to start using your magic, I'll teach you how to better monitor your mana. That might help you realize when your magic is leaking out." As though we agreed and it was decided, she nodded once and returned to the fire.

"But like shields," the boulder next to me said, "casting over a distance is harder."

The stone spoke, just like the amazing magical statue hidden under Fael Themar. Was that how the statue had spoken to us? Warder magic? "Manipulating structure" sounded an awful lot like carving statues. Maybe I didn't care so much about shields, or making rocks talk, but the idea of the art I might create with magic's aid appealed to me.

A groan of pain caused us both to spin to where Elliah and Hughelas sparred. She was on her knees next to his prone body, saying, "Sorry, sorry, sorry." Illiara was hurrying back from the fire to help them.

For whatever reason, the situation made Beldroth smile. "I also think you've shown enough control that you can be trusted to spar with the others." His eyes became distant once again, and his bright smile melted like butter in the sun.

Sparring. Wonderful. More sore muscles. But it brought with it the opportunity to learn to mold stone with my magic.

"Okay," I said. "So teach me."

Beldroth : 5

"It's not going to be easy," Skaljian told us. We had moved away from the campfire, just Skaljian, Illiara, and I. The stars and a dim magelight provided sufficient light and privacy.

Before Fael Themar, before hearing the message from the past, I wouldn't have cared. Or rather, easy or hard wouldn't have mattered. The Mother would have guided my steps. The Mother would have seen me through.

"I see the High Council didn't convey to you just how much our relations with the Alluvium had deteriorated," Skaljian said.

What did the Mother want? Was I meant to raise an army and fight the trolls? Was I meant to kill the Mother? Did none of our actions have meaning?

"The last envoy from the High Elves to the Alluvium never returned." Skaljian wanted me to respond. He needed some kind of acknowledgement.

"I understand," I said. A statement vastly untrue in the most important ways. I didn't understand if I did what the Mother intended, or whether the Mother had any plan for me at all. But I did understand what he was trying to tell me.

"You have to be our representative, not me," he said. "That is your mission's best chance at success. If they see a High Elf in charge, we might end up in prison… or worse."

I'd already told him I understood. Did he need one of my smiles? I tried. He cringed.

He pursed his lips and sighed. "I think it's likely to backfire, but I'll present our mission to them. We will reach Cenaedth tomorrow. You're in no shape to…"

He let the sentence drop. He was right—I was in no shape to advocate our mission. My mission. I'd sold the High Elves on it. Captain Skaljian was just along to ensure we reached Cenaedth.

"I can do it," Illiara offered.

"With all due respect," Skaljian said, "your heart isn't in it." He spoke as one presenting facts. "The Alluvium are a passionate race. They will see through you if you don't believe what you're saying."

I almost laughed at the idea that, after all the yelling Skaljian had overheard on our journey, he didn't believe Illiara to be passionate. But it came out as a grim chuckle, earning me a scowl from the woman who yelled at me as much as she kissed me.

"And you could do better?" Illiara asked Skaljian, her tone surprisingly gentle and curious. Overtly so, in fact.

"I do not know," he answered. "I am not a passionate speaker. My job is soldiering. But I believe things happen for a reason." He had surprised me before with short statements that indicated he believed and followed the Mother.

It galled that he held to his beliefs, even if they weren't as vocal as mine. He'd seen the pedestal. Why wasn't he shaken? It made me want to bring him down to where I was. "What of Trentius?" I asked. Skaljian cocked his head, creating furrows in his brow, thinking I asked whether Trentius should represent us. I clarified my question. "If things happen for a purpose, why is Trentius the way he is?"

Skaljian looked down at his feet for several bloated seconds. "Did you know that Trentius's father was on the High Council?"

That got Illiara's interest. "Who?" she asked.

"Todley," he answered.

Illiara sucked in a breath. "He was the one who engineered the aqueduct," she said, though I suspected there was something more behind her reaction.

"And an advocate for racial equality," Skaljian replied. "He used his own project as an opportunity to update labor laws, even though it cost him time and money."

"You know all that?" Illiara asked, which seemed odd, since obviously he did.

Skaljian ignored her question. "His death was a tragedy. A ruse set up to frame the Wood Elves for his death, and deepen tensions that were on the mend."

Illiara's mouth hung open.

"I married his daughter," Skaljian said with a small smile. "Trentius's older sister. Trentius was meant to follow in his father's footsteps. He spent half his time as a child playing with the Wood Elves. But, somehow, in the aftermath of his father's death, someone got a Hook in Trentius. His sister, my wife, removed it, but it had set deep and long, and it made him…" He waved back toward camp.

"Then she must know who did it!" Illiara hastened to answer.

Skaljian held up a hand. "My work brings me before the High

Council," he said. "I wouldn't let her tell me. I insisted she block off the memory even from herself." He smiled wryly. "Who knows whether she actually did, but since we still live, I suspect she walled it up. That information is a death sentence."

I shifted uncomfortably. "You use this as an example of the Mother's plan?" All the times people had pushed me on my beliefs bubbled up, and I wanted to tear his ideals apart, just as mine had been. "A man robbed of his capacity? Treachery? Murder?"

"Would you rather have a puppet leader on the council controlled through a Hook? His sister was in the right place to save him. I was there to look out for him. Not all of us have missions to save the world." He smiled. "Some of us just save a small, precious piece of it."

"Everything happens for a reason," he said, opening his hands like he didn't understand and didn't try to. "Perhaps, it's the Mother's plan. Possibly, the mechanics of the Universe. Or maybe... there's something even greater that guides our steps." He shrugged. "But *we* still have to take the steps."

The distant fire cackled, and insects buzzed noisily from the sparse trees of the foothills. Slowly, I nodded, not embracing my old beliefs, but willing to pull myself out of my glum despair and at least be accountable for having gotten us where we were. "I'll present us to the Alluvium," I said.

Skaljian nodded. "Okay. Let me talk you through it."

Elliah ~ 6

The main entrance to Cenaedth impressed me more than I wanted to admit. Hundreds of columns carved out of natural rock created an oddly striated but still cavernous entry chamber. Carved. It was incredible—they'd carved the cavern into the mountainside and left the columns. Unevenly spaced, the pillars of rock produced voluminous pockets of varying sizes, but they blocked visibility and required one to weave about to enter the mountain. From the outside, it resembled a long, open mouth with countless teeth... from the inside, the teeth continued into the space where a tongue should have rested. A cluster of pylons looked odd. Darker. Damaged? Mended perhaps?

If Alluvium magically worked stone, why was the cavern carved? Maybe they couldn't. My reference material was weak—Telana Talenforged had ghosts and maze tunnels. And Fire magic differed from Earth magic, though I was hardly an expert in how they differed. But Taegen had said the Alluvium that visited them had carved out the tunnel we'd walked through.

As we walked, I first became disoriented and then lost. The entrance faced the river and coastlands, so I failed to grasp from what attack the strange ingress defended itself. Occasional carts with enterprising Alluvium owners dotted the pockets between pylons, suggesting not only that the area did not see attacks, but that enough people must trek through it to warrant the vendors. They sold food and jewelry, mostly to Wood Elves, but I saw a sprinkling of Salt customers. The jewelry consisted of metals of various colors and gems of all sizes. While many bracelets and rings were simple loops, some took the form of skeletons of elves or animals. I spotted many such creations sported by the Alluvium, along with their simple leathers that tended toward burgundy or a darker red.

The Alluvium were as fascinating as their crafted jewelry. Though dark-skinned, they more closely resembled Wood Elves than they did Salts, Warders, or High Elves. I'd seen some from a distance as we'd passed the ports on the Flawless River, but I hadn't known which, if any, were true bloods. Apparently Wood Elves and Alluvium had been at the back of the line when the Mother handed out height. But Alluvium were more heavily muscled than Wood Elves, and looked much stronger than the spindly High Elves and Salts. When it came to strength, nobody held a candle to the Warders, but the angry scowls the Alluvium shot our way made their muscle disturbing.

If I wasn't mistaken, the scowls were directed at the High Elves. Captain Skaljian had warned us that tensions between the two races were high. *How much do I look like a High Elf to them?*

I gawked as I meandered through with Hughelas, having abandoned my mother's side ever since she'd revealed she'd previously ventured into Cenaedth. I couldn't believe she'd never told me before. She claimed she did tell me, when I was a small child about the same age as when she'd gone there, but I think I would have remembered that.

We'd traveled through foothills, skirting between the ocean and the mountain, finding a trail that grew into a road. It led to a crossroad that had sprouted an interesting town. We'd taken the eastbound road to Cenaedth, but the west led to the bay and Salts, while the north led to Wood Elves' towns. Shops like those in Themopolis dotted the road, the trees not grand enough to support raised buildings, but, again like Themopolis, they were mostly run by Wood Elves. Alluvium and Salts were sprinkled about, decorating the shops. I wished we could have sat at the inn on the crossroads and simply watched for a while, but we marched through without stopping. Beldroth's doing—something had lit a fire in him, though a grim one.

My mother walked with Beldroth, the two of them quietly chatting amidst the cavalcade of our entourage. Beldroth did not appear as awestruck as Hughelas and I, though the Warder had said he'd not visited before.

"Aendolin and other Warder cities offer similar spectacles," Hughelas explained, waving at the cavern. "While he has seen them, I have not."

"You haven't been to your own cities?" How had I not learned that?

"We lived in the ruins of Bellon, which is more of a waystation in a functional war zone than a proper city." The bewildering maze of columns lost their allure compared to Hughelas's past. He noticed my attention and elaborated. "It's the first city on our side of the mountains that separates us from the trolls. The woods there never regrow due to troll attacks, so the Roamers don't protect it. While it isn't the closest city to dragon lands, it is close enough. Aendolin, our capitol, lies farther south—it suffers less from direct attacks, and so it holds more of the wonders of our culture."

I mulled that over. I'd all along thought Hughelas more worldly than I. He'd come to our Wood Elf town, exotic and, compared to me, gregarious. Even though he'd said, many times, that he'd read a lot, I'd still attributed to him more travel than I'd experienced. But, in fact, outside of book-lore, he was just as raw as I.

The columns thinned, revealing a wide opening that the magelight from our party didn't penetrate. We were deep enough into the cavern that despite the huge mouth of the cave, very little light penetrated, and it stopped where we did. After a moment where I wondered if we might wait for some kind of Alluvium welcoming committee, Beldroth marched into the darkness. And we all followed.

We descended into the long throat of the mountain, some of our party keeping their magelights near us, while others sent theirs traveling up until they became pinpricks. They couldn't illuminate the sheer volume of the cavern. I expected it to get cold, but it didn't. I anticipated sudden chills or a cold touch on my cheek or neck, some passing spirit drawn to my warmth. If anything, the air became more humid… thicker. Wherever the ghosts were, it wasn't there. Nor were we in any kind of maze. I wouldn't have any trouble turning around and finding my way out… so maybe nothing hindered the ghosts escaping either, giving them no reason to linger and haunt us.

Then a noise drifted up from below: a faint screech or scream, assuring me that, even if they weren't at the entrance, ghosts haunted Cenaedth below. My mother's eyes pinched, which added to my nerves.

We hiked for a full minute, until we entered something even bigger, and emptiness engulfed us. It wasn't just dark outside our magelights… it was *vast*. Several lights still danced like wisps high above, revealing nothing but themselves. We halted like we'd hit an imaginary wall, the tail end of our party compressing, then expanding backwards or moving to the side to give everyone room. And I sensed eyes on me. I imagined spirits watching, and, shivering, I fancied I spotted the red eyes that haunted my dreams.

Hughelas and I waited expectantly—the captain had coached Beldroth and told the rest of us to remain quiet. The Alluvium's greeting of the High Elf cavalcade required a ceremony.

"Roots grow deep in the earth," a voice intoned from the darkness ahead. An elf voice. A female's voice.

Beldroth was supposed to respond—it would establish him as

the head of our assembly and give him authority to make the council's requests. Yet, I had a sudden concern that he'd forgotten his line. "What a splendid cave!" just wouldn't do. And why did a part of me want nothing more than to shout out exactly that?

Fortunately, Beldroth saved me from my self-destructive anti-benediction. "Which gives the trees their strength."

"Water feeds the soil and nourishes life," said the voice from the darkness.

"Leaves reach for the sky, dancing in the wind," Beldroth said. He looked tense, but he'd looked that way ever since Fael Themar. I imagined him picturing the Mother of Trees in his head, her crumpled form having no resemblance to his words.

"And Fire," said the woman, "clears the way for new growth, forging the path to the future."

Flames flared up around us, from the floor, from the walls, from the ceiling, dancing among far off stalactites... fire everywhere my eyes landed. A scream issued from the passage below, the ghosts doing their part to add their voices to the roar of the flames.

Stuff me in a hollow and leave me for dreaming!

It was a *lot* of magic! How had we ventured so deeply into the mountain that a cavern that vast could even exist? But it wasn't as empty as I'd believed when we'd walked to its center. While it contained no statues, no edifices to power, it housed hundreds of dark-skinned soldiers and mages, who had silently surrounded us. Unlike our exit from Fael Themar, our small cadre wouldn't stand a chance of leaving if the Alluvium didn't want us to go.

My eyes adjusted to the change in lighting, while my body recognized the uncomfortable warmth brought by the flames. None danced so close as to burn us, but it weaved across the floor in smooth patterns that my eye failed to discern while I resided amongst them. I imagined that if I perched from above, I would see them creating something magnificent. The flames on the floor stayed low to the ground, licking no higher than my ankles. Vines of flame clung to the walls, creating an abundant light source. The vines connected into a knot of fire high above, their conflagration no doubt bright, but their location so distant that they contributed little to the cavern's luminosity.

We had walked into a slightly recessed area, the very broad circle around us about waist high, minus the ramp we'd walked in on. A similar ramp went up and out the other side of the circle, and a tunnel, still quite large but smaller than the one we'd entered, descended deeper into the mountain. Ten elves could hold hands and walk down it side by side, and my nervous brain pictured exactly that.

I inched closer to Hughelas, and I realized we'd all scooted closer together. While the cavern had been mostly dark, its vastness had felt so open as to be almost outdoors, but the threat of the Alluvium and their Fire pressed in on us, making me claustrophobic.

One robed male, an Alluvium mage, along with a muscular Alluvium woman in leathers, marched solemnly into our midst from the lower ramp while I marveled at the cavern and the summoned fire. The mage wore a burgundy robe laced with patterns in yellow and red that reminded me of Beldroth's blue tattoos. Small jeweled trinkets adorned his body, but he wore no visible skin-art—though his robes hid much. He looked diminutive next to the High Elves and Warder, but he still stood slightly taller than I. The woman appeared unarmed, though her belt bore an empty sheath, and no bow sat upon her shoulder—but then how much purpose would a bow serve in a cave?

The patterns of the fires affixed to the floor undulated and shifted about, their design changing. When the pair of Alluvium entered our midst, a ring of fire closed around us, not tight, but there. I couldn't say for certain whether the High Elves were daunted, though their postures suggested they were, but the display cowed me.

"A Warder," said the mage, "leading a party of High Elves. Perhaps Gormar was right, and the end times are upon us." The woman made a scoffing noise beside him, and the mage grinned. "A clever ploy on the part of our big-headed cousins, but you were warned of your fate should you set foot in Canaedth." The ring of fire that wrapped us flared, a wave of furnace-heat washing over us, and in an instant, the atmosphere altered from intimidating ceremony to dangerous purpose.

While murmurs reached my ears from the High Elves, over the cheering of distant Alluvium, Beldroth spoke loudly. "I have never been to Canaedth," he said, eying the ring of flame dubiously. "And while I admire its entrance, I find the hospitality of its people to be less than I'd imagined." He still lacked his fanatical, beatific, disarming smile. In fact, I'd never seen him look so… disappointed. "We are elves. Enemies surround us, yet you would threaten your own kind?"

"*My kind?*" the woman barked, her voice loud and clear over the din. "High Elves *Compelled* Alluvium to fight against their wishes, in battles they knew they would lose. *My kind* died. Those who protested were the next to die! Lines have been drawn," she said, eying the blazing ring of fire. "And you're on the wrong side."

Elliah ~ 7

"I warned the High Council," the irate Alluvium warrior spat. "Any High Elves who set foot in Cenaedth would share the fate of my brothers and sisters used as fodder in the High Elf war."

The bright ring of flame on the ground inexorably tightened. High Elf mages attempted to counter the spells with their own, resulting in winds pushing at the flames to little effect. Several stared out into the Alluvium crowd. Hooks? The Compulsions which the Alluvium accused them of? Whatever they were doing, it had no noticeable effect. One High Elf charged and jumped the low circle. He lit up like the sun, and a smoking ruin hit the ground on the far side. The smell of burned meat assailed me, its implications nauseating. Several High Elves, including Skaljian, approached the two Alluvium inside the circle with swords drawn.

"Lower your swords!" Beldroth shouted. Then, he barked "Control!" at Marinna, who stood wide-eyed, clenching and unclenching her fists.

Most of the High Elves listened. One marched toward the Alluvium, preparing to strike, and he screamed, dropping the sword, which turned to a puddle of molten slag on the ground. He hurried backwards as he stared in horror at charred flesh that had formerly been his hand. I wanted to warn him not to back up into the other side of the ring, but I couldn't get the words out. Fortunately, he stopped on his own, dropping to his knees to wretch.

My mother rushed to him, casting her spells.

My mind spun. I had a chance against magic, but not against fire. What could I do to change the balance? My knife, unlike their swords, was made from bone. Did bone melt? My eyes flicked over to the charred remains of the High Elf who'd jumped the fire, the smell of his bad choice still strong—yes, ribs protruded. I wanted to puke, but I didn't have the luxury. The bones hadn't melted. But the black and smoking bone would still burn my hand. The hammer had a bone head, but the wood of its handle would incinerate.

Despite the closing circle of flame, the two Alluvium had a space around them that no High Elf dared to penetrate. Beldroth stood closer than any. "Please," he said. "Stop this." Sweat poured down his face—

whatever barrier the Alluvium wove to hold the High Elves at bay did not ignore the Warder, but he held his ground. "We must stick together." Beldroth growled his next words like a wounded bear. "The Mother has Blessed this quest."

The warrior woman made a scornful click in her throat.

I had to do something, or, just as the Mother predicted, everyone I loved would die.

I cast a glance that dragged on for an eternity at Hughelas, who attempted a spell of some kind—probably a spell to learn something from their spells, if I knew Hughelas. He saw my look, and though he couldn't know exactly what I intended, he nodded. I dropped my weapons and marched toward the two Alluvium.

"Elliah, no!" my mother shouted as I marched past Beldroth.

But the spell they used to create the heat that held the High Elves at bay didn't land on me.

"I'm sorry," I said to the wide-eyed mage. His warrior guard growled and lunged, but not before Beldroth's training paid off—cold-cocking the mage came to me with practiced ease.

I fell to the side from the warrior's shove as the Alluvium mage collapsed like a rag doll. The warrior and I rolled toward the ring of fire.

Would the magic housed in the circle of sorcerous fire incinerate me? My resistance to magic wasn't foolproof, and I'd burned through my luck. I shoved the warrior off with my legs, flinging her toward the ring. Maybe she had protection and maybe she didn't, but she was out for my blood, leaving me little choice. Yet we weren't as close to the ring as I'd thought, and she landed well clear of it.

We bounced to our feet, and the path to the ring cleared as High Elves screamed in pain, moving away from us with clothes smoking. I wouldn't be getting any help—whatever magic burned from the Alluvium warrior kept them at bay. I silently thanked Beldroth again for his relentless hand-to-hand combat training. Fortunately, the warrior also fought unarmed, though she quickly had me moving away from her as her fists flew like a hurricane wind. The High Elves around us shuffled to provide space—my retreat put more of them in harm's way. She was at least a hand taller than I, more thickly muscled, and filled with rage. Something oozed down my face, and my vision pinched in pulses from my left eye. I wasn't sure when I'd taken the hit, but I wouldn't have depth perception for long.

The rest of the Alluvium, those outside the ring, kept their distance. Mystical patterns of flame still danced across the floor between the slow-closing circle of fire and the audience. Could they not move through their own patterns? Or did they choose not to? I chanced a look at the charred remains lying outside the ring, repulsed but hoping for some clue. The corpse kept its secrets.

I put my back to the ring, which kept the warrior there too. That way, I didn't risk scalding my companions from the warrior's magic. She took advantage of my swelling eye and attacked with her right. I backed closer to the ring of fire, hoping for a moment to breathe. Relentless and not showing any sign of the weariness that weighed on me, the warrior closed the gap.

I didn't have a chance.

The warrior leapt forward, and I braced to take her weight without moving. I had no more room behind me. But she flopped into me—a clumsy fall and not an attack at all. Beldroth's hammer clattered to the floor, having hit the warrior along the way. We'd taken out the Alluvium inside the ring! That left just the entire arena of yelling Alluvium on the other side.

The thought had only a moment to register, because, panic-stricken by the sudden screams of the ghosts from the tunnels below, I fell, tangled with the Alluvium warrior, onto the ring of fire.

Elliah ~ 8

"Wake up, sleepyhead." My mother didn't sound angry.

So I resisted.

"Can't I stay home from school today?" I moaned, caught in a world of dreams. Varitan was such an arrogant ass. Couldn't I just skip for just one day?

"Sure," she said. "Anything that keeps you from having to cross rings of magical fire."

The memory of fighting crashed into my mind, shattering my hazy dream from the past, and my eyes shot open.

Cold stone.

I lay on my back atop cold stone, firelight dancing on the ceiling above.

I gasped, trying to process whether I was burned, injured, or about to be swarmed by angry Alluvium.

But the sound wasn't right. No voices echoed off distant walls. No crackle of a fire. And no smell of burning flesh.

"You're okay," my mother said. "I hope."

Her voice calmed me. I let out my breath.

I found I was wrong: a thin pallet separated me from the stone floor of a small room, my mother sitting next to me while a tiny mage-light glowed softly above us. Tilting my head forward to look past my feet, I found a third elf. Marinna. She sat with her knees up and her head on them, oddly reminiscent of the Mother of Trees when we'd found her in her silvervein. There was room for my mother and me to lie side by side without touching, and a third person to sit, but little more. At the moment, my mother sat cross-legged, leaning against the outline of a stone door with small openings above it that let in air but no light.

"I'm alive?" I gently touched my face—it was puffy and sore, my left eye swollen almost shut, but it still worked. My mother hadn't Healed me. Why not?

"For now," my mother said, sighing.

A rising sense of panic urged me to do something. I tried to push myself up, while muscles and bruises screamed in protest. "We have to get out of here!" I panted.

"Easy," my mother cooed. "When we're ready, we can get out.

We have Marinna, and both Beldroth and Hughelas are in a cell down the hall," she said with a wave at the wall. "These cells weren't designed to hold Warders. Just rest for now."

She helped me push myself into a sitting position and lean against the wall, like Marinna. Was she asleep? I moved carefully, sore in muscle and bone. I sighed when I finally achieved a stable and not-too-painful position.

"Did the woman I fought live?" I asked. I pictured the magical Fire consuming her... and cringed.

"She did. They're more angry than a clowder of cats with their tails tied together in a rainstorm, but I think her living is the only reason we aren't dead." My companions lived—the Mother's prediction hadn't come true. Internally, I'd loosened my grip on a rope tied to my fears, and a length slipped through my fingers. "Yet."

I grunted, grabbing the rope before it got too far. Yet. We were locked up. The Alluvium were angry. Death still stalked us. But my mother thought we could escape.

"They halted the spell when you and their leader fell atop their magical fire and didn't..." she gestured with her hands like smoke rising. The awful smell of charred elf filled my nostrils, then disappeared just as quickly. Horrid.

"Their leader?" I asked. I'd fought their leader?

My mother nodded. "The pair of them, I think. The mage you knocked out and the warrior, they lead together, if I got it right. I'm honestly not sure. They weren't exactly chatty as they led us here."

"Who died?" I asked. Whose charred body would I forever smell?

"Imbryl was his name," she said. "I hadn't spoken two words to him. Couldn't tell you a thing about him. And now he's gone. And at the hands of elves."

"Is that any different from what you feared the High Council was going to do to me?"

She shrugged. "Ironically enough, I feared the High Council would do exactly what the Alluvium accused them of. Compelling you, and me, to fight until we died." She shrugged again. "But it might not have worked on you."

We sat in silence for several seconds as I contemplated once again the weight she'd carried for my sake for so many years.

"Ultimately, no," she said. "No different. The only thing that differs is who wields the magic. It still offends me though."

I nodded my head, then winced at the pain.

She chuckled softly. "You fought well."

"Not well enough."

"You're young. She's had more practice."

"I'd be dead if Beldroth hadn't thrown his hammer." My hand fumbled for it.

"Tch," she said. "I threw that." I searched the corners of the room, hoping to find it. "It's not here. They kept it. It's why I couldn't Heal you. Without its magic... you've grown very resistant."

I sighed. It made sense that they'd taken our weapons, but I worried Beldroth would be disappointed when he learned I'd lost his hammer. Plus, its magic had made it easier for my mother to Heal me, and a bit of Healing would have watered my vine. The aches intensified, redoubling their effort, at my thought that the hammer was gone.

"I threw the hammer after my arrow incinerated. Oddly, the hammer's shaft didn't burn."

I smiled. She might not have liked the thought of elves fighting elves, but she'd chosen to save me long ago, and she still chose the same. No matter the price.

"Well, at least the Warders must be happy," I said. "Trapped in a cave. Probably the first good night of sleep they've had."

My mother chirruped with laughter. But then she wiped tears from her face. "I was scared when my Heals wouldn't land."

"You Healed me a month ago, even without the hammer."

She shrugged. "Possibly because you're lugging around that hammer all the time. Your body is learning to fight its magic? But it was getting harder to Heal you even before the hammer, so maybe just age?"

"Yours or mine?" I jibed.

She elbowed me in the ribs, but the pain was worth it.

"I do feel old," she said, putting her hand on her belly. Her bump had become noticeable, not that it would slow her down.

"Yeah, kids are a real pain."

"Tch." She put an arm around me. "Yes, my daughter. Yes, they are. If you do it right, they make you realize who you really are, and that can hurt."

That sounded deeper than I meant to go, but I found I didn't want to talk about what might happen next. Everyone would have died in that circle if I hadn't acted, but death still lingered. It still hovered, always ready. The physical pain I could live with, but I wasn't ready to once again face the thought of losing everyone. My tug of war with fate. So I avoided it, and instead, I leaned into the conversation my mother offered. "And who are you? Or who were you before me?"

I looked more closely at Marinna. She couldn't really still be asleep, with all the noise we'd made, but she pretended to be. My mother waved dismissively, unconcerned whether Marinna overheard or not.

"I am the daughter of Haryk Faelynn, the ruler of Heann'el, and I was a magist." For a moment, I forgot about all my pain. Finally—finally!—after eighty years, my mother was telling me about her childhood. I'd heard of Heann'el, a Wood Elf town at the north end of the Border Woods, but I'd never heard of Haryk Faelynn. I was both shocked and unsurprised at the same time. It came as no surprise that she'd run from somewhere, some former life. Raised by the High Elf Zoras, but obviously a Wood Elf herself. I hadn't imagined her pedigree to be quite so lofty, but she'd never talked about it, never made it important. And, truly, Heann'el was just another town—it wasn't like its ruler was king of the elves or any such thing. The whole idea of a former life for my mother was so incongruous, it was like she was talking about somebody else. Still, did it mean I had other relatives? Would I find a town, like the elves in Fael Themar, where everyone looked a little like me?

"That's not a word," she said conspiratorially, and I was momentarily confused. What word? I'd focused on her parents. My grandparents. What else had she said? That she was a… magist? "I believed that those with more magic were better than those with less." She grinned, looking at the far wall and not at me. "I know you haven't been around much magic to see, but while my magic isn't the most powerful, my mana recharges faster than anyone's I've met. And I chose one of the most gifted mages among the High Elves to mate with, in hopes of producing offspring who could fight back against the trolls."

"Wow." I really was astounded. Partly by her clinical frankness—choosing an elf to mate with based on his power? But I was even more taken aback, dragged out of thoughts of finding relatives, by the realization that she'd planned for a magic prodigy, and she'd ended up with… me?

"Oh, Elliah. I was so terribly, terribly *wrong*. Everybody likes to think what they have is special, but skill in magic makes you more delusional than, say, singing or writing, by granting you power over the things around you, gifting you a sense of control. But it isn't real. We aren't in control—something bigger is. Something larger than us has a plan."

"Now you sound like Beldroth." I smiled, but I was still a tad wobbly from the realization that my mother once would have scorned me, had I not been her problem to deal with.

"Maybe," she said. "But something is wrong with the Mother, and yet we march on. Don't tell the father of my child, but I think his zealotry is… misplaced. Not wrong, mind you. But maybe there's something bigger than a semi-comatose bundle of sticks hiding in a tree."

I giggled at her blasphemy, but my dreamlike memory of the infinity of time seen through the Mother's eyes contradicted her heresy. Yet neither was she wrong—something was… off… with the Mother of Trees. Still, the whole idea of who my mother had once been, and what she'd done, tore at me. Her revelation was like finding a tree fallen after a storm that you'd never realized was *hollowed out*. "Why have you never told me?"

"Tch. Told you what a monster I was?" She sighed. "I always thought I would. For a while I told myself you were too young. Then, that I should wait until you made a big mistake, when I would use my life's story to illustrate how we all make mistakes." She looked at me and grinned. "I would have been *so* comforting. We try so hard to make even our faults into glories." She turned back to our prison wall. "And then… well, I waited too long. I just… couldn't."

I leaned my head on her shoulder.

"Revealing your ugly truths is hard," she said. The magelight glinted off a tear that trickled down my mother's face. "Even to ourselves."

I didn't want to leave her in her pain. She didn't deserve it. Whatever she had been once, she'd done nothing but protect me for almost a hundred years. All the talk that made me question how well I knew my mother made me wonder how universal that might have been. "What were your parents like?" Zoras had parented her to adulthood, but she'd never deigned to tell me of her upbringing. "Your… biological parents I mean."

Silence reigned long enough that I believed her childhood would remain a secret. But then she surprised me. "I don't really know," she said haltingly. "I thought I knew everything." Another pause. "They were distant." Oddly, she looked over at Marinna. "Aloof." I waited again, letting her remember. "I'd led such a privileged life, yet I'd treated them so badly. They sent me away to Zoras when I was about your age. No.

Younger, I suppose. I used our family name to establish myself in Alenor. Then I embraced the delusional life I'd told myself was my right. I was horrible. Truly horrible. I'm so sorry."

My attempt to alleviate her pain had backfired. I didn't like how she beat herself up, but I didn't know what to say. Didn't know how to make it better.

A noise outside ripped me out of the conversation and back into the stark reality of our surroundings. My first thought was that some spirit banged around outside, in the maze of tunnels, searching for living captives. My mother jumped to her feet. Marinna's head popped up, and she rubbed her face and climbed to her feet as well. Had she really been sleeping? After I painfully realized I could not easily hop up, my mother helped me rise. Whether we found Beldroth and Hughelas there to break us free, a mob of angry Alluvium, or we were destined to confront ghosts… we would do it together.

Elliah ~ 9

Metal scraped on metal as the door nudged open. My mother let her magelight drop as a crack of light intruded. Was she afraid of spirits catching her using a spell? Could ghosts open doors? Did they need to? The door caught several times, and I heard a grunt. Dark fingers grabbed the inside of the door and pulled again. Those fingers didn't belong to a ghost, nor to Beldroth or Hughelas. With reluctance born of ancient rust, the door revealed a magelight floating in the hall beyond. If the situation hadn't been so dire, I would have found the slow, loud, and jarring door-opening amusing.

Finally, the owner of the hand stuck a leg into view, covered in a red robe. A mage then. The mage braced and lifted the door, scurrying to the side to get it opened.

"Need help with that?" my mother asked, and I couldn't help but snicker. Marinna did the same. When I smiled at her, she quickly looked down at her feet.

"I'm sorry," she whispered, so quietly I almost didn't hear her. My mother's ears had swiveled as well.

"And they…" the door-opener, male, paused to catch his breath. "… think I'm wrong…" Another pause. "… about the end times." His tone changed, as though he recited a verse: "The doors of fate shall be sealed, their hinges rusted and still." It was not a quote I knew, but it sounded like something Beldroth might recite. Surely our jailer wasn't trying to apply some grand foretelling of doom to our cell door. Was he?

What was Marinna sorry about? Eavesdropping?

The Alluvium held out his hand to forestall us while he alternated between catching his breath and glaring at the door.

Thinking to comfort Marinna, I told her, "Thank you for letting us talk."

She ducked her head, but shook it I, like I'd misunderstood. I'd sparred with her over the last few days. She understood what I was—a freak of nature who lacked magic. I understood what she was—a Wood Elf who had Warder magic and something she was running from. We'd bonded with a quiet, introverted, awkward camaraderie. I raised an eyebrow, but she shook her head.

Finally, the Alluvium nodded his head. "I'm Gormar Blackfoot.

Welcome to Cenaedth." He stepped into our cell, his magelight following and brightening the room. The cell was cramped when it had just been three of us in there—with the fourth person it became uncomfortable. My mother eyed the door, but I didn't know if she was considering bolting out, or if she just sought a little more space. We couldn't back up any more. Gormar looked at us curiously, then took a step back. "Oh, right. Wood elves. Personal bubble. I suppose it comes from having all that space in the woods." He shivered as though the thought made him uncomfortable.

"Greetings... Gormar," my mother offered hesitantly. "My name is Illiara, and this is my daughter, Elliah." I nodded to him. "And this is Marinna," she said. Marinna stood behind my mother and me. He looked at each of us in turn, until my mother finally asked. "Perhaps there's something we can help you with? A reason you're here?"

"You're just not what I expected," he said, his eyes darting between all of us. "The end times. The prophesied destroyer. I just thought you'd be... bigger."

A visceral memory of two red eyes boring into my soul made me shiver. When I dwelled on the memory, its anger and hatred became more real and present. "There *is* something out there," I said, though I probably should have kept quiet. "Something intent on our destruction."

The Alluvium cocked his head like a wolf hearing something unexpected. "There are many things out there intent upon our destruction. Always have been." My mother grunted in agreement. His eyes locked onto me. "But you're the one who's actually going to do it."

I tried to take a step back, but bumped into Marinna. "Wait, me? What? I'm not..."

"Not what I expected at all," he agreed, like he was finishing my sentence. Though that wasn't what I'd been thinking. "May I?" he asked, holding up his hands like he intended some kind of hug.

"No, you may not—" my mother snapped.

But he didn't listen. He wiggled his fingers, casting a spell.

Nothing happened. While I didn't appreciate having unknown spells of dubious intent cast at me, at least I hadn't been burned.

"Remarkable," he said. "You felt nothing?"

My mother scowled and stepped directly between us. "If you have to *ask* a woman, then, indeed, she *felt nothing*. And from the looks of you, that's hardly 'remarkable.'"

"Rude," Gormar said, staring at my mother. They were roughly the same height, and his door-wrangling exhaustion suggested he didn't have the musculature of the Alluvium warriors. He broke the stare first, looking down. "She's your daughter?" he asked. He reached toward my mother's belly, saying, "Does this one have the same father?" My mother slapped his hand, and he jerked it back.

Personal space!

"At least this should prove entertaining," he said, rubbing his hand. "Come on." He turned and walked out the door.

My mother and I looked at each other as his magelight slipped away. In a quick and silent exchange, we decided leaving the cell with the crazy jerk was better than staying in it, and we followed him. My mother preceded me into the hallway. I glanced back, and Marinna followed me with her head down. I pitied her. All she'd wanted was to learn to control her magic, and she'd found herself locked up in an underground prison. The corridor was even more narrow than the cell, barely wider than the door, and I had to follow behind my mother rather than step up to walk beside her. A whiff of relatively fresh air surprised me. The cell had been musty, though I hadn't noticed until I stepped into the hall. Looking over my shoulder, I saw shafts of light—sunlight—shining down through slats in the ceiling.

"Is that…" I began, fumbling for words. Gormar stopped, and we all had to halt not to hit him. He looked at me quizzically. "Is that really sunlight? We're that close to the surface?"

Gormar turned around and resumed his walk. "Of course," he said. "It would hardly be punishment if the cells were tucked deep inside the heart of the mountain, now would it?"

No. No, of course it wouldn't. Best to keep people captive *right next to the exit!*

My hopes of getting out alive increased dramatically.

The mage trudged down a hallway lined with more stone doors. Each door boasted a metal wheel the size of my forearms connected to vertical bolts that locked the door into metal plates fastened to the stone walls. *Are Hughelas and Beldroth behind one of those doors?*

As though reading my mind, my mother scraped a nail along a door on the left as we passed.

"I wonder if the baby you carry is also Bereft," Gormar said out of thin air.

My mother stumbled a step. Her lip curled. "Where are we going?" she asked, her words sharp and her gait slowing. Was she thinking it was time to make our exit?

"The Low Council," Gormar said. "They have questions."

"Low Council?" my mother asked, letting Gormar pull farther ahead.

The mage stopped and turned. "The High Elves have their High Council. We're underground, so..." He spun and resumed walking. "It's almost funny how our rebellion mimics those we rebel against."

"The High Elves don't... rule... other elves," my mother fumbled, letting him walk ahead into a room. "So, technically, I don't think you're rebelling at all."

"I'm taking these prisoners to the Low Council," Gormar said to someone we couldn't see. After an indiscernible question, he said. "Yes, they'll be back. Unless the council sets them free."

My mother turned back to look at me, and we had another unspoken exchange where she looked at the door she'd scratched and raised an eyebrow. If we were going to be back, I thought it might be better to escape when it was night out. Plus, the Mother of Trees needed an army. An audience with the Low Council might get Beldroth that army. So I shook my head no. She nodded and followed Gormar.

The corridor vomited us into a small room with a slightly larger hall leaving the far side. A soldier and a mage stood guard in the room, a magelight floating above them, but they did nothing to stop or question us as Gormar led us through. Pots of glowing purple fungi hung on metal hooks protruding from the walls. dimly lighting the corridor. The corridor bent to the left and down.

"How did you keep her alive?" Gormar asked.

"Screee!"

A distant scream came from ahead of us, and I froze. It wasn't from the cells behind us, so they weren't torturing my friends. But did ghosts lay ahead of us? The scream hadn't sounded remotely like an elf. Even my mother looked rattled.

"That's what they'll want to know," Gormar said, ignoring the scream that had died away after a couple of seconds. "I'm a little curious too, but I'm much more curious *why* she will kill us. *How* she kills us is interesting, of course, but *why*? *Why* is what plagues me." He stopped right in the middle of a four-way intersection, and I looked to the left and right, seeing more pots of fungi and curved corridors, even another mage walking away down one of them. Or perhaps a ghost. When I finally realized our guide waited on *me*, I gave him my full attention. He repeated his question. "Why do you want us dead?"

"Well," I said, genuinely appearing to consider my answer despite its absurdity, since it appeared we would stand there forever if I didn't answer. "You tried to kill me and my friends on our first meeting." They'd *killed* a High Elf, in fact. Imbryl, whose name I hadn't even known until he died. "Then you locked me in a cell."

"With your mother," he pointed out like he'd arranged that comfort. He hadn't even known she was my mother!

I rolled my eyes. "But despite all that, I don't find myself inclined to destroy the lot of you, even if I knew how to do so. I, frankly, have no idea what you're talking about! What makes you *think* I'm here to destroy you?"

He stared at me, head cocked to the side, and my mind tried to find something that would move the conversation along. "Interesting," he mumbled, then he turned and started back down the hall. "The prophecy of course."

Next, he said over his shoulder, in that voice he'd used for quoting verse, "But beware the rise of the army of the Bereft, for when the Destroyer awakens, the Bones of Cenaedth shall be consumed."

I looked at my mother, sorely tempted to grab her and run down one of the side tunnels. Of course, that was absurd. We wouldn't leave without our companions. And the Mother needed an army. Yet a prophecy about an army of the Bereft, when I was there to help Beldroth recruit an army, unsettled me.

"Do you know your way around?" I asked my mother. She'd said she'd been there before, after all. I wanted to know, if we did make a run for it, would she know where to go?

"I was here as a child much younger than you. So I have no clue where we are or—"

"Tch," I commented, irritated at… everything. It was a sound she'd made often enough, and I'd never quite mastered it. Before that moment, anyway. What was happening to us wasn't fair. The Mother of Trees. The magic under the swamps. *And now this?*

"Ladies," Gormar said from behind my mother, startling us both. "I know the tunnels can be confusing. Please try to stay close." He turned his back to us and walked off.

My mother gave me a queer look and followed the crazy mage.

"Tch," I said, again, for emphasis, and hurried to catch up, Marinna on my heels.

Illiara - 6

As we beelined through the labyrinthian tunnels of Cenaedth, the temperature rising as we descended, I wondered how much the Low Council mimicked the High Council. Did the Alluvium take pieces of the High Elf proceedings and turn them on their heads? I doubted that was possible except in trivial expressions of difference. One still needed order. Procedures still reigned.

"Screee!"

I jolted, the shriek cutting through the air, closer and louder than before. It died out in seconds, fading to eerie silence. We had ventured deeper into the maze. Nearer to the ghosts?

What ghastly spirits did the Alluvium torture? The sound haunted me from my childhood visit. We hadn't stayed long—the meeting had been much more utilitarian than ceremonious. A handful of Alluvium had met us in the chamber where Elliah had fought, and led us through a side passage with many forks, twists and turns, to a small room where my father, leader of Heanin'el, had brokered an arrangement with Cenaedth. He hadn't explained the details, though I noticed Alluvium around our town after. I'd been excited to see the "rivers of lava" I'd heard about, but the screaming had scared me more than my curiosity drove me, and we'd left via the maze through which we'd entered. My nerves flayed with the screams of the undead, like I was once again a small child.

Just as before, Gormar didn't react at all. Why would he? They were the spirits of *his* world. *His* people. We approached a well-lit room and the buzz of chattering elves. At least, I hoped the chattering was elves. *Living* elves.

"I won't accept your claim of eminent domain," said a woman loudly enough to overpower the general murmur, "even while I acknowledge your expertise in the field as demonstrated by the public use of your bedroom." I paused at the entrance, the first words that greeted me contrasting sharply with my expectations.

Raucous laughter, both male and female, greeted the speaker. Opposite of the High Council indeed.

The cavern, a clean-cut, square room three times the height of an elf, held about fifty Alluvium. A mix of fighters and mages, many sat on benches at stone tables that held about six elves each. Others stood. Fire rimmed the wall around the ceiling and blazed in a ball from above, creating a near-day level of light, but with shadows darting about wildly. I wondered why they chose fire over magelight, but it wasn't the time to ask. The Alluvium wore red and black, robes or leathers, with sporadic dabs of yellow. They'd strewn the tables with papers and mugs and bits of discarded food. The scent of the room put me in mind of the taverns we'd passed in Telloria'ahlia. Side conversations bubbled as a female warrior garbed in black leathers and a woman in red mage's robes stood on benches and shouted at each other over the noise.

"That cave stands between Cenaedth and the thieving Enaed. For the security of our people, we need to fortify that passage!" shouted the warrior.

"And the ruby-rich walls have no bearing on your interest, you cave-grabbing—" The mage, the woman's voice I'd heard as I entered, stopped shouting when her eyes landed on me.

The noise died down as people noticed either our entrance, or the cessation of the discussions around them. Gormar walked to a table and filled clay mugs from a similar pitcher as I stood by my daughter under the scrutiny of the Alluvium leaders. Marinna hid with her head down behind us. I empathized with her while I simultaneously wanted to shake her and tell her to look more alive. We had stepped into what was essentially the center stage of the room.

Gormar returned with three mugs, handing them to me, my daughter, and then reaching between us to hand one to Marinna. The drinks smelled of alcohol and… mint? "Welcome to the Low Council," he said, and pandemonium ensued.

People rose, fists pounded on tables… drinks slammed down, some to the demise of the clay vessels, creating wet papers and puddles. An otherworldly scream resounded above them all, and while it sent chills up my spine, no one else stopped anything they were doing. Gormar ambled back to his table as the screaming vanished, but I lost him in the movement of people who shouted and shoved at one another. Small fires literally flared up around the room, then quickly extinguished.

"Mother of rutting Trees," I breathed, unable to digest the totality of the bedlam. I glanced at Elliah, whose eyes were enormous, and smiled. When in Cenaedth…

I took a sip of my drink. It proved to be as strong as it smelled, and the mint overpowered the alcohol. But I looked forward to its anticipated effects in the overwhelming chaos.

I watched the Alluvium shift about and resolve into two groups, one mostly mages, and the other mostly warriors, but a good mix in each group. Some sat, but most stood. The bedlam decreased from shouting to loud discussions, and the volume continued to decrease until the discussions seemed almost civil.

"Why is she still alive?" a woman finally shouted. My head spun, and I found the warrior Elliah had fought against in the circle of magical fire. The one I had assumed was their leader. "She made fools of us! For that alone, I would kill her."

"If we killed everyone that made a fool of you, the caves would be empty," a mage from the other camp said loudly.

My eyes widened, and I sipped at my drink, taking comfort in its proffered bite. The Alluvium operated *very* differently from the High Council.

"You sided with me when it was the High Elves making fools of us," the warrior bit back.

"*I* didn't," another mage shouted. "And more the fool I am for not fighting harder against it."

"Gah!" the warrior shouted, grabbing a mug like she intended to hurl it, but holding back.

"What I want to know," shouted one of the handful of warriors from the mage camp, "is how the Wood Elf *lived*!"

"She's Bereft," a mage from the same camp said, not as loudly, because the noise had diminished. *Yes*, I wanted to say, *my daughter lacks magic*. But to say she lacked magic didn't paint the true picture. She absorbed magic. Like the trolls. A condition that had caused us to run and hide her entire life.

"So we've been told," said one of the few mages in the warrior camp. "But that's impossible."

"See for yourself." Gormar's voice, I recognized. He sat, where most of the others still had not settled.

I tensed as some twenty-ish mages began chanting, and I quickly stepped in front of my daughter.

"Not all of you at once," Gormar groaned, and the mages let their spells fizzle. "Illimar, you doubt her. You do the honors."

"Don't I get a say—" Elliah started.

I stalked toward the mage who I suspected to be Illimar, wielding my mug like a weapon and snarling, "Keep your filthy spells off my daughter!"

I never reached the mage. Two Alluvium warriors grabbed me before I came close, relinquishing me of my mug and pulling me out of the path.

"Screeee!" The noise came in louder than ever, from directly out the main doors behind the Alluvium council members' backs.

Elliah jumped at the sound, her eyes fixing on the entrance from which the scream came. Then her head snapped back to the mage, glaring, and I knew it was too late for more protests.

The mage, Illimar I presumed, nodded his head. "The spell didn't land. She's Bereft."

The noise level rose again, and Illimar, head down in thought, left the warriors and joined the camp of mages. Another mage followed. The one group of Alluvium dwindled while the other grew.

"Back to my question," a warrior said. "I wasn't asking how she survived the deathfire. How does she *live*?" Deathfire. The flames that instantly incinerated the High Elf Imbryl were called deathfire. But I didn't understand the question.

That's when I realized that the council's eyes had turned away from my daughter… to me.

The warriors holding my arms let me go, and I growled and stomped back to Elliah's side, retrieving my mug on the way for good measure.

I looked Elliah over to be sure she was unharmed, but also to buy time. The room had actually grown quiet. Elliah placed a hand on my shoulder. "Mom, I'm fine." I took another sip. "Mother," Elliah said. "Their question is for you."

I knew that, but I didn't understand what they wanted. "What was the question?" I asked, pretending like I'd been so worked up that I hadn't been listening.

"How did you keep her alive?" the same mage asked.

"Our Bereft die in infancy," another mage stated, a man with a forlorn face. "I've lost two children."

"Every one of mine are Bereft," a woman in mage's robes said angrily, then choked on a sob as she said, "I've lost them *all*."

"How does she live?" one warrior asked.

"What did you *do*?" said another.

I held up my hands as more murmurs erupted, hoping to forestall more questions. Though I finally understood what they asked, I didn't know how to answer. "I'm sorry, but I don't *know*. We don't even know what *causes* their condition, much less—"

"Wait!" the warrior who had it in for me shouted. "Who doesn't know the cause? Wood Elves? High Elves?"

"Anybody," I said, cocking my head in consideration.

The room again buzzed with noise, and I caught enough of the mocking tone and bits of statements like, "know-it-all High Elves," and "so obvious," and, "how could they not know," that I realized the Alluvium *knew* what caused children to be born Bereft. They shifted again, mages moving back over to the camp that largely held warriors, including the angry woman who had lost all her children. The split looked biased toward the warriors.

"So what causes it?" I shouted over the din. What made Elliah Bereft?

"Why should we tell you?" my nemesis countered.

"Maybe if I *knew*," I said, "and we all talked about it like *reasonable people*, we might figure this out." I looked at the angry mage who'd lost all her children. "Maybe we wouldn't have to lose any more."

The mage looked down, put a hand on her belly, and shuffled back to the other mages. A couple more drifted back amidst quiet discussions and a low murmur of voices. Was all the shifting an indication of picking sides? Voting? For what? Gormar still sat at the table where he'd first planted himself, drinking and refilling his mug, rooted firmly in the middle of the room.

"That's no answer," I said, referring to the way the mage who was presumably pregnant had shifted seats. I was dying to know what made Elliah Bereft, and from her eager, wide-eyed look, Elliah felt the same.

"We are not here to answer your questions, fool!" the pregnant mage snapped.

Elliah took an aggressive step toward the mage, but I held out a hand, stopping her. Oddly, a warrior nodded at Elliah and shifted over to the mages' camp.

"Why *are* we here?" I asked, giving Elliah my best rein-it-in look. She gave me the look right back. Fair, I'd lost my temper too.

"You're on trial for your lives," Gormar said, grinning as he set his mug on the table. "Did I fail to explain that?"

Hughelas #7

"What if the Mother doesn't have a plan?" my father asked, startling me.

We'd sat in the cell for hours. He in his sullen thoughts. Me, reading the journal Felaern had provided me. Fortunately, I'd had it in my robe and not in my pack. The Alluvium had found it there, but didn't think it threatening enough to throw in with our weapons and packs. Thankfully. Because my father had been as talkative as the surrounding stone.

We'd exchanged words briefly, noting how easy it would be to break out of the cell, but not knowing whether we needed to take the risk. He'd decided we would wait, and I half wondered whether it was because he wanted some sign. Some signal from the Mother to prove he wasn't misguided.

"Mother?" I asked, stupidly. Who else? But, my mind had been elsewhere. In fact, I was quite excited. I thought I understood what the troll Warlord in the magical statue was trying to say. The "five-dimensional spherical cage." And if I was right... well, if I was right, we'd made one really bad decision. "Dad," I said. "I think we may have a problem."

"If she didn't have a plan," he said, "then all of my years of leaning on her for comfort have no meaning."

I brightened my magelight, so that he would be able to see the picture I'd stared at for the last hour. Cross-legged, with my back to one wall, I faced my father, who leaned against the wall opposite, his legs straight in front of him but bent at the knees so he could fit. I spun the book around, making it right-side up for him. "Dad, look at this. I think we shouldn't have given her the hammer."

"The thought that taking solace in the Mother is unfounded opens a hole in me," he said.

"I think it might be killing her," I said.

My father's face clouded. "The idea that Lyrei is *gone*... in a vast and meaningless Universe..."

The floor literally began to rumble.

I'd rarely seen my father lose control. Just like the last time, it hadn't been a moment of battle, but in the dark times after a deep loss. When our mother died, he'd buried the carcass of the dragon who'd killed her, hiding its body deep underground, just for spite. He'd told me in Zoras's manor that he regretted that, and I'd promised him we would help dig up the bones when we returned.

The only ones who would be buried if he lost control in the cells of Cenaedth would be us.

Slate and shards!

"Dad!" I said, leaning forward and placing my hand on his arm. I hadn't even been listening! But I'd heard his moping all the way from Fael Themar, and had a good sense of where his head was. To my discredit, I'd enjoyed seeing him struggle. His unflinching confidence in the Mother in the face of the reality of her existence had driven me absolutely cave-bat crazy.

"Breathe, Dad. One-two-three..." I counted in a whisper as I inhaled.

My father growled, deep in his chest, and the floor rumbled with him.

I was an idiot. I'd pushed him away ever since our encounter with the Mother, frustrated by his conviction. Then I'd reveled in his discomfort when his ideals had fractured. It had all been about me and what I'd wanted, and I'd lost all sense of empathy for my father. Buried it like my father had buried the dragon in Bellon.

It was awkward, but I unfolded my legs, kicking my prized book into the corner, so that I sat by his side. I put my head on his chest like I had when I was a child. Though uncomfortable at first, his earthy smell, that close, brought back old memories, and it wasn't hard to let myself slip back in time to a child who needed to be held.

The rumbling in his chest stopped first, then the floor followed. He reached up his massive arms and gently hugged me.

But he needed more. Irritated with myself for how I'd acted by making him suffer through weeks of my bad attitude, I tried to make it up to him.

"Have you considered," I murmured, "that the dragon in the buried city made its choice, hid itself away in death, for a reason?"

"Yes," he said, "I'd considered that. The bespelled stone had implied as much, that the dragon wanted to save their bizarre message for the future."

Knowing I might very well be cursing myself to deal, once more, with the overconfident Warder-on-a-Mission, I suggested, "Maybe the one that killed Mom did it for a reason too." I recalled how the boney tail of the dragon had wrapped the pedestal, and how the dragon we'd fought in Bellon had wrapped its tail around my mother the same way.

Coincidence?

Something changed in my father's hug, a sigh of relaxation that made his rocky muscles inexplicably softer. "Thank you, Son."

He held me there, and I wondered which of my fathers I would find if I looked up at his face. The beatific smile of unflinching faith, or the sullen frown of shattered hopes. I wasn't sure I wanted to know. "Fate," he said, "brought us a message of doom, preserved by ancient magic: kill the Mother of Trees." A few seconds passed before he continued. "But fate and magic are the Mother's brushes and paint."

Elliah ~ 10

The physical split of Alluvium in the Low Council, the shuffling between groups, took on meaning. They'd chosen camps, picked sides, decided whether my mother and I would live or die. I quickly tried to count the elves on each side of the room. I failed. When had they moved? What had been the topics where they'd shifted? My heart beat in my ears and I couldn't think. I had the useless and defeatist thought that Hughelas would have discerned the intent of the Alluvium… would have worked out a plan.

"Any more questions?" Gormar asked. But he wasn't asking me, or my mother. He asked his fellow members of the Low Council.

The biggest shift had occurred after they'd confirmed I was Bereft. Had that, as with the High Elves, condemned me? For some reason, my mind returned to the single warrior who shifted sides at the end when I'd lost my temper.

No one spoke. My mother scanned the room, then squinted at me. She wasn't sure which way the room balanced either. Marinna continued to try to go unnoticed behind us.

"Very well, then." Gormar stood and walked over to the group dominated by mages, accompanied by the groans of the other cadre. "Let's get on with the End Times!" He clapped his hands once, loudly.

His declaration caused another eruption. I heard mutterings of "stupid," "unbelievable," and "of all people." I wasn't sure what any of that meant beyond a generic complaint about losing, and perhaps a specific complaint against Gormar. The fact that the opposing group seethed with vitriolic venom had me thinking my mother and I had won our case, though I frankly wasn't sure. What if they were excited to declare our sentences of death?

Gormar wormed his way through the tables and the bickering Alluvium, heading our way. My mother took the opportunity to pour more of the minty alcohol into two mugs she'd somehow procured.

"Drink up," she said, handing a mug to me and another to Marinna. "We just dodged an arrow we didn't see coming. That deserves a toast."

My upbringing did not include an education in drinking traditions, but my mind had shot into overdrive with trying to sort out all the details of the meeting in the Low Council, then calculating how close we had come to death. I suspected, from the uproar, that Gormar had been the deciding vote. So he wanted me alive… because he thought I was prophesied to destroy them all? That made no sense! And yet, our lives had hung on that thread. I took the mug and drank, coughing and wheezing after an overenthusiastic gulp of the harsh liquid. The stuff burned!

"What of our friends?" my mother asked Gormar, who'd dodged my cough and joined us.

"Are the High Elves your friends?" Gormar responded.

"I was thinking of the Warder and his son," my mother replied. "But there's at least a couple of the High Elves I wouldn't push into your infamous rivers of lava. Where are those anyway? This is my second time to Cenaedth and I've yet to see them."

"Magma rivers," Gormar said. "Not lava rivers. Anyway, the prison cells are meant to be cold," Gormar answered. He grinned. "We don't send criminals to a spa." Spa? What was a spa? The lower caves were far too warm for my comfort.

"Were we criminals before we went on trial?" my mother asked. "You're not so different from the High Elves as you think."

Gormar's narrowed eyes and scowl added to my worry about what they would do with everyone else who'd arrived with us. But my mother wasn't wrong. Our room in the Luminarium had been more gilded, but still a cage.

"Let's start with the Warder and his son then," my mother said. "They're not High Elves."

Two Alluvium approached. One was a male warrior, the one who had switched sides when I lost my temper. Gormar and my mother had their backs to him. I took a sip of my drink, careful of its kick, then another, while trying to determine whether the warrior meant trouble.

The other Alluvium was the pregnant mage who'd said all of her children had died. From being Bereft, like me. That deserved another sip.

"The Warder proclaimed himself leader of the party," Gormar said to my mother, ignorant of the approaching duo. "Undoubtedly a High Elf tactic to prevent the spilling of High Elf blood, but as the supposed leader, he will suffer their fate."

My mother scowled.

"And the son?" I asked. My mother's eyes went wide, but I wasn't giving up on Beldroth; we needed Hughelas's brain to help us argue our way out. Still, my tongue had sped a little ahead of my thoughts, my longing for Hughelas overcoming my common sense. "He's neither High Elf nor leader."

Gormar cocked his head at me. "You are... correct. We can consider—"

"Zoras," the warrior blurted, startling my mother and Gormar. "What news of Zoras?"

Gormar's eyes flared at the newcomer, but he kept quiet, biting his lip and standing straighter.

"Who are *you*?" my mother asked.

The man didn't answer. Didn't say anything else. He just waited. The pregnant mage stopped next to him. Were they together?

"He died," I said. I hadn't meant to say that. It had spilled out before I'd caught it. I pursed my lips and took another sip of the spicy drink.

"How?" he asked, nodding his head and offering a tight, sad smile, apparently unsurprised by the news.

"Protecting me," I blurted, despite a cautioning look from my mother. Her eyes drifted to my mug, and she reached for it, but I turned slightly to defend it. "He helped me break in to see the Mother of Trees, so that I could prove to the High Elves they shouldn't kill me, and so Beldroth could get her Blessing and come recruit an army of Alluvium." My mouth ran well ahead of my brain. I knew I'd said more than was wise, but a few more words would fix that. "I'm not allowed to know more of the plan than that." There, that would put a stop to my babbling. "Because something evil got into my head when I communed with the Mother of Trees and they're afraid it might happen again."

My mother maneuvered to get in front of me while I'd talked and she snatched my mug away. She grabbed a hunk of cheese off a table and shoved it in my hands. "Eat!" she demanded.

"Beldroth?" the warrior asked.

"The Warder," I said, sampling the cheese. Spicy cheese? Still, I was a little hungry.

The warrior turned his piercing gaze on Gormar. "And you want to kill him? A Warder with the Mother's Blessing?"

Gormar squirmed. "*I* don't want to kill him. That was the Low Council's decision."

"You want to kill everybody," the warrior said. The woman next to him smirked.

"*I* don't want to kill anyone!" Gormar yelped. "I just said I've seen our deaths. Even the Pyre's Reckoning says as much."

The warrior's lip twitched in a snarl, the first sign of emotion he'd displayed, and it disappeared so quickly I wondered if I'd imagined it.

"Fire lies," he said. As Gomar stammered, the warrior continued. "Free the Warder, or you'll regret it."

"Don't threaten me, you puffy... relic."

The corners of the warrior's mouth pulled up the height of an ant. "Relic," he said, savoring the word. "It wasn't a threat, young Gormar. Just wisdom. 'The Flame Bearers must gather, their hearts alight with the Fire of Cenaedth.' The Warder comes to gather the Flame Bearers, does he not?"

Gormar slapped his hand over his mouth. Then he eased it off. "You know the Pyre's Reckoning? That's for the ears of Red Prophets alone. Your speaking it is heretical!"

"Then perhaps Elandra should not have prophesied it in my presence," he said.

Gormar's hand flew back to his mouth.

Elandra? Why did that name ring a bell?

"Fire lies, Gormar," the warrior said. "Believe me."

"I've seen the visions," Gormar replied with passion. "Elandra will return and lead us through the final battle. She is the ancient, the old guard, hidden away... for the day of battle against *her* army." He spat the last at me.

"*My* army?" *What? Wait, he wanted me alive to fight me?*

But Gormar didn't answer me. Instead, he stared daggers at the stoic warrior. Slowly, Gormar's anger melted, then he cocked his head at the warrior with a newfound curiosity. "Let me speak with Vesryn and Almathara," Gormar said, and he shuffled away.

Leaving us with the warrior and the female mage.

"I do not know if many will miss young Zoras," he said. *Young Zoras? Zoras was ancient.* "But I count myself among them."

"He raised me," my mother said.

His ghost of a grin returned. "Your deft avoidance of acknowledging whether you will miss him confirms your heritage." The smile died. "Fire lies, but Zoras did not. Though the strands of truth might stretch thin and find themselves braided with beautiful and distracting ornamentation."

My mother barked a laugh. "I've never heard a description more apt."

"Red Prophets," the warrior scoffed, shaking his head. "Alluvium used to interlace magic and muscle. At some point while I was away, these Red Prophets built a sect around the writings of Elandra, calling her visions prophetic. I'm no Zoras—my attempts to dismantle their beliefs only encouraged them. They're fools, but, believe me, I know how convincing Fire can be."

The woman next to him put a hand on his forearm, an acknowledged connection, though she wore the robes of a mage herself. Were all mages Red Prophets?

After a brief pause, my mother said. "I am Illiara. This is my daughter, Elliah, and our companion, Marinna. Zoras raised me for several decades, until I woke the Mother of Trees and then spent my days running and hiding."

"Ah," the warrior said. "I know the story. Zoras probably even told me your name. He loved your mother."

My mother's mouth dropped. That was news to her.

"Everything changed with her," the warrior continued. "Zoras had to learn to process *feelings*. Things he only understood as levers up to that point. I didn't hear from him much during the years he had you in his home. But his words flowed like lava, slow but inexorable, once you ran off with your daughter. Zoras was a complicated man, but he had many years to cope with his feelings."

"You're Wynruil," my mother said.

Wynruil? A name from legends! "Wynruil Embergrove—" I slapped my hand over my mouth, the gesture much like Gormar's. I was embarrassed for having called him by a name he couldn't have been happy with, but if it bothered him, I didn't read it in his body language. Embergrove. The elf who went mad and burned down the Faeltic Forest. He was the reason Bellon was destroyed, and he created the situation that caused Beldroth and Hughelas to train Warders to defend the Blasted Lands.

"I am Brittanie," the woman next to him said. "We need to talk." She put a hand on her belly. "I need to understand."

As I digested the enormity of the staggering effects one elf had created, and the possibilities that a discussion about Bereft might unveil, Gormar returned. "We will free the Warder and his son, but the High Elves will remain in custody."

Beldroth and Hughelas would be freed! What would Beldroth do to the man who had burned down his homeland?

"Those High Elves have likely never even seen the war," Wynruil said to Gormar.

"They serve the same leadership," Gormar replied with a dismissive wave.

"Do you destroy all the bricks in your kiln when but one shatters?" Wynruil asked Gormar. "You condemn them as a race for condemning us as a race."

"They started it," Gormar replied. "We merely play by the rules *they* established. Fair is fair. How do you even keep your seat on the council with your constant votes against Alluvium prerogatives?"

"You are young, Gormar," Wynruil replied. "You mistake passion for wisdom." He turned his gaze to my mother. "I heard you ask about the magma. Come, we can wait for your friends there and talk more privately." Only then did I notice that a good deal of Alluvium lingered. "When they arrive, bring them to the Molten Gorge Overlook, Gormar."

Gormar looked like he'd rather chew rocks than do as Wynruil asked, but Wynruil gestured for us to follow him out the main doors, and as we did, Gormar stayed behind. Brittanie came with us.

Moving once again brought out my aches and pains, and my thoughts turned to my hammer. Beldroth's hammer. I'd gone from wishing I had it so that my mother could land a Heal, to having a hammer-sized longing in its absence. Was that how Beldroth felt without it? How could I miss carrying around that weight? And while I recognized it was impertinent to ask to be armed after having barely been allowed to live, my tongue had other ideas. "Can we get our weapons back?"

"Eat some more, Elliah," my mother said, nudging my hand that held the cheese. Rude.

"From what I saw, you are armed even without your weapons," Wynruil replied, still walking out. "When Gormar returns with your friends, I will send him to fetch your weapons."

"Can we get them now?" I asked, the hammer's absence aching like a leg that had fallen asleep.

"I don't know where they are," Wynruil said. With a ghost of a smile, he added, "I'll make it Gormar's problem." The hall we walked was wider and warmer than the ones leading to the prison cells. Six elves could have walked side by side, and the tops of the walls sported a more luminescent plant, brighter than the dull purple from the prison halls. Occasional magelights from others sojourning down the hall added to the light. Metal pipes ran above the plants, and the occasional drip of water revealed their purpose. In contrast to the rough walls near the cells, the surrounding walls were smooth save for the occasional engravings of unfamiliar scenes. Foot-traffic had etched a groove in the floor, black granite with crawling white veins, heavy with quartz. *How many elves over how many centuries had created that groove?* I imagined a time long in the future, when the floor would become so deep that the engravings loomed high overhead instead of at eye level.

"I'm sorry I didn't help," Marinna whispered. My mother and I both turned to look at her. "When you fought, I should have helped. The magic was there. Pounding. Calling to the rock. It was all I could do to keep it in. Beldroth told me to keep it under control."

My mother put an arm on her shoulder. "You did right, Marinna. Losing control while we're *inside* the mountain. That sounds like a *very* bad idea."

"But I was scared," Marinna said. She looked like she wanted to say more, but struggled to find the words.

"We were all scared," my mother said.

"You weren't," she said, meeting my eyes.

Hadn't I been scared? I was scared about everyone I cared about dying. That still scared me.

"I was scared," I said. I'd been scared a lot in my life. Always on the run, afraid of being found out, of being caught, of being noticed. "I guess... these days... I'm just more frightened of the consequences of *not* acting."

Wynruil grunted. We'd been speaking softly, but he'd still heard.

That seemed to be enough to stop Marinna from pursuing the topic. She nodded thoughtfully, pursing her lips. But not lowering her head. I was glad she kept her head up.

Red light brightened the end of the corridor, and the air thickened with heat and moisture, as sudden as stepping through an invisible wall. The corridor opened into a vast chamber, glowing red from below a stone balcony that blocked further progress. The balcony hugged the side of the cave, with many elves following it to other entrances into the mountain, but ahead of us, the deck appeared to cantilever out into the void. A banister of black glass marked the edge.

I held my breath as we neared the overlook that would reveal the scene below. A river of magma flowed beneath us, coming from the far end of a truly vast chamber and disappearing sluggishly beneath the platform on which we stood. Tiny rivulets formed tributaries here and there, disappearing into passages along the side of the cavern. Balconies decorated the walls in various places on both sides of the cavern. It brought up memories of looking down at a river flowing through the mountains, but the colors were wrong—reds and blacks replacing blues and greens.

"How…" I began, my head spinning from the heat and height. I closed my eyes hard. A hand on my shoulder made me open them again. Marinna, trying to steady me. It helped. "How does it not all *melt*?" I finally said.

"Do you see those whitish-gray lines running near the magma?" Wynruil pointed to long lines stretched all around the granite below, like bones knitting together muscle. "Those are pipes. That metal has a higher melting temperature than granite. Water courses through and cools the granite, resulting in the lovely humidity of the air." He inhaled deeply, closing his eyes. Sweat trickled down my nose and dropped past the rail. It would evaporate before it reached the magma. "Granite forms naturally when magma cools slowly, creating crystals. Learning to work Fire is not only about flames, but also cooling. Repairing breaks in the containing walls of the magma river is part of Alluvium magical training."

"Where does the water come from?" my mother asked.

"From the Witless Tarn," he answered, and my mother cringed.

Wynruil continued. "I know. The High Elves believe the water to be tainted by the trolls. So they built on the Flawless. But, your own people—your mother included—have towns built on the Witless. They survive just fine. In fact, I suspect the trolls add to the rich minerals we value."

My mother stuck her tongue out, disgusted. I lacked experience in the topic, but my skin crawled at the thought that the air I breathed was plump with moisture packed with troll waste.

"SCREEE!"

The screaming, louder than ever, came from below. I searched for the army of ghosts that must have haunted the indomitable red river. What I found was pipes spewing steam into the air. Lids slammed shut, and the screams died down.

"That scream is from *steam*?" my mother asked, genuinely surprised.

"Yes," Brittanie said. "Water heats, pressure builds, and it is released."

"So not ghosts," I said, both relieved and oddly disappointed. After all, if one couldn't believe Talena's adventures, then what could one trust? As my adrenaline dissipated, weariness settled back in like a wet blanket.

"Ghosts?" Brittanie responded. "No." Was she smirking?

"But you do talk to the dead," I said, slumping against the black glass bannister.

"Talk to the dead?" Brittanie asked. "Some Red Prophets believe their visions come from ancestors who have passed away and gained insight into the future."

"You don't think that?" my mother asked. I did a quick check, and while Wynruil wore no jewelry, Brittanie did. Most notably, a bracelet of golden bones connected end-to-end in a circle.

"I think Fire lies," he said simply. Brittanie held up the hand my gaze had locked onto, but she tilted her head at Wynruil and nodded her head, agreeing with him.

I didn't know if it was the heat and humidity, the troll waste I was breathing, or a result of the drink, but I didn't feel so good. I leaned against the rail, letting the heat bake my face, and quietly pondered whether vomit evaporated.

"Elliah!"

I spun at the sound of the familiar voice. Hughelas jogged toward me, leaving his father and Gormar behind. His smile fell as he neared... I must have looked as bad as I felt. He hugged me, then put his hands on my cheeks and gently lifted my head to look into his eyes. His hands cooled my cheeks in the steamy chamber, and I closed my eyes, enjoying the sensation.

My eyes flew open when his lips touched mine. I looked over to my mother as I started to push him away self-consciously, but she smiled and laughed a little, then took her eyes off me to hug the Warder. I glanced at the stoic Wynruil, but he stared politely over the balcony. Gormar scowled at us, but I cared not a whit what he thought. *Army of the Bereft to destroy his people!* Marinna and Brittanie watched us as well, and the need in Brittanie's eyes made me self-conscious. Even though I wanted his kiss, I pushed Hughelas gently away. Thankfully, he didn't look offended. Just concerned.

"I need to know how she survived," Brittanie said, her voice urgent. Wynruil returned his attention from the magma below. "I'm sorry," she said to Wynruil. "I know there are other important questions, but this means *everything* to me." Wynruil nodded, and she nodded back, then turned to my mother. "I'll go first. Let me explain *why* she is Bereft."

She had my entire attention, as well as my mother's.

"It's very simple," she said. "I can't believe the High Elves haven't figured it out." She paused, squinting at my mother like she didn't trust that we were being honest about our lack of knowledge, but whatever she saw, she relented. "The more powerful the parents are in magic, the more likely the child will be Bereft."

Despite my being excited to hear the answer, when I heard it, it was like the whole world had dropped away. Sounds grew distant. People faded from my senses. It was just me and my thoughts.

My mother had mated with a calculating High Elf in order to create a child powerful in magic. Who was I kidding, she'd been calculating too. They'd wanted a powerful child. It was consistent. But did it make sense?

"You said all of your children were Bereft," I stated.

"I can melt the balls off an ice dragon from a mountain away." Brittanie looked wistful as she spoke.

"Dragons don't have balls," Beldroth said distractedly.

"It's a saying." Brittanie's words held no venom. "Like 'hotter than a lava lizard's piss' or…" She looked around and gestured toward my mother. "'Hornier than a Wood Elf in a moonlit glade.'"

I gasped, but my mother just shrugged and nodded.

"Point being," Brittanie went on. "My spells have kick. I must be right at the threshold. Even mating with a man weak in magic pushes my babies over the limit. So," and she looked my mother in the eyes, "you and her father were powerful enough together to cross the line. Are there not many Bereft among Wood Elves?"

My mother considered the question before answering. She looked at Beldroth, silently communicating *something* with a look. "No. They are not so frequent as to make your conclusion obvious. The Alluvium are clearly the most powerful race of elves when it comes to magic."

Brittanie and Gormar both sighed like felines settling in a beam of sunlight.

Then Brittanie's eyes locked with my mother's. "But how did you keep her *alive*?"

My mother paused. Again, considering. Hughelas had taken my hand somewhere during the conversation. I'd been so preoccupied, I hadn't noticed. But his cool grip soothed me.

Finally, my mother answered. "I am better at Healing spells than many, though not the best. But I can also—"

"Her father?" Brittanie interrupted.

My mother squinted, probably having hoped to avoid the topic of my father. "Mind magic," she said, avoiding the direct statement that he was a High Elf. "Powerful with magic, yes." Gormar, Brittanie, and Wynruil all turned intent gazes on me, measuring me up. Taking note of my longer neck, no doubt, but I balled my free hand into a fist so that they couldn't see my long fingers. Gormar nodded like it all made sense. Of course being High Elf would make it more likely I would raise an army to crush his people, right?

"That explains only *why* she's Bereft," Brittanie said. Neither she nor Wynruil looked particularly bothered by my parentage. "You both had strong magic. Possibly yours was not so strong that, with a weaker partner, you would have produced a Bereft, but together you had sufficient power. It doesn't explain how you kept her alive. We may not be Wood Elves, but we can muster Heal spells, and still our babies died."

My mother grimaced. "I can only think of two things that might be different about our situation. One, when Elliah was born, the Mother of Trees held her. Elliah... chewed... on her bark."

I had? I'd eaten a piece of a goddess?

The Alluvium mage scowled at that. "And the High Elves keep the Mother to themselves."

"The second is that I recharge mana faster than most elves."

"Much faster," Beldroth affirmed.

"That's my real strength." My mother looked sheepish. "Where other mages tire out, I do not. When Elliah was sick or injured, I just kept casting and casting. Spells eventually land."

Brittanie looked puzzled. "It is not a matter of spells landing or not. Yes, we can eventually land spells. Healing from an injury or sickness... we manage those, though, as you say, it takes effort, usually multiple spells cast at once by different mages." She pursed her lips. "Please, visit our nursery. Let's see if there's... anything."

"Absolutely!" my mother responded, putting a hand to her belly. Brittanie noticed and smiled sadly.

Oddly, Hughelas's hand-holding had triggered a desire in me. A desire ridiculously out of place, yet one I couldn't ignore. While my mother asked about how many Alluvium children were born Bereft, I maneuvered Hughelas so that his back was to them, providing us a modicum of privacy.

Then I stood on my tippy toes and pulled him down into a kiss, relishing it as much as I had his touch. With Hughelas holding me, I was safe... the problems of the world manageable. I relaxed into the kiss. Fears washed away, and my aches and pains, while still there, mattered less. We were in Cenaedth, speaking with leaders. There was at least a chance the Mother of Trees would get the army she needed. Hope flourished. And with hope came *energy*. I felt better, less sore, recharged.

A vibration underfoot startled me and we pulled apart. We weren't the only ones looking around. The fact that the Alluvium looked just as apprehensive worried me further. A rumble echoed through the cavern, and though I had trouble placing it, the Alluvium all turned to look at an entrance to the cavern to the right. Wynruil darted in that direction. I grabbed Hughelas's arm and pulled him to follow after Wynruil, but his arm fell from my grasp.

Halting, I looked back, surprised that he wasn't eager to investigate. I was even more surprised by what I found. Hughelas, down on one knee, his light skin turned gray, dark bags under his eyes. "What did you do?" he eked out while climbing to his feet.

I stepped back to Hughelas, helping him up, my newfound energy taking on an ominous overtone. I felt better. Hughelas looked worse.

What did I do?

Beldroth : 6

"I'm okay," Hughelas said, waving off Elliah's helping hand, though his voice trembled with barely concealed irritation.

"What happened?" I asked, lifting my son up from under his arms.

He pushed me off, standing on his own. "I'm okay!" he snapped, eyes flaring at my help. A far cry from the connection we'd reestablished in the cell.

He didn't look okay; he looked like he'd been smacked around by a troll. On our journey through the labyrinthian tunnels of Cenaedth, he'd been pensive, but not battered. Elliah looked better than when we'd walked up, her eyes more clear and the puffiness in her swollen eye reduced. I didn't know what that meant, but it didn't bode well. Had Hughelas tried to tell me something about a problem with Elliah and the hammer?

"Come on," he said, jogging toward the big passageway to which Wynruil and many other Alluvium ran. The source of the noise. I stood straighter, proud that he charged toward the danger. Many of the dark-skinned elves ran the other way, or ran past the passageway. I shouldn't have counted that as fear... they might have been running to help family members or gather weapons. Like a kicked ant pile, Alluvium went everywhere, but most charged into the passageway that led to the noise.

My son didn't sprint. I could have easily passed him. But I stayed behind, letting Elliah get by his side while Illiara and I watched from behind. I exchanged a quick, worried look with Illiara. From her subtle head shake and shoulder shrug, I didn't think she knew what happened either.

The Alluvium, in their dark burgundies, blacks, and splashes of yellow, almost looked like flames as they charged about. But the difference was very clear when a gout of flame tore through the Alluvium entering the passageway ahead of us, lighting them and the granite beneath them afire. A moment later, a red dragon, only a little bigger than an elf, flew out of the tunnel and into the large cavern, diving and disappearing from sight.

Dragons!

I sprinted ahead, reaching for my hammer and snarling about its absence. I hadn't even had it that long before I'd given it to Elliah, but it had grown on me in that short time and I missed it. But I'd fought dragons before I'd crafted the hammer, so I reached for my sword. Also gone. Confiscated.

To my relief, the large hallway was not filled with dragons. Alluvium, both mage and warrior, ran up a sloping hall that opened to another chamber lit by fire.

I spotted a sword in the grip of a downed and burning warrior and kicked it free. I tore off my tunic and used it to grab the sword. The little dragon that had gotten through would have to wait; the trembling ground took on ominous meaning.

As I charged up the slope, another small dragon slipped into the hallway, sticking near the top as it glided down the way I had come. It spat out its fire as it went, but some mage in the crowd was ready for it, and coerced the magical flames to stick to the upper part of the hallway. The flames, confined for space by the spell, surged ahead of the dragon, but to my chagrin, the dragon flew through them without harm.

Another dragon for later.

The din of battle reached me as I ran up the passage, entering a familiar chamber—the room where Elliah had fought for us. There must have been a hundred dragons roughly elf-sized spinning around the room. The scrape of metal on dragon scales, the yells of men and women, and the roars of the dragons created a familiar cacophony of battle. The smells of burnt flesh and earth assaulted my senses. Alluvium cast spells at the dragons, trying to pull them down by means I didn't understand. Several corpses, both dragon and elf, already littered the floor. In addition to the handful attempting to reach the inner caverns through the main passage, some wolf-sized dragons slipped out a side passage. I wasn't sure, but I thought it was the passage that led to the prison cells. We certainly hadn't gone down the large main passage that led to the lava river when they'd escorted us away.

The bigger threat wasn't the hundred small dragons; it was the three colossal beasts, each one towering three times the length of an elf, their scales glinting ominously in the firelight. Two were on the ground, drawing most of the warriors' attention, and one flew above, creating trouble via mighty downpours of magical Fire.

The floor shuddered and my eyes flew to the far side of the room just in time to see Wynruil darting up and out, toward the entrance to the mountain. I wished once again I had my hammer.

The hammer.

I wanted to charge after Wynruil, but I'd just had the most horrifying of thoughts. And my gut told me it was true.

Turning back, I searched the incoming fighters and mages for my friends. When I found them, I cringed. What were they thinking, running into a battle with dragons weaponless? Hughelas, exhausted? But I was pleased to see Gormar, the disgruntled Red Prophet, with them.

"The hammer!" I shouted toward them. I'd almost yelled out *my hammer*, but I'd caught myself.

Illiara looked at the sword in my hand, cocking her head, but then the body of a warrior flew between me and my allies, compelled by some blow or force I hadn't seen.

I shook my head. I didn't need a different weapon. "Hide the hammer!" I yelled, and my son nodded. He, at least, understood what I was thinking. The dragons were there for the hammer. I created a personal Shield and picked a path through the treacherous battle to reach the other side. Nothing I'd seen yet explained the mountain shaking. With a deep sense of dread, I suspected Wynruil would need help. Though the words had no audience, I explained, "Dragons collect their dead."

Hughelas #8

Dragons collect their dead.

I was tired—I didn't have the mana to summon even a mage-light, not that one was needed in the fire-lit cavern. Even my thoughts crawled sluggishly about or misfired, like I'd gone a night without sleep.

But they didn't move so slowly that I misunderstood my father's train of thought.

"Where did you put our weapons?" I turned and asked Gormar, right at the entrance to the vast chamber.

He ignored me, mouth agape at the mayhem before him.

"Where are our weapons!" I shouted, grabbing his shoulders. Elliah, Illiara, and the mage, Brittanie, all stopped with me, though Illiara's eyes followed my father dodging through the room.

Gormar shook his head quickly. He didn't know.

Brittanie swept her arms out, and Fire shot forth. I ducked, and a small dragon plowed through the space where my head had been, Brittanie somehow bending the fire to push the dragon up and away.

"They're in one of the cells near where you were being held," Brittanie said. "Do you have something that would help fight *this*?" A bout of flame came at us from above and she waved her arms, creating a bubble around us much like a shield.

"We may have a way to make them lose interest," Elliah said, catching on.

Brittanie's eye twitched, uncertain of something. Probably our intent—would we take our weapons and run, or worse, help the dragons? Maybe she paused because she questioned her value as a guide versus fighting dragons. Anyone who could "melt the balls off an ice dragon" was needed to confront the dragons. But, in the end, she nodded her head. "This way," she called, waving us around to the right. "Gormar, stay in the colosseum! Don't let those dragons into our home." The colosseum… the room where Elliah had fought the Alluvium, and the Alluvium fought dragons. A place for battles.

Gormar nodded, his eyes wide and his mouth hanging open.

We skirted around the edge of the room, avoiding trouble for the most part, though we had to dance around a smoking corpse at one point. A group of Alluvium mages and warriors stood guard around a heavily muscled warrior who cranked a wheel on the pipes in the wall. I spun back at a roar from one of the larger dragons. It was the one in the air, and it shook its wings like a wet cat and dived toward the hallway leading to the magma rivers. Alluvium scattered, and I jerked when something hit my head.

Drops of water quickly spread into puddles as we continued toward our goal. The wheel—a valve for water. We reached the side hall, and Brittanie raced into it. I took one last look back at the battle. In places, the water fell as ice, and in others, ice had formed on the floor. But the only effect it had on the dragons was pulling them out of the air. I knew from experience that red dragons didn't mind the cold. But I doubted the water was there for dragon attacks—likely they used it for ending their greeting murder ritual ceremony.

Then I disappeared into the corridor behind Brittanie with Elliah right behind me. Not that I'd memorized it when they'd taken us down it the first time, but the narrow passage and purplish lighting from the sporadic plants seemed the same. I tried to summon magelight, but still didn't have the mana to do so. After scraping the wall several times, I yelled back, "Can you summon a magelight, Illiara?"

But it was Elliah who answered. "She stayed behind."

Great.

She probably went to help my father. Without a weapon. And me without magic.

Just great.

Nevertheless, a magelight appeared, more or less over my head. And it tracked with me as I hurried to catch up with Brittanie. We passed a couple of side tunnels, then turned down one, and entered the guard-chamber of the prison cells. How long had that taken? A few minutes?

Long enough. The two guards lay dead on the floor. The mage we'd passed less than an hour before lay with his entrails on the wrong side of his body, and the warrior's head was nowhere to be seen.

Cursing, Brittanie raced ahead. And I followed, though I grabbed the sword from the ground near the warrior as I left.

It was a foolish vanity. I had no magic, and the hallway was too thin to wield the sword effectively, not that it had done the warrior enough good in the guardroom where he could have swung it. But Elliah didn't even have a weapon, and she followed behind. As though to emphasize my foolishness, the mountain rumbled as it had before. Something even bigger than the dragons we'd left behind?

But getting to that hammer, using Elliah to hide it from the dragons... from what I'd learned, that solution to our dragon problem might have been hastening her toward death. Though a hint of mana returned, my gut told me that Elliah had slurped my mana away when we'd kissed. Her anti-magic competed with the magic of the hammer. Using her to hide the hammer from the dragons had made her resistance stronger. Without the hammer, she'd needed to consume magic from elsewhere to survive. She'd fed on mine.

It didn't take long before the corridor ahead blazed with light. I nearly ran into Brittanie, who had stopped suddenly. I looked over her shoulder to see a red dragon with its back to us, breathing fire onto the metal bolts of a door. It paused and beat its head against the door, the passage too narrow for it to turn its body to pound on the door with its feet.

"I think the dragons want something you brought," Brittanie whispered. "Your things are in that cell."

Though Brittanie whispered, the dragon turned its head to look back over its shoulder. It crawled up the wall and dropped down to face us. Then it backed up two steps, turned once more toward the door, and breathed more fire on the hinges.

It didn't want its back to us, but it cared more about getting in that door than killing us.

Good. At least for the moment, we were safe.

"Hughelas!" Elliah yelled, and I turned back to see another dragon looking our way from the guardroom.

Illiara - 7

"I'm not the one running *toward* dragons."

Those were Elliah's words when I'd told her I was going to help Beldroth, and for her to get the hammer. Ultimately, hiding the hammer was something only Elliah was able to do. If the dragons were there for the hammer. What had seemed good fortune in the prison cells being close to the surface, so that we could have escaped if we'd needed to, might have backfired—the dragons sensed the hammer near the entrance to the caves. It wasn't buried deep enough, like the dragon in the swamps.

I'd grabbed Elliah's arm before she went in. "Get the hammer," I'd said. "I'll keep Beldroth alive."

She'd hesitated.

As did I.

"Don't die on me," I'd said.

"I'm not the one running *toward* dragons," she'd replied. Then, with a final smile that didn't conceal the worry in her eyes, she'd turned and ran after Hughelas.

When I turned around, Marinna was there. I'd practically forgotten about her. She looked down the small tunnel Elliah had taken, then at me. Waiting for me to tell her what to do? After I'd gotten over my initial shock of how Beldroth had introduced her, I became indifferent to her. Then, the night Beldroth had gotten drunk off his ass, she'd told me about her family problems. She was desperate to get away from a father who'd been absent during her childhood, but had shown untoward interest in her as an adult. While the long lifetimes of elves made interfamily mating non-scandalous—elves older than half a millennium had adult great-grandchildren that looked the same age as them—a father-daughter pairing was not okay. I'd insisted we help get her out of the swamps. Her presence had given Beldroth something to do, which was better than his moping about, but I'd built a mild resentment about the time Beldroth spent with her.

"I'm going to help Beldroth," I said. "If you come with me, be prepared to fight." She could do what she wanted, but I wasn't going to spoon feed her.

Then I ran around the circumference of the chamber, staying as far from the main fighting as possible, to reach the passage up and out of Cenaedth. I dodged deeper into the room at one point to snatch a sword from near a body that no longer needed it. The owner must have been heavily muscled, because it weighed a *lot*. Marinna had made her choice—she'd followed me.

We continued around the rim and the mountain rumbled under my feet again. The fighting lessened as we neared the hall that led out of the mountain, the combat being heavier at the other end of the chamber, where the dragons were trying to push their way into the passage that led to the magma rivers.

I dropped the sword at the bottom of the ramp leading back to the entrance chamber. Beldroth didn't need me to be armed; he needed my Heals, and the sword was heavy. To my surprise, Marinna picked it up. I heard her cast a spell as I ran up the empty ramp. The passage to the entrance was not short, giving me time to second guess myself. Sending Elliah into the maze was likely a safer play than having her fight amongst the dragons and Alluvium, but what if I was wrong? What if Elliah needed me more than Beldroth? What if Elliah *died* because I wasn't there to protect her?

I slowed, breathing hard, but not because I'd been running uphill. I'd taken a million tiny steps toward letting Elliah go. Getting her off the High Elf shit list had been the last tether of caution that tied us. She was her own person, who would live and die by her choices. But that didn't make it easy to let go. I calmed my mind and my breathing. Realistically, Elliah was safer than Beldroth. Elliah had Hughelas, and the Alluvium mage who had competently protected them.

"You okay?" Marinna asked.

Elliah was probably safer than I. Definitely safer than Beldroth. "Tch," I responded, and picked my pace back up.

At the top of the ramp, I stopped, jaw dropping, just as the floor trembled again. An enormous red dragon, one too big to fit between the stone pylons decorating the room, had pounded its way through the center, one mighty column at a time. As I watched, it crawled forward over rubble, such a massive beast that it couldn't stand completely upright in the cavernous chamber. It reached the next pylon blocking its path, inhaling.

It breathed its magical fire onto the column while I searched madly for Beldroth. Had the dragon already roasted him? Surely he hadn't taken it on. Even in those close confines, there was no way of taking on such a beast.

What was the dragon even doing? So what if it got through the columns? I looked back at the passage I'd just climbed. Okay, it might squeeze through that one, but once it got to the chamber where the others fought, it would be stuck!

I suppose we had no way to communicate that information.

There! Movement on my side of a column helped me spot Beldroth. It looked like he was focused on casting a spell. More searching revealed Wynruil behind a different column, also working magic. They each looked at the pillar the dragon blasted. Wynruil siphoned away the heat while Beldroth reinforced the structure?

The dragon's breath ran out, and the last flames licked against the stone. Since the beast couldn't stand upright, it remained in a crouch, rocking on its elbows to pound its head against the column.

When the column didn't fall, the dragon narrowed its eyes and sniffed the air. That's when I realized the smell of charred meat had followed me up. Remembering the vendors we'd passed on our journey in, I had a sinking sensation that the smell had beat me there. The dragon's eyes narrowed even more, and its reverberating growl shook me from several columns away. Only a few stone sentinels stood between that beast and the passageway to the Alluvium home.

Lightning-quick for such a large creature, the dragon swiped like a feline at the column Beldroth hid behind, its claw bending when its arm hit the stone such that its claw reached behind it. Beldroth went flying from his hiding space. He lay there as the dragon inhaled. I cast a Heal, and I heard Marinna casting next to me as the dragon's Fire engulfed him.

I may have screamed. If I didn't, it was only because I poured my magic into a Heal at the fiery inferno where my Beldroth should have been. The flames suddenly jumped up from Beldroth and shot my way, and I dove to the side and took shelter behind a column. Even so, the magical flames singed me.

I peeked around the far side, and Beldroth was gone. Were the flames of such a huge dragon powerful enough to incinerate bone?

The dragon returned its attention to the column, weakening it with fire, and I searched the chamber. The columns created many obstacles, but Marinna still stood where I left her, and I moved back toward her, trying to follow her gaze. I held my breath as I searched, hoping beyond hope that Beldroth had somehow survived the blast.

Finally, I found Wynruil and—*thank the Mother*—he pulled Beldroth from a hole in the ground.

"Yes!" Marinna hissed. "I did that," she said, but not to me. She said it to herself. "*I* did that!" Then she saw me and blushed. More meekly, she said, "I made the hole."

I nodded, grateful—she'd saved him from the flames by breaking the mountain beneath him, tucking him into safety—but my attention had already returned to the pair of fighters.

Beldroth squatted, clearly injured. Heal spells were not as effective at a distance, but I had the luxury of mana that refilled faster than anyone I knew, so I cast and I cast, and while the dragon battered down the next column, Beldroth recovered.

He looked my way and smiled.

As the dragon crawled forward, Beldroth and Wynruil moved closer to me as well.

"Go!" Beldroth shouted. "We can't stop it. We're only slowing it down. Get the next chamber cleared!"

Leave him behind?

Yet I found myself taking an involuntary step back down the ramp, following his desperate command. Clear the chamber! But the chamber had been full of dragons and Alluvium. How in the world would I clear *that*?

Elliah ~ 11

There was no way out—the one dragon was focused on the cell door, and the other cocked its head at us from down the hall.

"What's in these cells?" I shouted to Brittanie as I grabbed the metal wheel that controlled the locking mechanism on the door in front of me and spun it.

"Sleeping High Elves," Brittanie answered, easing back toward me.

Oddly, the dragon who had been melting the wheel on the door that guarded the hammer stopped and watched what I was doing. The other approached cautiously. When the metal bolts on my door freed, and I pulled it open, the dragon by the door that held the hammer reached up a claw and spun the wheel on its door.

The wheel spun once, then thunked to the floor, the hot metal clearly damaged. The top metal pole slid out of its bracket and clanged against the wheel, startling the dragon back a step. But the bottom pole sat secure. Meanwhile, both of my bolts came free.

I slipped into the cell as the dragon growled. The sounds of the dragon banging against the other door followed me in; gravity had kept the lower bar of that door in its bracket and the door remained stuck. Hughelas and then Brittanie jumped in behind me, Brittanie swinging the door closed as best she could as she darted through. There was no handle to pull it closed from the inside, but something on the other side pushed it the rest of the way shut.

I hoped the dragons wouldn't turn the wheel and lock us in. Or maybe I wanted them to... wouldn't we be safer locked in the cell?

Brittanie's concentration hadn't been enough to usher in her magical light, but she created a new one. Two High Elves lay sleeping on the floor, not stirring by our entrance, even though we must have bumped or stepped on one of their legs. We'd chanced upon the cell that held Skaljian and Trentius.

"Why are they sleeping?" I whisper-hissed, unsure why I kept my voice down. Perhaps in vain hope that the dragons would forget we were there?

"We drug them," Brittanie said. "Can't have them working their mind magic on us. Even when they wake, they're too out of it to Compel us."

Compel.

"That's it!" I whisper-shouted. "The High Elves can get the dragons to back off!"

"Dragons are resistant to magic," Hughelas said. "But... for dragons that young, it might work."

He didn't whisper, and I felt a little silly.

"Okay," I said, raising my volume to almost-normal volume. "How do we wake them?"

"Why should we wake them?" Brittanie answered. "Let the dragons get what they came for and leave." After a pregnant pause, she added. "I don't trust waking them."

Okay, fair point. I wanted the hammer, but the dragons did too. *Dragons collect their dead.* Giving it up was a viable solution. I knew Beldroth would be angry, but surely he would agree it wasn't worth the deaths caused by keeping it.

"What's in that cell," Hughelas explained, wringing his hands, "is a magical hammer, and it's the key to keeping Bereft alive. If you want your children to live…"

What was he talking about? I hadn't had that hammer as a child. I couldn't believe what I was hearing. My heart sank with the realization that Hughelas wasn't the elf I thought he was. He was willing to manipulate a life and death situation just to save something he thought his father would want.

But Brittanie was already convinced. She'd stepped toward their heads, stooped down and placed a hand on each of their faces. The room heated and sweat broke out in both men.

"What are you doing?" I asked Hughelas behind Brittanie's back, my eyes wide and appalled.

"Trust me," he mouthed back. "Please."

She didn't know I was talking to Hughelas, and she answered, "I'm burning the drug out of their bloodstreams."

With a gasp, first Skaljian, then Trentius, sat up.

Marinna 2

I'd saved Beldroth! I'd done *exactly* what I'd wanted to do with my magic and I'd saved him!

"Come on," Illiara said, grabbing my arm.

"I should stay and help!" I said, pulling away.

Illiara nodded her head, agreeing that I was able, but her words conveyed a different message. "You need to clear out the next chamber."

"What?" I said dumbly. "I... I'm not leaving. He needs me!" Thanks to him, I was in control. I wasn't about to jump in front of a dragon, but it wasn't right to leave him.

Illiara grabbed my shoulders. "Listen to me." I tugged away, but she repeated. "Listen."

I watched Beldroth and Wynruil jump out and strike at the dragon's flank. The tip of a claw went flying, and the dragon snapped at them, catching only air, but halting its strike against the stone pillar. The duo disappeared in the maze of obstructions.

"I can't clear that room, Marinna," Illiara said. "You can. How will I get their attention? Grow a flower sweet enough to draw the eyes of every elf? You can use that spell to project your voice. Warn them. Get them out!"

But Beldroth needed my magic.

"You know he would want you to save them," Illiara said.

And she was right. The same way he'd saved me.

Grunting, I turned and started back to the other chamber. As soon as I realized she wasn't following, I stopped, fear grabbing hold of me. She wanted me to go by myself!

I wasn't sure why that surprised me nor why it scared me so much. Obviously Illiara's Heals were important to keep the two warriors able to slow the dragon. Her staying made sense. But why was I so frightened to be alone? I'd basically been a loner my whole life. My dad had been out of the picture, until he was suddenly back in, but for all the wrong reasons. I'd had a few friends, but most had distanced themselves when my "accidents" started up, except for poor Nesterin.

But as I shook off my fears and started downhill again, the fear gripped me tightly. I didn't stop, but my weeks of training with Beldroth helped me recognize that my control on my magic was slipping. I slowed so that I could calm my breathing, and tried to isolate what thought triggered the fear. It wasn't being alone.

No, the real fear wasn't about facing this challenge by myself. It was the weight of being solely responsible for the lives of others. The decisions I made, the actions I took, might mean the difference between survival and catastrophe for them. That truth pressed down on me like the mountain above me. If I failed, it wouldn't just be my own life I'd lose—it would be theirs. And that... that was a fear far harder to escape.

But recognizing it was enough for me to get it under control. Beldroth had taught me enough. I didn't have to master my fears, just keep their effects from spilling forth. I sped up and reached the entrance to the colosseum without incident.

The mayhem had intensified. One of the bigger dragons lay unmoving, but only one other medium-sized dragon—it had been a big dragon before I'd seen the one Beldroth fought—remained in the room. That meant one had gotten away and entered the magma chamber. Several smaller dragons lay unmoving. But so did many Alluvium. Water puddled on the floor in spots, mingled with pools of blood, but had stopped raining from above. Much of it had vanished, drained by some mechanism I hadn't noted or evaporated in the heat of the magical flames.

The bigger problem? Many still fought in the colosseum.

Illiara expected me to get everyone's attention in *that*? Looking at the heated—literally heated—battles, I thought not.

The room shuddered, and as close as I was to the entry hall, I heard the stone crash like an avalanche a second later. Another column had come down. Everyone was running out of time. I had to do something. One more shudder... one more crash of sound, and the enormous dragon would have access.

I had to try.

I crouched and placed my hand on the ground.

The stone was an extension of me.

But I needed the finger movements Beldroth taught me to work my way through the magic. Mnemonic devices to help connect from the simple magic that created a magelight to the forms of Earth. I finished my spell and whispered to the stone beneath me.

The stone whispered back!

Or at least I thought it whispered back. It was very hard to hear with all the yelling, clanging, groaning, and whooshing of flames.

The room shook with another column crashing down. Maybe we would get lucky and the roof would collapse atop the dragon.

I wanted to lie down, have even more surface contact with the stone beneath me. But I didn't think I'd be able to cast the spell like that.

Only then did it occur to me that, if the Alluvium fled, there would be nothing to stop the dragons. The battle in the colosseum kept the dragons from invading the Alluvium home. While the enormous dragon might get stuck, all the others would be let loose. Was I even doing the right thing?

Another rumble—far too quickly on the heels of the last. Had Beldroth fallen?

Shooing the distracting thoughts from my mind, I repeated my spell, but I didn't hold back. I let all my crackling worry and annoying self-doubt pour through my hands as I shoved my palms down onto the stone. I shouted, and the entire floor of the room shouted back.

"Everybody RUN!"

Even the dragons jumped.

Not everyone stopped fighting, but they all looked around. As if on cue, Illiara sprinted down the entryway and dived to the left, rolling past me as the enormous red dragon announced its presence with a spout of flame that created a river of slag out of the entrance ramp.

The Alluvium retreated. Not all, but most. As they gave ground, they did their best to keep the dragons contained.

The giant dragon slid down the molten granite claws first, splashing liquid rock like heavy water. Illiara, somehow quicker than me, yanked me up, and we ran toward the side passage her daughter had taken. The dragon's head emerged, spewing flames. I wouldn't have made it out the exit everyone else took.

Any Alluvium who'd held his or her ground in the colosseum got roasted, the dragon's fire more than their individual magic could handle. The group holding the dragons back from the magma chamber fared better. Their combined magic must have deflected it.

With just its head and front legs partially in the room, the dragon thrashed. It scrambled madly, splashing magma with its flailing, and it inched its way forward. At least, I consoled myself, the beast would have nowhere to go but back out the way it came.

Unless it melted and widened the passage to the next room.

My immediate problem was getting out of range. Once it had its front legs fully free, it would be able to reach me. Casting the spell had taken a toll, and I was breathing hard.

A cool energy, smelling of flowers and soil, flowed into me. I looked over my shoulder and Illiara nodded. I breathed easier, and I knew it wasn't just her magic renewing me—it was relief.

Illiara had taught me how to evaluate my mana, so I checked as I ran. I hadn't depleted it all, but I'd used quite a bit.

At the entrance to the side passage, I stopped. The dragon's front half was entirely out of the tunnel, and it strained to pull the rest of its body through. Taut muscular forelegs, thick as trees, pushed against the wall, and with a pop, the dragon broke free, soaring uncontrolled across the colosseum and smacking its head against the far wall in a room-shaking impact.

Nothing living remained in the colosseum as the dragon shook itself like a wet cat. Except me and Illiara. It occurred to me that the passage we planned to escape through was long and straight—perfect for melting a pair of fleeing elves.

The first thing the dragon did, after clearing its head and issuing an echoing roar almost as loud as my magical shout, was turn around and blast the passage it had slid down with Fire. Gouges on its haunches ran with blood. Either the squeeze through the cave had taken its toll, or Beldroth and Wynruil hadn't wasted the opportunity when the tunnel had imprisoned the dragon.

To my shock, Beldroth and Wynruil strolled through the flame and magma, Beldroth's arm wrapped around a limping Wynruil, the red shimmer of a Shield clinging to them as the flames danced to avoid them.

A low, slow growl reverberated throughout the chamber as the dragon waited for them.

As though I wasn't shocked enough, Beldroth addressed the dragon. "I wish to thank you, dragon."

The dragon cocked its head. "You *do* owe me thanks," the dragon replied. *Dragons can talk?* "But it would shock me if you knew *why*."

Beldroth paused, not as shocked as I, but puzzled. "Why do you *think* I should thank you... dragon?"

"Because we are setting you free," the dragon rumbled. *Free? Free from what? The bonds of life?* "But you took something of ours. Something of *us*. My mother wants it back." *Its* mother? *Muck and mire!*

"You should have asked," Beldroth said. "Instead you killed innocent people. So I thank you. Because I felt guilty. And I intended to go dig out the rest of the dragon I *buried* so that dragons could collect it. I thank you because I no longer feel guilty for hiding that dragon's corpse... nor yours."

Elliah ~ 12

Brittanie squatted, her face even with the two High Elves whose eyes slowly focused. "Let me be *very* clear," she said, articulating her words slowly and carefully. "I just woke you by burning out of your bloodstream the narcotics that kept you asleep. But at the first sign that one of you tries to Compel me or another elf, I will finish the process and boil out the blood."

Skaljian and Trentius unconsciously inched backwards on their bottoms, in vain hope of putting distance between themselves and the angry Alluvium. The room was small and crowded, and though cooler than the lower caves, with five elves and little airflow, it smelled of sweat and panic.

"Are we clear?" Brittanie asked, and the High Elves nodded vigorously, then tried to backpedal even more when one of the small dragons in the hallway bellowed.

"That's what you're here to help with," Brittanie said with a wicked smile. "There are two dragons in the hall, and we need to get into the room they're trying to break into before they do."

The High Elves slowly climbed to their feet, rubbing stiff and sore muscles and trying to shake off the effects of their sleep.

Skaljian tried to speak, coughed, then tried again. "And if we refuse to help, is it the same threat? Blood boiling?"

Brittanie narrowed her eyes. "I'm not threatening you. That's simply what will happen if you use your magic on us. I won't force you to help us. There's life-threatening danger involved, and you should be allowed to make your own choices." Her words were very pointed, an eyebrow raised to be sure they caught the significance. "That said, there are other lives at stake. There are dragons in Cenaedth, a significant threat in their own right, but they also seek something that will save our sick babies." She directed the last at Hughelas.

He nodded slightly. I grimaced. How could he mislead her like that? Especially when she was trying to show them how greatly she valued choice. It made my stomach twist. Was it possible he thought the hammer really would help the babies?

"I've heard magic doesn't work on dragons," said Trentius. His eyes reflected clarity, his shoulders relaxing as he accepted the situation for what it was, but doubt in himself still drew his brows together. Skaljian still knotted his shoulders and frowned, not even ready to accept the reality of the dilemma.

"The small ones are not as resistant," Hughelas told Trentius. "Their resistance grows as they age, or as a result of their size."

Brittanie raised an eyebrow.

"Bellon sits near the DragonLands," he said in answer to her implied question. "Dragons spill over the mountains that separate us from time to time. Trolls from the Witless, dragons from the DragonLands." He shifted from foot to foot, impatient but having no outlet.

"It doesn't sound very safe," Brittanie said. "Why do people live there?"

"There's sheep," Hughelas said absently. He looked pointedly at the door. "Besides, I haven't found any place I've visited to be particularly safe."

A scraping on the door warned us, and we somehow melted, even in the small and over-packed cell, away from the door.

The door swung abruptly outward, flying open so fast that it banged against the hallway wall and partially shut again. I couldn't help but contrast it to the door of the cell my mother, Marinna, and I had been stuck in. Of course we would hide in a cell whose door was well oiled. What I could see of the hallway was empty.

Then a dragon popped its head into view. It must have swung the door open from the side. It scurried forward, turning its head from side to side. Trying to decide who to fricassee first?

"Fair enough," Brittanie said. She readied a spell as the dragon took a deep breath. Its magical Fire never reached us, folding back around the dragon, and out the door. The dragon shook its head and body, confused.

Its scaly brows furrowed, angry. Its haunches tensed as it readied to try a more physical attack.

Then it froze. It settled back on its haunches, cocking its head once again in curiosity, as Trentius said, "Gotcha."

Beldroth : 7

And just as I'd done with the white who'd killed Lyrei, I distracted the red with theatrics... while I brought down a stalactite from above.

While I talked, keeping the dragon busy, I worked my magic on the stone high above. It almost returned my faith in the Mother. My battle with the dragon in Bellon had prepared me.

Only... the physiology of red dragons was different from that of whites. Whites had flattish heads, something like a viper. Reds had wide jaws made for chewing rocks. Not literally, but powerful mandibles. Their heads, however, were not as flat, and they had dermal plates that ran from head to tail.

The stalactite crashed down right on the dermal plate, breaking into pieces and tumbling to the ground. The dragon's head bobbed, but unlike with the white, the stalactite did no serious harm.

I rushed us out of the magma, because I was going to have to let go of Wynruil, dropping the Shield which magically wrapped us, and that would be the end of his fancy black boots. And the important bits inside them.

The dragon glared at me. "First," it said, "I'm going to kill you." It pulled itself forward, towering over us. "And then I'm going to burrow my way into this mountain, and make it my home. It's... cozy."

It didn't breathe more flame at us. Wynruil would have blocked that. It raised a mighty clawed fist.

We'd barely hobbled out of the magma when I had to switch to a bubble Shield. The boots weren't going to make it, but our feet might. And the pounding from the dragon? I didn't have the magical strength to hold back many blows. The first rained down, hitting the bubble and stopping, but the bubble popped, and we went flying to the side.

We pushed ourselves up, sheltering behind a piece of the fallen stalactite.

My mind spun desperately. "I understand you were a brilliant tactician," I said to Wynruil. "Before you went mad." He put more weight on his foot, sighing. I couldn't see Illiara, but she must have been out there somewhere, doing her thing. I realized Illiara was far superior a Healer to even Anlyth, the resident missionary healer back in Bellon. It wasn't that she knew the most complex aspects of Healing, but what she did know, she could repeat over and over again. Quick little Heals kept you from ever needing anything more complex.

I renewed my bubble Shield. It may not have held, but it offered us a moment's protection.

"Yes," he said. "I have a plan." Another giant fist slammed down upon us, and we went flying again as it popped. As we pushed ourselves up from the ground, he said. "The next strike, you go left, and I'll go right."

"That's your plan?" I asked, incredulous. I'd hoped for something more brilliant.

"Yes," he said, "that way we die one at a time instead of both at once."

He had a point.

"Brilliant," I said, not favoring complicated plans anyway. "Ready?"

As the fist came down, he said, "Ready." I dropped the Shield and ran.

Marinna 3

"Did you do something to me?" I asked Illiara, confused by a strange sensation washing over me.

"Of course," she said. "Still am."

She didn't even look away from the men, who had run in opposite directions after several failed attempts at hiding under a Shield.

"*What* are you doing?" I asked. "To me," I specified. She obviously cast spells at the men being battered.

"I dunno. You tell me." She still didn't look at me.

I smelled water lilies. Obviously, there were no water lilies, but their sweet fragrance nestled... inside me. I felt... better.

I wasn't hurt. So there wasn't anything left to Heal. Yet she was casting something on me, repeatedly. Something that improved me in a way I couldn't put my finger on.

The dragon followed one, then turned its head to follow the other, like a giant cat deciding which mouse would be more fun to catch first.

"Ah, you've come out of your cage to play," the dragon said. "If only we all could."

I needed to help them. I checked my mana. To my shock, I had plenty!

"You've recharged my mana," I said.

"Good," she said. "It's a spell I've been working on."

"You just tested a spell you've been working on?" That was a recipe for death. "On *me*?"

"I tried it on myself first. I lived."

"You can make your own mana recharge faster?"

"Questions later, Marinna. If we live."

Right.

I had mana.

What to do with it?

I didn't have time to think. I knelt and cast a spell, placing my hands on the ground with the final sequence of hand gestures. It was a simple spell, letting loose all the magic Beldroth had trained me to contain—all my frustration, all my fear, all my anger, focused into that which Beldroth taught me not to do. It was surprisingly easy. I blew out all my mana in one spell. But would it work?

The dragon chose a target—it followed Beldroth. My spell would take a few seconds, and Beldroth didn't have that much time.

"Shield, Beldroth!" I yelled. I couldn't Shield him. Didn't know how to from a distance, and didn't have the mana to if I'd known.

He dived down the steps *toward* the dragon, who sat in the deeper section in the middle. A very thin red Shield popped into place around him.

By getting closer to the dragon, he'd made its downward blow tougher, difficult to land with any force. But he was right under the dragon, and instead of raising its forearm for another blow, it simply shifted its weight. Beldroth held up the weight of a behemoth—it would be like being buried under an avalanche. He would be crushed.

I looked up, watching for the effect of my spell, worried that, at worst, it would add to the problem. Beldroth had dropped a single stalactite.

I dropped them *all*.

Stone needles pierced the dragon's leathery wings, ripping holes in them, tearing off swaths. For the most part, they bounced off the dragon's scales, though a few found purchase. The dragon bellowed, and it shifted forward from the weight of the assault. If Beldroth yet lived, he might have gained a moment's respite. Rock that had hit the dragon or the ground flew around the room, and Illiara pushed me down and covered me, protecting me from harm.

The effort cost her. I wiggled to get out from under Illiara and the debris—she lay unmoving, her left arm bent in a way arms weren't meant to bend.

To my horror, something dashed toward me from the side passage we'd targeted. A small red dragon. It must have circled back or gotten lost in the labyrinthian tunnels. I pushed harder, but I was pinned down by more than Illiara's weight. There wasn't enough time.

I covered my head with my arms as the dragon came out, not that it would make any difference.

Nothing happened.

I opened my eyes to see the dragon had gone past, ignoring me. Behind it came a High Elf. Trentius!

"Let me help with that," he said, as others emerged from the passage behind him. Hughelas. Elliah. Brittanie. The weight above me shifted, causing a moment of sharp pain in my side, and I scrambled from beneath, surprised to see the small red dragon shoving the rock that had pinned us to the side.

Elliah and Hughelas flipped Illiara over, pulling her closer to the wall. We'd lost our Healer.

But we had more immediate problems—the damage my magic had done was nowhere near enough to kill the monstrous dragon. It stood back up, spreading out its legs and stretching its wings. They had holes and tears, but it wasn't like the dragon needed to fly to kill us all. It shook, and some of the stone thorns fell out, adding to the rubble on the floor.

"Where did you go, little elf?" the dragon said, lifting its forearms one at a time.

There were plenty of rocks larger than Beldroth on the cavern floor. The dragon stomped its foot on one, creating a cracking explosion of rock.

"Not there," it said.

It picked up another foot and repeated its show.

"Not there either. I hope you haven't left. We have unfinished—"

The dragon stiffened, then bent its long neck and tried to reach its forearm up as though to scratch it. I immediately saw why. The stalactites that remained, thorn-like, in its body, had begun to melt. Molten rock poured into the dragon. Its arms couldn't reach.

Wynruil!

As though my thought made him appear, I saw him helping a limping Beldroth lurch haltingly from rock cover to rock cover, trying to put distance between them and the dragon. Casting such a spell to melt the rock while helping Beldroth was truly impressive.

Then I looked behind me and realized Brittanie was casting. Illiara was somehow revived, and she too worked a spell.

"Wow," Trentius said. "Brittanie Boils Behemoth's Blood," he said, moving his hand like the words were on a sign in front of him.

The ground shuddered one last time as the dragon collapsed.

Elliah ~ 13

Of all the things to cheer about, learning Hughelas hadn't lied brought me the most joy. Thinking he was the kind of person that would manipulate a frightened mother had cut deeply.

The Alluvium created an odd, surprisingly non-gruesome, but what had to be a much livelier, nursery. They formed cribs from dragon ribs, hung mobiles of shattered bones held in place by string, used two larger dragon skulls as changing tables, and lined the walls with longer leg bones. Cleaned of its meat, then purged of any remaining organic material by magical fire, the bones had become white like the head of Beldroth's hammer. Most peculiar of all, the dragon bones released a light floral scent that soothed even me.

Though the magic of bones from the red dragons did not have as strong of an effect as the one from the hammer, coating the room in them produced a cacophony of crying babies and mothers weeping with joy. A stark difference from the quiet shroud of death that had hung in the room when we'd brought in the first bones.

It was like the way spells would land on me if the dragon-bone hammer were in my possession, I supposed. I hid the magic of the bone with my anti-magic, but the hammer also reduced my resistance to spells. It didn't explain how *I* had lived through infancy, but my mother was a pretty amazing Healer. Or maybe my Mother kept me alive to serve Her purpose.

I sat outside the caves with Hughelas, where I enjoyed the fresh air—Hughelas seemed equally content in a cave or outside—as Alluvium drove their slug-creatures to haul out dragon remains. "Your Bereft children will conceal the bones in the nursery," Hughelas had told them, "while the bones keep them alive. But you've got to get the rest of the bones out. Other dragons will come looking."

"Dragons collect their dead," Gormar had chanted in reply.

I was glad to see Gormar had survived, even if he did believe I intended to destroy his people. For Gormar, it seemed a matter of curiosity more than a death wish. He was as fanatical in his beliefs as Beldroth had once been, though they believed different things.

Beldroth had recovered a hint of his former zealotry, though it was easy to read the fleeting doubt that would sometimes rob him of his smile. His plan, the Mother's Blessed plan, had worked—the Alluvium intended to send an army to Alenor. Wynruil refused to lead an army, like in the days of legend, but he was willing to lend his support to Brittanie, who had the honor of leading the first army of Alluvium in generations.

We sat at a crossroads in the small town we'd traveled through on the way to Cenaedth. The one where I'd wished we could have sat and people-watched. There was not a lot of traffic, though the little town that had grown around the crossroad was lively enough. I'd needed to get away from the stench and the confined space, and Hughelas had humored me.

Hughelas studied his book, thumbing back and forth between sections. Several times, he had seemed to want to tell me something, but had paused and flipped to some other part of his book. He would tell me when he was ready, and I was content. I watched the people. Alluvium. Salts. Wood Elves. No Warders or High Elves. A few elves that might have been of mixed blood. Oddly, there were fewer there than near the High Elf capital. One would think there would be fewer near the place it was frowned upon.

We'd found the perfect little spot. Someone had built an inn right on the corner of the crossroads, created a covered area in front where they served food outdoors. And drinks. They'd built it for people-watching, or perhaps for clientele who might profit by seeing who went where with what goods.

"Learning anything?" I asked, as a group of Salts took one of a few free tables remaining. It was interesting to see the other half of Hughelas's bloodline again. They were all thin and light-skinned with white hair, like the crew of the Knoll. Their clothes and jewelry tended toward the pastels, or possibly colors once bright which had faded.

I was entranced enough that It took me a moment to realize Hughelas hadn't answered. "Hughelas," I said a little more loudly, but his eyes were zipping across the lines of the page before him.

"Helloooo, Hughelas," I said, raising my voice even more, but he still didn't respond.

I didn't really have anything important to say or ask, so I let it go and went back to people-watching.

I cocked my head in curiosity as two Salts got up from their seats and headed our way. One female had striking blue skin markings on her angular face. There wasn't anything on the other side of us except the street. A quick glance revealed nothing obvious they might be seeking beyond us, though they could have simply been heading to another shop.

Thud! My eyes darted back to Hughelas, who had slammed the book closed and looked intently at me. "I think I understand," he said, the excitement in his light blue eyes electric.

"Understand what, my mixed-blood genius?" I was so thankful he hadn't lied to Brittanie.

"Why you're Bereft. How you're alive. What a..." he tried to mimic being larger than he was. "...five-dimensional spherical cage is." He leaned in, tapping the book. "I think I understand what's going on with magic."

"Hughelas?" a woman's voice said.

A Salt stood right behind him, the other coming around to my side of the table. They looked friendly, but I put a hand on my dagger anyway.

"Son of Lyrei?" said the woman. "The captain of the Knoll spoke of you."

Ah, they'd talked with Captain Edraele.

"Yes?" Hughelas asked, though I was willing him, just that once, to lie. Something was off.

"Well," she said, looking back at the table she'd left, all of whom had stood. "That was easy." She twirled her finger in a circle, then pointed west.

A sudden wind pushed me down while raising Hughelas and whipping the table onto its side. Hughelas's book went flying, pages swirling out like a devil made of paper. I reached for the hammer on my back, but the wind fought me. I had to get rid of the hammer, so that their magic wouldn't work on me.

Hughelas tried to yell, but only a muffled groan escaped the magic.

Alluvium, Wood Elves, and Salts alike jumped up and drew weapons. The wind stole my yells. I sat, a helpless fool.

"This man is a fugitive," the woman shouted. "He is wanted by Jade Galefinger, Daughter of the Nine Winds, for *theft!*" Wait! Wasn't that the title Beldroth had used for Hughelas's mother?

I tried again to get to the hammer, but it was like being stuck in a wet blanket. The crowd grudgingly parted to let them through. I recognized no one there. None of the Alluvium there knew Hughelas's role in saving their home, in saving their Bereft babies. No one would stand up for him against the Salt woman's authority.

"You should never have revealed yourself, son of Lyrei," the woman said to Hughelas. Then she leaned in and hissed menacingly in his ear. "Deara keeps its secrets."

Author's Note

Want more? Book 3, Secrets of Deara, will follow Hughelas and Elliah into the waters of the Salts.

If you enjoyed Bones of Cenaedth, please leave a review on GoodReads (https://www.goodreads.com/book/show/219093443-bones-of-cenaedth) and Amazon (https://mybook.to/trb2), Bookbub (https://www.bookbub.com/books/bones-of-cenaedth-an-epic-fantasy-thaumatropic-roots-book-2-by-steven-j-morris), etc. Ratings definitely encourage folks to give my books a shot, and reviews, even a few words, help people understand whether they're going to get the fantasy they're hoping for. Help other readers connect with the stories they want.

If you didn't know, this series, Thaumatropic Roots, is a prequel to The Guardian League, and Urban Fantasy that takes place here on Earth (assuming you're on Earth). That story begins with The Guardian of The Palace (https://mybook.to/lkIH).

Sign up for my *newsletter* (https://pages.sjmorriswrites.com/ebook-landing-page) to receive updates on my writing, as well as early views of artwork and exclusive short-stories that give you glimpses into characters from The Guardian League and Thaumatropic Roots.

http://sjmorriswrites.com

Thanks,
Steve

Acknowledgments

I just reread my acknowledgments for Book 1, and I see that I said I needed to find a new cutline for Book 2 because it was too long. Kinda funny, since it ended up being the shortest book I've written so far. But I was pleased with how it turned out. Originally, what is now going to be Book 3, Secrets of Deara, was in Book 2, but it really didn't work. I now have to rewrite Book 3 completely, but the foundation of the plot it there already.

Let's get to some thanks. First, I'd like to thank Oksana Marafioti. I found her on Reedsy, and she brought my story up to the next level. She edited this book and provided structural feedback, but she also coached me on many things that I think helped increase tension, give the characters more depth, and connect the pieces of the story better (the latter being my primary ask). She also provided advice that I couldn't incorporate—not because the advice was bad, but because I wasn't mature enough in my writing skills yet to incorporate her suggestions in a timely manner. But I plan to think about her suggestions which I couldn't wrap my mind around in my future books. If you're looking to bring your actual writing up to the next level, consider Oksana (http://oksana-marafioti.com).

I've gathered a crew of writers that have provided good feedback on a lot of the ancillary things that go with the book... blurbs, ad content, the best vodkas for writing. Thank you for the support June Levy, Eric Margerum, April Gomez, Simone Lindberg, Heike Theis (get your dang next book out), Toby LeBlanc, B.K Greenwood, Marla Taviano (also my copy editor), Edith Pawlicki, and Erin McPherson. Anyone looking to get started as a writer, and want someone to hold your hand, consider Erin.

I want to thank Matthew J. Holmes for his marketing classes. His experience and knowledge on FaceBook advertising has helped me connect with new readers and grow my writing business. Ultimately, that gets me more time for writing, and gets you more books. :)

Which leads me ultimately, to you, my readers. Without those of you willing to like/rate/review indie writing, there would be a ton of cool fantasy that would die on the vine. So thank you for reading, for rating/reviewing, and for supporting indie writing!

Prologue for Secrets of Deara

Every dawn aboard a ship reveals a new world.
— Captain Jade Galefinger, Daughter of the Nine Winds

If we don't catch a wind today, I'm feeding week-old sea cucumbers to the lot of you until you pass enough gas to fill the sails.
— Captain Jade Galefinger, Daughter of the Nine Winds

Author's note - good chance the details for the prologue will change. :)

Elliah

I felt a terror unlike any I'd felt before as I stared into the twin pools of night on the enormous head of an ancient black dragon. As though casually reading a story instead of living it, a tiny bit of my brain noted the difference between the soul-sucking fear of having a monster inside my mind versus the very visceral terror of seeing the booted foot of a High Elf caught between two lower teeth of a maw big enough to engulf Beldroth, while the jaw worked with an alarming chorus of bone-snapping crunches.

I might have giggled as I took a step backwards... a maniacal little chirp at the absurdity of my situation. I stepped clear of the puddle created by the betrayal of my bladder, as though having good purchase for my feet would matter. Running wouldn't get me far.

"Interesting," the dragon said, its voice peculiarly resonant, like multiple pitches came out at once, a chord of tones. I stopped my retreat, shocked.

"Who meddles in the affairs of elves? Be it Shaythyl?" Out of fear of what other remains might hide behind it, I couldn't take my eyes off the bloody stump of a leg protruding between two sharp teeth. A pointed tongue snaked out along the lower teeth, finding the leg and popping it into the maw. I shivered at the quick crunch and swallow.

"Do you understand these words of mine?" It asked. "Or has the language of elves changed too much since the Breaking?" Since the Breaking?

"I... I understand you," I stammered.

It paused, its tongue looking for any more treasures and finding none. I slowly backed up, though I had little room to do so.

"You cannot conceive how great is my irritation." The dragon's black eyes, like a Universe empty of stars and life, narrowed.

Well, maybe I could, after what we'd done. We'd stolen the dragon's egg! And then Pyrravyn had sprung his trap, disappearing in a blink of light with the purloined egg and leaving us to fight the angry parent alone. Leaving us to die. No witnesses. Jade had been right.

"Stay here," it said. "My children need food." It leaned forward, and I jumped back, jarring my lower spine painfully against the ship's rail, then falling onto my face. The dragon turned its head and picked up the prone form of the other High Elf, slinging it into its mouth, then it pushed away from the ship, rocking it like it was a toy. It spread its wings, scooping water up on the backs of its wings and splashing it on the ship as it took off.

At least the water put out most of the flames.